Acclaim for Jon Clinch's *Finn*

Named a best book of the year by the) the *Christian Science Monitor.*

Named a *Notable Book* by the *American Library Association.*

Winner of the *Philadelphia Athenaeum Literary Award.*

Shortlisted for the *Sargent First Novel Prize.*

"A brave and ambitious debut novel… It stands on its own while giving new life and meaning to Twain's novel, which has been stirring passions and debates since 1885… triumph of imagination and graceful writing…. Bookstores and libraries shelve novels alphabetically by authors' names. That leaves Clinch a long way from Twain. But on my bookshelves, they'll lean against each other. I'd like to think that the cantankerous Twain would welcome the company."
— *USA Today*

"Ravishing…In the saga of this tormented human being, Clinch brings us a radical (and endlessly debatable) new take on Twain's classic, and a stand-alone marvel of a novel. Grade: A."
— *Entertainment Weekly*

"Haunting…Clinch reimagines Finn in a strikingly original way, replacing Huck's voice with his own magisterial vision—one that's nothing short of revelatory…Spellbinding."
— *Washington Post*

"His models may include Cormac McCarthy, and Charles Frazier, whose *Cold Mountain* also has a voice that sounds like 19th-century American (both formal and colloquial) but has a contemporary spikiness. This voice couldn't be better suited to a historical novel with a modernist sensibility: Clinch's riverbank Missouri feels post-apocalyptic, and his Pap Finn is a crazed yet wily survivor in a polluted landscape…Clinch's Pap is a convincingly nightmarish extrapolation of Twain's. He's the mad, lost and dangerous center of a world we'd hate to live in—or do we still live there?—and crave to revisit as soon as we close the book."
— *Newsweek*

"An inspired riff on one of literature's all-time great villains…This tale of fathers and sons, slavery and freedom, better angels at war with dark demons, is filled with passages of brilliant description, violence that is close-up and terrifying…Everything in this novel could have happened, and we believe it…"

— *New Orleans Times-Picayune*

"Finn brims with tension, fueled by sentences as taut as a cane pole wrestling a catfish in muddy waters. Considering the heady literary terrain Clinch hopes to master, the novel succeeds better than anyone but its author could have hoped. It offers a jolting companion to the mischievous antics of *Huckleberry Finn*."

— *Christian Science Monitor*

"In Clinch's retelling, Pap Finn comes vibrantly to life as a complex, mysterious, strangely likable figure…Clinch includes many sharply realized, sometimes harrowing, even gruesome scenes…*Finn* should appeal not only to scholars of 19th century literature but to anyone who cares to sample a forceful debut novel inspired by a now-mythic American story."

— *Atlanta Journal-Constitution*

"What makes bearable this river voyage that never ventures far beyond the banks is the compelling narrative Clinch has created. He writes exceedingly well, not with the immediacy Twain imbued to Huck's voice, but with an impersonal narrator's voice that almost perversely refuses to take sides. Masterful."

— *Fredericksburg Freelance-Star*

"Disturbing and darkly compelling…Clinch displays impressive imagination and descriptiveness…anyone who encounters *Finn* will long be haunted by this dark and bloody tale."

— *Hartford Courant*

"Every fan of Twain's masterpiece will want to read this inspired spin-off, which could become an unofficial companion volume."

— *Library Journal* (Starred)

"An important work that would be regarded as a major novel, even if *Adventures of Huckleberry Finn* didn't exist."

— Kent Rasmussen, author of *Mark Twain A To Z*

Acclaim for Jon Clinch's *Kings of the Earth*

Named a best book of the year by the *Washington Post*.

"In his masterful and compassionate new novel, *Kings of the Earth*, Clinch borrows from a true-life case of possible fratricide. Three elderly, semiliterate brothers live in squalor on a ramshackle dairy farm in central New York state. The prismatic narrative shifts time and point of view, and Clinch easily slips into the voices of his diverse cast of characters—a nosy, good-hearted neighbor, a police investigator struggling to do the right thing, and the brothers' drug-dealing nephew. Through evocative descriptions of the landscape—'a countryside full of that same old homegrown desolation'—and by imbuing these odd men with a gentle nobility and an 'antique strangeness,' Clinch has created a haunting, suspenseful story."

— *O, The Oprah Magazine* (Lead Title, Summer Reading List)

"True feeling seems to be out of fashion in contemporary fiction, and fiction is the poorer for it. Disaffection and irony may be the tenor of the times, but too much of it can leave you estranged and lonely. Then along comes Clinch, and we are once again safe at home, in the hands of a master. *Kings of the Earth* recalls the finest work of John Gardner, and Bruce Chatwin's *On the Black Hill*. It becomes a story that is not told but lived, a cry from the heart of the heart of the country, in William Gass's phrase, unsentimental but deeply felt, unschooled but never less than lucid. Never mawkish, Clinch's voice never fails to elucidate and, finally, to forgive, even as it mourns."

— *Washington Post*

"Clinch's literary alchemy results in a stunning book. Because each chapter releases essential information, the book moves easily toward closure, but an intricate knot of story lines plays out through them. Recalling William Faulkner's *As I Lay Dying*, each short chapter is broken into a section that is told in the first person. Not only do we get the brothers' voices, we hear an entire rural chorus: the dead father and mother, neighbors, the sister, brother-in-law, lawyers and the police."

— *Dallas Morning News*

"The power of *Kings of the Earth* lies in the intricacies of the relationships among the Proctors; neighbor and childhood friend Preston, who serves as something of a guardian angel; the drug-dealing nephew, and the police. Clinch is canny enough to move his characters through their own understated lives, hinting where he needs to as he skirts the obvious, and refusing to overlay a sense of morality on their actions. The landscape informs the story as much as the internal terrain of the characters does, giving *Kings of the Earth* a grounding that is missing from many modern novels. We know the events that lie behind Clinch's novel were real, and that the novel is not. But the realism here is no less, with writing so vibrant that you feel the bite of a northern wind, smell the rankness of dissipated lives and experience the heart-tug of watching tenuous lives play out their last inches of thread."

— *Los Angeles Times*

"It's the sort of book you race through then read again more slowly, savoring each voice. Preston, the kindly neighbor who cheerfully admits he doesn't entirely understand the Proctors, says, 'Where a man comes from isn't enough. You've got to go all the way back to the seed of a man and the planting of it, and a person can't go back that far ever I don't think.' Clinch goes back to that seed and that planting, and readers will eagerly go with him."

— *Seattle Times*

"This is a gritty but warm-hearted and beautifully realized novel about three old unmarried brothers who live together on a rundown dairy farm in upstate New York. Clinch addresses one of Faulkner's favorite themes in this novel—our ability to endure—and explores it in ways that are inspiring and poignant. Enthusiastically recommended for readers of literary fiction."

— *Library Journal* (Starred)

"In Clinch's multilayered, pastoral second novel (after *Finn),* a death among three elderly, illiterate brothers living together on an upstate New York farm raises suspicions and accusations in the surrounding community. Family histories and troubles are divulged in short chapters by a cacophony of characters speaking in first person. Alongside the police troopers' investigation, each player contributes his own personal perspectives and motivations. Clinch explores family dynamics in this quiet storm of a novel that will stun readers with its power."

— *Publishers Weekly* (Starred)

Belzoni Dreams of Egypt

A Novel

Jon Clinch

unmediated ink™

Visit jonclinch.com.

ISBN: 0692220879
ISBN-13: 978-0692220870

Version 1.0

FOR DR. HENRY W. JONES, JR.

BELZONI DREAMS OF EGYPT

PRELUDE:

The Letter

"Those were the great days of excavating.
If there was a difference of opinion with
a brother excavator, one laid for him with a gun."

— Howard Carter on Belzoni, 1923. Quoted in
Glyn Daniel, *150 Years of Archaeology*, Cambridge, 1950

*

Hospital of the Holy Cross
Porto Novo, Benin, Africa
5 December, 1823

Sra. Sarah Belzoni
In Care of the British Museum
Great Russell Street
London, England

My dearest Sra. Belzoni,

It is with high personal regard, terrible reluctance, and a nearly inex-
pressible grief that I advise you that your beloved husband's life has
lately come to an unfortunate end here in our village. *(Fear not for my
wisdom or my tact, by the way: I have good reason for daring to insert the
term "beloved" into the otherwise clinical statement above. All shall be revealed in time.)*

Sr. Belzoni's fame most surely preceded him to our remote outpost, of that you can be certain. What man on Earth, even in a place as removed from civilization as this, has not thrilled to the adventures of The Great Belzoni? Yet—*and I hope, Madame; nay, I pray, that I am not overstepping the bounds of either ordinary human compassion or simple good taste when I mention it*—there was not a man in the village capable of recognizing your husband at first sight. The fault was not ours. Having learned by heart the tales of his triumphs in London, his mighty works in Cairo, and his historic discoveries in the Valley of the Kings, to witness the Great Belzoni so pitifully reduced was a shock beyond our imagining. He who had once shouldered stone relics weighing many hundreds of pounds could now barely raise his own limbs, although with the help of a pair of burly seamen he managed to descend the gangplank and make his way up the lane to our little hillside hospital. He would not under any circumstances permit himself to be carried.

A stomach ailment had been his companion throughout his passage from England, and his bodily reserves were woefully depleted. I did for him all that I could, but his recovery was slow and frustrating. I determined that he should remain under my care until fully recovered, and I advised him accordingly, but he would have none of my caution. Your husband, as you know, was a man possessed of a powerful will. He insisted from his very hospital bed that he intended to discover the source of the Niger, and he assured me that the expedition he had assembled would brook no delay.

And so, contrary to my orders, he vacated the premises and set out. Barely three days had passed before his band of fellow adventurers returned, bearing their leader's cold form upon a stretcher. I intend no exaggeration when I say that they proved themselves, to a man, overwhelmed by the variety of grief that can be predicated only upon boundless admiration and, dare I say it, great love. "Let the source of the river remain a mystery," said one of them, an ancient foreigner with dirty white mustaches and a turban to match. "If it cannot be found by Belzoni, then it should not be found at all."

His fellows nodded their sad agreement.

*

Your husband left little in the way of personal effects, the chiefest of which I enclose. The remainder shall follow at our earliest opportunity for shipment, along with the sea chest in which he conveyed them.

The first item here is a leather-bound edition of Jean d'Outremeuse's *The Voiage and Travaile of Sir John Mandeville, Knight.* I have no doubt that it will be well known to you, for it bears within it your signature and handwritten inscription. Your husband spoke passionately to me of that book more than once during our brief time together, explaining that its outlandish visions had inspired him to test his merely mortal accomplishments against standards that can only be described as the products of legend and fancy. He assured me, however, that even had the book not borne that particular significance to him, its simple status as a gift from you—*it was bequeathed to me by my beloved Sarah,* he would sigh as he cast his eyes upon it—was sufficient to have established its worth as beyond any earthly measure.

The second item, a packet of pages dictated at sea to a junior naval officer who proved himself quite handy with a pen, can only be understood as Sr. Belzoni's final testament. *(Here, Sra. Belzoni, I must beg your indulgence. Had I known how transported I would be by the thrilling nature of his adventures and the resonant timbre of his voice, I should never have begun reading! The fault is thus mine, although perhaps not entirely.)* The narrative, you must understand, is in certain ways larger and more encompassing than even the Great Belzoni himself could have meant it to be. It begins as the story of how a boy became a giant. It becomes, by and by, the story of how a giant became a man.

I hope and I trust that these documents will bring some comfort to you in your hour of grief, I beg your forgiveness for the plainspoken nature of this hasty missive, and I assure you that I remain,

Yr. Ob'd'nt Servant,

James P. Rutherford, M.D.

P.S. Within the opening pages of *The Voiage* you will find a third document. Your husband was quite insistent, first to the junior naval officer and later to me, that this set of papers—complex and befuddling as they are, and filled to bursting with lists and instructions and spidery diagrams got up in India ink—be delivered upon his death to a certain James Curtin of London.

That name, and that individual, will no doubt be known to you as well.

J.P.R.

CHAPTER ONE:

Rome

"Belzoni emerged from his mother's womb already marked for his Great Work, weighing 6.5 kilogrammes unclothed and measuring 43.9 centimetres from head to toe."

— Rudolph C. Mütter, *Verloren in Ägypten,* Munich, 1845

*

I MAY HAVE BEEN BORN IN PADUA, but my life began in Rome.

We rattled into the great city—my mother, my three brothers, and I—in a wagon driven by my father, the illustrious barber Giacomo Lorenzo Belzoni. I remember the cautious way that his hands held the reins, barely touching them, holding them out at arm's length as if fearing they might develop a will of their own and rise up to strangle him for having abandoned his natal city.

"I would suppose that hair grows just as reliably in Rome as it does in the Veneto," he had sighed as we piled our belongings onto the wagon. My mother, not always the stronger of the two but surely the more stubborn, had convinced him at last to return her to the city of her childhood. He would never again be entirely happy, regardless of what might transpire in the capital city. Or at least he would never admit it.

I was seven years old, and already as big as a man.

Whether I was a child or an adult or something else altogether, my memories begin on that day, with my father's delicate meticulous hands,

hands smaller than my own even then, and a pair of reins winding around them as treacherous as snakes. Before that moment, nothing.

Perhaps it was the quality of the Roman light. It was sharper than the light at home, it was cleaner somehow and less forgiving, and it made every detail of every object stand out in sharp relief. The light in Padua possessed that dreamy Venetian vagueness, as if it were forever trying to lull you to sleep.

More likely, it was the quality of the Roman darkness. There was a furtiveness to it, something dense and secretive and alive. As a boy I could almost see it—the darkness, I mean—I could almost see the darkness, as if it were a living thing readying itself to be revealed to me by the power of the little candles that burned in every window, within every niche, around every corner. When night fell in Padua, nothing remained but you and the stars. When night fell in Rome, a world of possibility flickered everywhere, blooming like a secret garden.

I've known many varieties of darkness since then. The chiaroscuro of a torchlit Mithraic temple and its bloodstained altar, the echoing black belly of a freighter bound for Malta, a single gleam of torchlight in a tomb filling ever so slowly with poison gas. But none of that darkness compares to those first long nights in the capital city of Rome, when I was seven years old and the world was new.

*

I AM PREPARED TO DIE ON THIS EXPEDITION—if not from the disease in my belly, then from some peril that awaits me in the green depths of the jungle. No fate could surprise me less. I have, after all, spent my lifetime studying death in all of its varieties.

When my end arrives, history and time will lose an individual who drained the Nile with the help of an orphaned Irish boy, who silenced the singing statue of Memnon with a handful of indigestible desert rations, and who helped his own father shave the eminent neck of a Pope.

With my last breath I shall exhale all of these memories and more, a fate which troubles me not in the least. No one understands the transient nature of the human spirit better than an individual who has made his bed so happily and so often among the corpses of kings.

Listen, then. Listen, while this warship tacks beneath the wheeling stars toward the distant coast of Africa.

*

IT WAS FATHER MULLOOLY who first took me underground. He was a Dominican, a gaunt giant of a raw-boned Irishman living out the exile that his forefathers had undertaken in 1667. Exactly how the Irish Dominicans have managed to retain their national character century after century is a puzzle to me even now. They don't reproduce, at least not for the record. There must be a hidden spring of good Irish Catholic boys in Dublin or Limerick or somewhere out in the lush emerald countryside, a secret place where freckle-faced boys with red hair on their heads and the love of God in their hearts emerge from the ground itself and rise up to fill the ranks of the exiled Irish Dominicans. If such a place there is, I would be the man to find it. I, who first ventured underground at the impressionable age of nine or ten, escorted by Father Mullooly into the basement of the church of San Clemente. There was water running down there, now that I think of it. I could hear it through the limestone walls, and I can hear it still in my fitful sleep. Perhaps it was that secret spring of Irish Catholic boys, rushing its recruits southward to fill the empty boot of Italy.

As the body of Christ hung upon the cross, so the sinew and the muscle of Father Mullooly hung upon his bones. He walked as if he were built of crucifixes strung together with wire, making his way down the aisle with a jangling kind of comical arrhythmic lurch that the scamps of the neighborhood struggled to emulate. He was not old; I believe he was probably a year or two younger than my father, who in those days was barely into his thirties. He had hair the color of sand, and a long narrow face from which mischief gleamed if he weren't careful.

"After Mass," my mother whispered to me one sabbath morning in the silence of the gleaming sanctuary, "see if Father will show you the splinter of the One True Cross." She knew all about the splinter of the One True Cross. She had grown up in the church of San Clemente, and she knew every inch of the place as thoroughly as the Devil knows the Psalms. I wonder now: was it possible that she had gone to school with Father Mullooly? Or had he just emerged one day from the water pipes, fully grown and ready to submit to his vows? Another mystery that I shall take with me to my grave.

When Mass was over I shadowed Father Mullooly to his office behind the chapel and rapped at his open door. *"Giovanni Battista!"* he cried when he turned and saw me filling the doorway. *"John the Baptist!"* It was Father Mullooly who gave me my first English, by the way, and it was another Irishman—poor orphaned James Curtin, whose ultimate fate my mightiest efforts could not improve—who equipped me with the rest. God bless the pair of them for setting me upon my cosmopolitan path.

Father Mullooly put out a hand and placed it upon my shoulder, giving me a friendly little shake. For all the movement it produced, he may as well have been accosting the statue of St. John in the chapel. Probably nine or ten years old, I was already as solid as a monument. "John the Baptist," he repeated, for translating my name into its biblical equivalent gave him no end of delight, "what keeps you indoors on this fine day? No doubt your little brothers are already out making trouble in the streets."

I was the youngest in the family, but what was the point in explaining that to Father Mullooly? "I've come about the splinter, sir," I said, and left it at that.

"The splinter?"

"The splinter of the One True Cross, sir. I've come to see it."

"Aha!" He raised his eyebrows and tilted his head. "Easier said than done."

It was always easier said than done with the Dominicans. I'd likely have to learn some catechism and parrot it back to him before he'd show me the splinter—either that or perform a daylong set of filthy and Herculean chores to earn just the tiniest glimpse. He must have seen the way my young face fell, because he offered a sympathetic look and said, "Don't worry, Giovanni. I'm sure you're up to it. And if you get stuck, you can count on me."

He ushered me back out into the sanctuary, where old Signor Monteverdi was sweeping up. The caretaker was a little gray grasshopper of a man, always bent double over a mop or a broom or a bucket, forever muttering away about the good old days in his long-lost Venice. He was deaf as the striped post to which a gondolier ties up his boat, and he talked to himself at a volume that never failed to startle. Father Mullooly smiled at him and limped up to the apse, signaling that I should follow.

"Look up, boy."

I stumbled up the steps behind him, catching myself on the altar and looking where he pointed—at the Lamb of God in the mosaic above, with twelve sheep divided on either side of him. Jesus and his Disciples, I knew. But try as I might, edging closer and tilting my head and squinting into the light that winked from the gilded mosaic tiles, I couldn't for the life of me locate the splinter of the One True Cross.

"You can't see it with your *eyes*," he said. "You're going to have to use your *brain*." He tapped on his temple with one long woody finger.

The lesson was about to begin after all.

"Do you see the text up there, in the mosaic above the sheep?"

It was in Latin, of course. "Yes sir, I do."

"Good. Can you read it?"

I shrugged. "No sir, I can't. Not all of it anyhow." If Father Mullooly wanted me to acquire more Latin just to get a peek at a sliver of old wood, especially on a sunny day like this one with the light practically exploding in through the high windows, he was about to be disappointed. I didn't care if he had the whole oaken crossbar of the One True Cross hidden somewhere, plus a handful of nails with the Savior's blood still on them. Today was not the day for devoting oneself to a dying language.

"Fine," he said. "That's fine. I'll translate it for you."

What a relief! Perhaps there would be no lesson after all.

There were four phrases in the mosaic, separated one from another by little cruciform shapes. He read them off one by one: "'*This vine will be a symbol of the Church of Christ,*'" he said. "'*The remains of the wooden Cross and of James and Ignatius.*'" He paused for a heartbeat or two just to let that part sink in, and then he went on. "'*Rest above the writing in the Body of Christ. Which the Law causes to wither but the Cross brings to Life.*'"

He cupped his chin in his hand "What do you make of that?"

My shoulders drooped. "I don't understand it at all." I'd had my heart set on receiving step-by-step instructions for locating the splinter within that Latin text—some treasure map sent down from God himself—but it was all nonsense. Undiluted, frustrating, Latinate nonsense.

"Cheer up, John the Baptist. There's always hope."

"It mentions some kind of writing on the body of Christ," I said, picturing the Son of God tattooed like a heathen Turk. "But that's got to be pure malarkey." (*Malarkey* was a word Father Mullooly had taught me, and I enjoyed showing it off.)

He hmmmed. "I see your point. But what if there's a secret to it instead? What if it's a code? A trick? A puzzle?"

Now he had my attention. I'd never been much for the kind of thinking that gets done at a desk—my legs were always cramped and sticking out every which way, for one thing—but a puzzle was a different article. Suddenly the outside world and its bursting spring sunlight were a million miles away.

"Well, Giovanni?"

I barely heard him. I was fully engrossed already, rearranging the words I recognized and those that I thought I'd gathered from his translation, trying them out backwards and forwards. I took an involuntary step, drawn toward the mosaic like a magnetized needle toward the pole.

"It's easy once you know the secret." He produced a bit of paper, tore it into quarters, and scribbled the translation on it, one phrase to each slip. "Here. Put the first and last together, as one sentence." He held them together before me, and I tore my eyes away from the mosaic.

"'This vine will be a symbol of the Church of Christ,'" I read, "'which the Law causes to wither but the Cross brings to Life.'"

"Sounds good," said Father Mullooly. "Now. Do you see something up there that looks like a vine?"

The vine was obvious and everywhere, a dense winding net of greenery that covered a good portion of the golden dome. I hardly knew where to point, but point I did.

"Exactly. The Tree of Life, symbolizing the church. So far, we'd seem to be on the right track." He handed me the two remaining slips, and I held them up before me like two segments of an ancient map. "Read these aloud. The two middle phrases. Read the pair of them as if they were a single sentence."

"'*The remains of the wooden Cross and of James and Ignatius rest above the writing in the Body of Christ.*'" I suppose my eyes must have grown wide, for the words seemed at last to have made some kind of sense. But one more reading proved that I still had some distance to go. "I don't understand, Father. What's this about James and Ignatius? And where's the writing in the body of Christ?"

"San Clemente is blessed with relics of St. Ignatius and the Apostle James, too—and they share a hiding place with the splinter of the One True Cross."

I nodded, understanding but not yet illuminated.

"As for the writing, young Giovanni..." He enclosed the two last slips in one of his long hands and made them vanish as if by magic, freeing my eyes to return to the mosaic on the wall. "I'm afraid the writing is directly in front of your eyes."

Of course. The mosaic referred to itself! The mosaic *was* the writing! And above it, at the center of the Tree of Life that spread everywhere, hung none other than the crucified Christ. I saw it all in a flash, and I understood. "They hid the splinter in the mosaic, didn't they?"

"Aye, that they did."

"That's how it 'rests above the writing.'"

"Exactly."

"'In the body of Christ.'"

"Just so."

I was proud of myself, but I was a little disappointed as well. "So you can't show it to me, then. You can only show me where it is."

"Sorry. Some mysteries we can solve. The rest we must take on faith."

He gave me a long steady look, but I couldn't bring myself to return it. I was afraid he'd see in my eyes that I wanted nothing more than to return in the dark of night, raise a ladder, and smash at the body of Christ until I'd gotten my hands on that splinter.

There would, of course, be opportunity enough for that kind of rough work in the years to come.

*

UNLIKE FATHER MULLOOLY, my own father wasn't much for taking things on faith. He had only one belief, and that was in the vitality of human hair. "Can you feel this, my boys?" he would ask each morning as he woke us one by one with the fierce caress of his unshaven chin. "As surely as the sun rises, the stubble appears each day upon the cheek of every man on earth. Thus does mankind's curse prove to be the barber's blessing!"

Sometimes, lingering over olives and cheese and coffee at the breakfast table, he would describe the beard as no less than a recurring and highly personal sign from God—something on the order of the rainbow that He'd hung in the sky after the Great Flood, except that this time His reassurance was directed exclusively toward men who made their living with razors and mugs of soap. I gathered that barbers must have required more encouragement than other tradesmen, for my father never mentioned any daily signal that God might have established for bricklayers or woodcutters or smelters of iron.

"Even at the darkest hour of the night," he would say, "the barber is never far from God's reassurance. Imagine that some sound rouses you from your sleep. You sit upright, you sniff the air, you prick up your ears like a dog's. But it's nothing! Your wife and your dear children are all asleep in their beds! All is well! And as you settle back down and return to your dreams, you cannot help but notice how your jaw scrapes against the pillowcase. Aha!" He waved a bit of cheese for emphasis. "Aha! In that scraping, a barber detects the tender hand of God." He finished eating and sipped at the last of his coffee. "It is a well-documented fact that every barber on God's green earth sleeps like a baby. Every single one of them. And now you know why."

One morning in particular, as he was explaining how in the persistent pattern of stubble on a man's cheeks can be charted the inexorable advance of God's armies across a heathen world, my father had an idea. "You other boys are too small yet," he said, "but Giovanni is just about ready to become my apprentice."

I surreptitiously felt my cheek with the back of my hand. Nothing. No encouragement whatsoever. Perhaps that too was a sign from God.

*

MY FATHER'S SHOP WAS a spotless little mouse hole off a curving lane behind the Campo de Fiore. "Do you know what people say?" he asked as we drew near on that first morning. "They say that Julius Caesar was slain right here—right in this building where I am privileged to shave the faces of men both great and small. Imagine that. Julius Caesar himself."

I could hardly believe it. The high walls were gaily painted and densely festooned with clotheslines and flower boxes. Smells of cooking rose from kitchens and cafes. And in the distance, beyond the curve of the long high building where my father worked, the market square of the Campo de Fiore exploded with flowers. It was a scene for a festival, not a murder.

"Where?" I said. "Was it upstairs someplace?" I squinted against the light into the open windows overhead. Framed within one was an old woman preparing to hang out her wash, and I imagined her bare feet treading on tiles that had once run red with the blood of a king.

"Oh no no no. This," he waved his hand, taking in the building, "this is all new." It was probably five centuries old, crumbling and decrepit, but if I were doomed to learn nothing about being a barber, then at least I would get a lesson in the relativity of time. My father shuffled over and put his hand against the wall, kicking at the foundation with the gleaming toe of his little black shoe. "These stones here, though— *these* stones are plenty old."

"I see. So they murdered Julius Caesar in the cellar?"

"You could say that, Giovanni. Only in those days, it wasn't the cellar."

I scratched my head.

To rid me of my ignorance, he explained how everything in Italy was built atop something else. Plant a shovel in the ground, he said, and you're halfway to the fifteenth century. Dig a grave, and you're back in the Dark Ages. Sink a foundation for a new building, and you've opened a window into the unimaginably remote past.

As I sat that day in my father's shop, watching him going about his meticulous business, enduring his introductions to customer after customer, I felt like a man afloat in deep water. Who could say what mysterious creatures lurked below, frozen in time, reenacting their static history? When the door opened and the little bell rang to announce the arrival of Sr. Frazetti or Sr. Capote, and my father arose from his chair and signaled with a curt wave of his hand that I should rise as well to greet his visitor, I was as unsteady as a man regaining his legs after a long sea voyage.

Since that day, of course, I have visited dozens of other places where Caesar met his end. I have seen thousands of fragments of the One True Cross as well—enough to hang a score of saviors and a hundred thieves to boot. But each new rumor and each new relic still sets me off balance. I cannot help it. Such is my weakness for history.

How I grew to hate those days in that little dark den of a barber shop! Whenever my father had a new customer, I went on display: the obsequious boy in the body of a man, bowing and scraping and hardly daring to utter a word. And the very instant we were alone again, my father yanked off his clean white apron with a motion that set me spinning like a top. He'd take up a position in his big chair, half asleep and precariously nursing a cigar, while I swept the floor and swept it again and boiled water and poured it out and boiled some more and pelted down the street to fetch another batch of cigars and a newspaper and stacked up the clean towels and rearranged his instruments as fastidiously as some German bookkeeper.

Now and then I would study his case of medical tools—clamps, tongs, pliers, odd ominous forked things with forged screws and shining levers and handles of bloodstained oak—and I would pray that someone would come through the door with a toothache so that I could see exactly how these complex devices worked. But in all of the time that I spent in my father's shop, I was never to enjoy that good fortune.

One afternoon, the sweeping done and the instruments aligned, I asked my father if he would please show me how to handle a razor. He responded with a stricken look. "The apprentice must begin at the bottom!" he said, as if that were a lesson I had somehow missed. "Only by proving his devotion with the broom and the mop can a boy earn the right to take up the razor." To illustrate his point he chose the shiniest one from the table, flicked it partway open, and held it up before his breast like a lopsided crucifix.

Clearly, this was not going to be a satisfactory position for an impatient boy like me. And if the tedium weren't stifling enough, the instant my father had mentioned starting at the bottom my mind had gone racing down to the basement all over again. That was the place for me—down there underground, where the rats crawled and the roots erupted and the dead past lived.

I knew it then. I know it still.

*

FATHER MULLOOLY CONFIRMED IT for me at confession. I was accomplished at making confessions by then. I was nine or ten years old, as I've said, and I'd spent two or three years at large in the streets of Rome. Under those conditions, any boy who hasn't discovered a smorgasbord of sins is plainly lacking in imagination and drive. (My eldest brother, Mario, was in truth the confessional virtuoso of the family—but only because he had recently stepped across the threshold of puberty.)

Alas, though, my list that week was thin. Not only had I spent each day cooped up in my father's shop where the opportunities for wrongdoing were scarce, but I'd had to walk there tagging behind him like some oversized dog. What kind of trouble could I possibly have gotten into? Luckily for me, the Roman Catholic Church was well prepared for such emergencies. They'd devised so many kinds of sin that a man who'd been lying on a straw pallet with his hands tied behind his back all week long could have come up with something to confess. (I say this without exaggeration and from personal experience, for during my time at Sadler's Wells it was often my lot to ferry a certain Victor the Human Snail to some neighborhood church where he could make his own largely theoretical confession. I'd bundle him up in his black perambulator and off we'd go, the Patagonian Samson and the Armless Legless Boy. We'd stroll through the crowds with all the innocence of a mother and her infant child, but the things that he told the priests would have made a statue cringe. What an imagination he had! What a mind! Victor the Human Snail. I haven't thought of him in years.)

Occasions for actual sin notwithstanding, come Saturday I found myself in the dim little booth at San Clemente, whispering through the screen: "I've dishonored my father," I said. It was the best I could do.

"How so?" The answering voice belonged to Father Mullooly. I could have drawn any one of the Irish Dominicans who took turns hiding behind that screen, but this time my luck held. As a confessor, Father Mullooly was unsurpassed. First, because he had a special genius for helping a boy build a few small transgressions up into an edifice of evil. Second, because he generally went light on penance.

"How so, Father? Why, I scoffed at his work."

"Did you scoff out loud?"

"Oh no. In my heart." I knew that it made no difference. I was already a sophisticate in the finer points of sin.

"Why would you want to do that?"

"He's trying to teach me his trade, but I don't think I'm cut out for it."

"Barbering doesn't suit you?"

"He hasn't even let me try. Mostly I sweep the floors. Sometimes I run down the street for newspapers and cigars."

A little laugh rumbled in Father Mullooly's throat. "Custodian, errand boy, and tobacconist. That's not much of a trade. But it's something to fall back on, I suppose. In a pinch."

"I should make the most of it, I know." I bowed my head, perhaps a little too meekly.

"Sometimes that's easier said than done."

"But I've broken a Commandment."

"Which one? *'Thou shalt not sweep up the barber shop'? 'Thou shalt not fetch cigars by the handful'?* Please, Giovanni. You love your father. You're just cut from different cloth." He paused. "And believe me, you're not the first boy to have encountered *that* problem."

Never before had I found myself on the verge of failing so miserably at confession. So I gave up on my crimes against the Fifth Commandment and brought out the heavy artillery: in my desire to see my father unpack his surgical tools and perform some blood-drenched operation, I said, I'd prayed with all my heart that some stranger would stagger into the shop nursing a rotten tooth. How heartless I was! How cold-blooded! And hadn't Christ warned us that whatever kindness or cruelty we did to a stranger, we did to *Him?*

Father Mullooly didn't seem to be paying much attention. "Tell me something you liked about helping in the shop," he said.

"I hated it all. I was so miserable that I spent most of my time wishing a toothache on the Son of God."

"He forgives you. Trust me. Now *think.*"

I sat for a minute, as silently as if I were listening to Father Mullooly's confession instead of the other way around.

"There must have been something. The smell of the soap? The way the light comes through the window in the afternoon?"

I shook my head. I was obdurate. I was a confirmed sinner. I was all but beyond redemption.

"The people hurrying past your father's door? The women with their babies, the men with their loads of bricks?"

I shifted my feet.

"The stalls of flowers and fruit in the campo?"

He had the whole day to spend in that booth, and it was obvious to me that he was not above using it. So I gave in and made my real confession, straight from the heart. "They murdered Julius Caesar in the basement," I said. "I liked that very much."

Moments later, he had me doing my penance with a spade.

*

SOME OTHER DOMINICAN TOOK Father Mullooly's place behind the screen, and we headed straight for Sr. Monteverdi's toolshed. The caretaker dozed outside the door in the afternoon sun, muttering to himself at great volume, utterly unaware of our presence. We located a box of candles on a high shelf—Monteverdi must have required a stool to reach them, but it was no problem for me—and helped ourselves. Father Mullooly checked in his pockets for friction matches, ushered me back inside the church, and led the way down a set of stairs hidden behind a moth-eaten tapestry.

He tossed words back over his shoulder as we descended. "If you liked your father's cellar, you're going to love this one."

"I didn't exactly *see* my father's cellar, sir."

"No matter."

"I think it may be filled in with dirt."

"Precisely why God invented shovels."

I could hardly wait for Father Mullooly to show me whatever pile of dirt he wanted moved, whatever hole he wanted dug, whatever stone wall he wanted obliterated. I possessed the impatience of a boy and the strength of a man, an explosive combination if ever there was one.

A long and narrow storeroom opened at the bottom of the stairs, running what seemed to be the width of the sanctuary over our heads. It might have gone on farther, but our two candles didn't provide enough light to say for certain. The walls were plastered and freshly whitewashed at the near end, and as we moved along and our shadows leapt alongside us—mine adjusting the shovel where it lay over my shoulder, Father Mullooly's lurching onward into the dark with his unmistakable wooden gait—I noticed how the paint on the walls grew thinner and thinner until, about halfway along, it gave out altogether. Soon the plaster disappeared too, with a few last lackadaisical smears that still showed the hasty marks of a trowel. Beyond that point the walls were great square blocks of unadorned stone.

It was plain from the cobwebs and the rat droppings that no one came down here. The floor back by the stairs had been strewn with crumbling furniture, some dusty glassware, and a big damp sloping pile of broken-backed books, but at this end our footprints were the only signs of mankind's existence. Father Mullooly stopped when he came to a pile of crumbled limestone half as tall as I was. "My little hobby," he said with a wave of his hand, and then that same hand swept out to show me where the pile had come from. In the wall was a narrow slot just large enough for a man to step through, split at the top by a crack in the stone that gave the impression of winding all the way up to the sanctuary above. "Have no fear," he said. "That crack has been here for centuries. I've just widened it a little."

No sooner had I craned my neck to see if I could make out anything through the hole, than Father Mullooly turned sideways and slipped through it. "Watch your step," he called back as he disappeared, and his words were followed by a little scuffling noise that suggested he had failed to take his own advice.

As I followed him through, I was taken by surprise by an odd geometric transformation. First, I scraped my shoulder against a rock wall that jutted up where I had had reason to expect just empty air. Second, the floor upon which I stood was several inches below the floor in the hallway. It was as if the place I now occupied bore no connection to the place I had just vacated. The two of them were adjacent but completely without relation to one another, like two dead men long asleep in neighboring graves, and slipping from one to the other was like entering into some alternate world. To risk a single step in that revealed place—illuminated now by a third candle that Father Mullooly had lighted and set into a crevice in the rock—was to move willfully into a condition of unutterable *difference*. My young heart raced until I feared that I would suck the air from the room and extinguish the candles. Even puberty would never prove half so thrilling.

"Welcome to the fourth century," said Father Mullooly.

How did Michelangelo's heart sing when he first raised a chisel to a wall of mute rock? I know. What thrill coursed through Vivaldi's breast when he first heard the touch of a bow upon a violin? I know. For in that one instant the universe opened up to me, revealing my life and my love and my destiny. I was thirty feet below the known world, down where history keeps its secrets and time stores its potential. And I was *alive*.

I fear that the failings and filigrees of memory will prevent me from accurately describing the vista that opened out before my eyes. Can that dim subterranean vault really have surpassed any scene that I was later to behold—colossi buried to their necks in sand, mummified kings and queens buried in their gilded coffins, chapels built entirely of bone—scenes that it seems to me unfolded directly from that first dim chamber as if down a series of winding passages whose connections only I could follow? So it appears from this extremity.

If only I could return to that spot today, if only this ship upon which I have taken passage for Timbuctoo could reverse course and drop me at the mouth of the Tiber where I might make my way upstream and return to the sub-basement of the church of San Clemente, there I would happily surrender to the stomach ailment that has been my companion and my ruin since the day we crossed the equator. Let me meet my end where my life began, let me make of myself one more relic in that place of relics, and I shall die contented.

The walls were frescoed from ceiling to floor, huge images of saints and sacrifices gone black with age. Not a single painting was complete, and their missing fragments lay moldering on the floor, damp nesting places for the rats that moved audibly in the shadows. I looked up, squinting into the remote dark, and saw how on one side of the chamber a row of marble columns marched off into the darkness. Their regularity made me curious, so I took my candle and moved from one of them to the next with my little circle of light to keep me company. There were piles of rubble around their bases, some fallen from above and some heaped there by Father Mullooly's shovel. I kept moving ahead, trying to guess just how long he'd been working down here all by himself, until after a few more paces another wall materialized before me. There was a great eerie scene of judgment frescoed upon its surface, a dozen robed figures gazing out at me from the flattened and dimensionless past. Light bloomed around me and my own shadow rose up like a ghost as Father Mullooly approached from behind. I studied the wall and ceiling, hoping to discover another crack like the one he'd enlarged to give access to this place. I pressed upon the fresco with a tentative hand, knocking bits of it to the floor and sending Father Mullooly into a sneezing fit.

"You're right to suspect that there's more behind that fresco. I'm certain of it, too." He wandered away, keeping close to the wall. His candle bobbed with his unmistakable gait. "I've measured the distance between the columns, and it doesn't make sense that they'd stop there."

I prowled off in the other direction, studying my own stretch of wall.

Father Mullooly went on. "I've also compared the layout down here with the layout up in the nave. It seems to me we're less than halfway along, assuming that they built the new church directly over the old."

I looked over my shoulder and saw Father Mullooly's face draw near to the wall as if he were about to give it a kiss. He was squinting at something in the candlelight, rubbing at it with the index finger of his free hand. And after a few seconds he paused, took a deep breath, drew the candle back a bit, and blew air at the wall as hard as he could. Dust billowed up, and another sneezing fit brought him to his knees.

"Blast!" he cried, and it was by far the harshest language that I would ever hear him use. He crouched, balancing himself lightly on his fingertips, and continued studying the wall. "I thought I'd found a crack."

Another rat scuttled off into the darkness, and in his frustration Father Mullooly tossed a handful of pebbles after it. "Let's go," he said, rising to his feet and setting off. "Get your shovel, and we'll see if we can clear out some of the rubble from along the east wall."

*

IT WAS A WEARY LITTLE GIANT who sat at the breakfast table the next morning, my head full of darkness and my muscles full of knots.

Father Mullooly had pushed me to my limits, and then I'd pushed myself *past* my limits, and in the end the pair of us had removed about five centuries' worth of crumbled rock from beneath an imposing stone arch. By then we'd used up our energy and our candlelight, so we shouldered our tools and made our way back up the stairs. Father Mullooly rounded up a dinner of hard bread and cheese which we ate in the rectory kitchen without daring to sit down or even to touch anything, for we were both as filthy as coal miners. And finally, long past dark, he walked me home and explained everything to my mother. Would she mind my assisting with his excavations a few afternoons a week? There were saints on the walls down there, and martyrs, and something that was starting to look a great deal like the Madonna and Child. He promised that the exercise would be as much spiritual as physical. She gave us her blessing.

My father, I learned over breakfast, had different ideas. "I have great plans for you, Giovanni, *great* plans indeed. And they don't require you to bruise your knuckles like Samson amid the columns of antiquity." He pointed a finger at me, and it trembled like the palsied digit of a far less self-possessed individual. No customer planning to expose his neck in my father's big reclining chair that day would have been entirely comfortable to see how that hand shook. (At this late date I reconstruct the moment and wonder if perhaps he trembled not from ordinary anxiety but from some supernatural stress—for in likening me to that biblical

25

hero he was conjuring the future as surely as any of the Vestal Virgins whose temple Father Mullooly and I had hurried past the night before.) "The hands of a barber are tools of the utmost delicacy," he went on, concealing his own two beneath the table. "You must learn to care for them properly."

A boy of my forthright character might have wondered out loud why, in that case, I should be spending my days hauling coal, sweeping the floor, and fussing over buckets of boiling water instead of polishing my nails and practicing fancy maneuvers with a razor. But I was a respectful boy—we were all respectful in those days—and so I kept my own counsel. Besides, I had my mother on my side. Otherwise, how to explain the compromise that he offered without my even asking: I would stay on as his apprentice in the mornings and, so long as I passed along the complexities of my job to my oldest brother, Mario, and guaranteed that he would be out of bed in time to pick up where I left off, I could spend my afternoons underground with Father Mullooly.

This turned out to be a fine bargain for Mario, because the coal hauling and the cleanup that came after it had to be complete before the shop opened. All through the long afternoon I would picture him lounging there in my stead, inhaling the scents of my father's cigars and pomades, sweeping the floor now and then, leaning out the window and making eyes at the prettiest of the passing girls. But what did I care? Father Mullooly and I had come to a turning in the passage underneath the arch, and I was sure that any day now we would find ourselves behind that first frustrating wall, the one frescoed with the scene of judgment, the one beyond which the progression of columns surely led. Each shovelful might be the one that broke through. Each rock might be the one behind which lay an opening. Each subsequent breath might be drawn from air that had not passed through human lungs since the days of the Visigoths.

Sometimes Father Mullooly and I would stop to rest, collapsing upon a big block of limestone with our candles and a jug of water. He would give me a little lecture on some fresco or other, explaining how the arrangement of figures suggested this or that. He would tell me how some saint whose likeness I could barely discern had been hounded and scourged and finally martyred in the service of the Almighty. I listened only enough to report back home about the spiritual lessons I was receiving under Father Mullooly's direction. And then I'd race him back to the wall beneath the arch.

*

SO IT WAS THAT DAY AFTER DAY my brother loafed in the barber shop, smelling of soap and yearning after girls, while I labored in the darkness under San Clemente, smelling of rat droppings and scaling heights of yearning that Mario could not begin to imagine.

My father, of course, had a plan to change all that. "Tell Father Mullooly that you won't be playing in the dirt with him tomorrow afternoon," he called as I left one day. "Tell him you have an appointment to see his employer."

I turned in the doorway. My father sat in his big reclining chair, feet up, smoke from his cigar ringing his head like a halo in the sunlight that poured in through the door.

"An appointment to see his employer?"

My father clamped the cigar between his teeth and nodded once, just so, spilling a little avalanche of ashes onto his shirt. He parted his lips into a cunning yellow smile.

"What do you mean?"

"I mean exactly what I said. In case you've forgotten, we practitioners of the tonsorial arts tend to be a little more plainspoken than your theologians. We don't note which head is bowed in such and such a way in such and such a fresco in order to represent such and such an idea. We see a bowed head, and we inquire as to how much its owner would like taken off around the ears. It's as simple as that."

But I could tell by the way he held himself that it wasn't half so simple as that. There was bound to be more. So, as desperate as I was to run off, I folded my hands behind me and stepped back inside. "When you talk about Father Mullooly's employer," I began, "you'd be meaning..."

"Does the name *Gianangelo Braschi* mean anything to you?"

I had to confess that it did not.

"What on earth do they teach you at San Clemente?"

I had to confess that I did not know.

"Have you no sense of history?"

I protested that I did indeed. I allowed that my sense of history was in fact growing at a prodigious rate, although for some reason it did not include any information whatsoever regarding Sr. Braschi.

He extracted his cigar and aimed it at me like a brand. "This," he said, "is what you get for spending your time in church basements! All of those afternoons gone to waste, all of that digging in the dark, and still you aren't acquainted with the birth name of Pius VI, The Vicar of Christ."

I swallowed hard. "The Pope?"

"None other." The cigar went back in, and around it my father produced that smug yellow smile of his once more. "Tomorrow afternoon, at the stroke of two o'clock, my apprentice and I shall present ourselves at the Papal Residence—where we shall proceed to trim that blessed individual's most holy head."

My jaw dropped.

"This," he said, "is the kind of honor that God reserves for his beloved barbers." And then he reached for his newspaper, and I went flying off toward San Clemente.

*

"THE MAIN THING," said Father Mullooly, "will be to kiss his foot."

"Really?"

"Oh yes. Everyone does it."

"Should I kiss it right away, or should I wait a little?"

"Do it as soon as the opportunity presents itself."

"Will he lift it up so I'll know? Or will he put it on a little table or something? A footstool?" I imagined that the Pope must have special appliances for every purpose, including this.

"You'll kneel. For his part, he'll pretend that he doesn't even notice what you're doing. He'll be very offhand about it, as if it happens every day of the week. Which it does."

Aside from that, Father Mullooly couldn't tell me much about what to expect from my meeting with the Pope. It was as if I'd asked him what to do upon encountering a vampire or a talking fish or maybe even God Himself: garlic, three wishes, repentance. No particulars, only protocol.

And no, he didn't know of a single barber who'd ever before been invited to cut the hair of a Pope. And no, he didn't know of a single barber's apprentice who'd ever before been invited to go along. And no, he couldn't say how my father might have been selected to receive this honor—although Monsignor O'Toole might have had something to do with it. Long ago he had won Sr. Monteverdi the opportunity to muck out the stalls where the Swiss Guards keep their horses, although as Father Mullooly recalled it the adventure had not ended well. Monteverdi was already deaf at the time, and he had been so busy keeping his head respectfully down that he'd backed into a bucking horse, gotten kicked from the stable, and wound up bedridden for a month. (Had I noticed the crook in his back? That was a souvenir of his day with the Swiss Guards.) Once he was back on his feet, Sr. Monteverdi had begun to prize that crook of his as if it were a holy relic. He was known to hope—and Father Mullooly trusted that he wasn't giving away any secrets here—that one day his bent skeleton might prove worthy of being interred beneath an altar somewhere. Perhaps even right here in San Clemente.

We talked as we worked, down there in the sub-basement where I had come to feel so much at home, and Father Mullooly primed me with most everything he knew about the Pope's background. Cultivated as a prince and humble as a shepherd, Gianangelo Braschi was the son of impoverished nobility, born in Cesena, educated in law by the Jesuits. Had I known that just before entering the priesthood he had been engaged to be married?

No, I had not.

"It very nearly happened. But in the end, his fiancé took the veil."

I nodded like an old sage. "Once Braschi had made up his mind, what else could she have done?"

Father Mullooly leaned his shovel against the wall. "There's more to it than you might think," he said. "The truth is that *she went first.*"

He could see my quizzical look in the dark.

"She *preceded* him," he said. "The girl."

"You mean *she* entered the convent..."

"*Before* Braschi joined the priesthood. That's correct."

To a child of my innocence, the notion of a young man so lovelorn that he would seal himself into a monastery was beyond imagining. I have since learned, of course—I have learned time and again, through the educational power of my own first-hand experience—that love can cause a man to attempt things that are far more difficult than entering the priesthood.

*

OVER SUPPER MARIO DEMANDED to know why it was I, the youngest brother of all and the one who had declared himself the least interested in barbering, who would get to meet the Pope.

"Because he's the most impressive, that's why," said my father, and my mother seconded him with a nod.

"But look at those fingernails!" Mario countered. "And that mop of hair! I hope he can wash the filth out of it before you set off tomorrow." He rolled his eyes in my direction, but not in the same way that he rolled them at girls who passed by the shop window. Not at all.

My father drained his wine glass and sniffed. "Do you honestly think I'd let my son meet the Pope groomed like a barbarian? In the morning, I shall close the shop and devote all of my energies to making your brother fit to be seen in public."

I studied my reflection in the little kitchen window as we finished supper, deciding that he had plenty of work to do. My face was as black as the night beyond the wavy glass and my hair was blacker still, thick with a stubborn mixture of sweat and grease and grit. I'd combed it with my fingers, as usual. It would take a mad genius to make me presentable, and I feared that Giacomo Lorenzo Belzoni was just the fanatic for the job.

My mother put me to bed—she still put me to bed in those days, for within my oversized frame there still beat the heart of a little child—with a word or two of advice. "Keep your eyes open tomorrow," she whispered. "You might just get a glimpse of your future."

I assumed that she was talking about cutting hair.

*

COME MORNING, MY FATHER woke me early. He roused Mario, too, and we hurried to the shop at twice our usual pace, my brother complaining all the way. "I hate being up at this hour," he said. "I'm not supposed to start work until noon." The truth is that he'd been counting on having the whole day off, since my father and I were scheduled to be at the Vatican during the afternoon hours when he normally placed himself on display in the shop window. But today it was his turn to haul the coal and rake out the stove and light the fire and generally give himself an uncharacteristic but not entirely unbecoming (to my eye, anyhow) patina of grime.

I sat in the big chair, studying the text on various bottles of soap and tins of pomade, watching my father go about his preparations. And once Mario had the fire going and the water on the boil, Giacomo Lorenzo Belzoni started work in earnest.

I felt like royalty, I felt like a condemned man, I felt like a bride.

No hummingbird ever darted around a flowerbed with more fevered enthusiasm than my father lavished upon me that morning. He was everywhere at once, omnipresent as God Himself, and he could not have worked more furiously if he had been born with six pairs of hands. By the time he was finished I was a new boy altogether—a new man, more likely, since to judge by my stature I could have been his much younger and far more handsome brother—and Mario was agape in his spot by the window. I could hear the thoughts racing through his head: *What if one of the girls gets a glimpse of that brother of mine? How can I possibly compete with an oversized Adonis like Giovanni?* Fair enough questions, one and all. But in return I wanted to say, *Calm down, Mario. I am yet a boy, and I am interested only in digging my way through the sub-basements of San Clemente in the company of a wild-eyed Irishman.*

My father swept the cloth drapery away from me like Michelangelo revealing some massive sculpture, and there I sat in an unaccustomed cloud of talcum powder and perfume. On each side my long black hair lay fitted closely against my head like the helmet of a centurion, and in front it was pushed forward and up into a high cliff that leaned out over my forehead in the manner of a ship's prow—a style my father had adapted from images of the Marquise de Pompadour. Mario would have closed the shutters if he could, to keep the girls from looking in and spoiling his game. "Thank you, Father," I said, sighting down my nose to examine myself in the mirror. "Thank you very much."

We left Mario behind to tidy up, and set out for the Papal Residence upon a pair of borrowed horses. There was a stable around the corner from the shop, where the name of Pius VI produced a handsome matched pair on the condition that we mention the kindness to someone in a position of authority at the Vatican. Whether that authority might have to do with forgiveness, intercession, or the requisitioning of livery services, I cannot say. Regardless, I had never before seen the city from so fine and elevated a perspective. I would grow into this point of view as years went by, of course. Yet even today, as I pass through some bazaar or marketplace with my head a foot or two above the crowd, I recall that fateful morning when I headed off in a billowing cloud of talcum to address the neck of the Vicar of Christ.

We picked our way through the streets, galloped across the Tiber, and soon found ourselves at the entrance to the magnificent Piazza of St. Peter's. My father nosed his horse to the left around the edge of the mighty colonnade, and I turned my head to watch the central obelisk disappear and reappear between the columns as we trotted past.

A phalanx of Swiss Guards met us at an iron gate and helped us down from our horses. The most senior of them—a taciturn Sicilian with a furrowed brow, the hide of a crocodile, and a devilish black goatee—escorted us up a winding path to the Papal Residence, but after the first turning or two my father stopped short. "Wait!" he cried, striking his forehead with the flat of his palm. "I've forgotten my instruments!" He turned and started back, and then recovered the presence of mind to send me in his stead. "You'll find them in the saddlebag, Giovanni. And be careful! Even in their padded case, they must be treated with the caution you would reserve for handling your own life."

"They won't be needed," intoned the crocodile. He stopped me with an iron grip, and explained things to my father: "He keeps his own."

"He keeps his own instruments now, does he? The Pope?"

The crocodile lowered his eyelids to half-mast in a slow kind of affirmation, and then worked them open again.

"He keeps his own razors and scissors, his own Corinthian leather strop?"

The gaze that the guard fixed on my father was predatory, in a sleepy sort of way. He'd lost interest in me, though, and had let go of my arm.

My father kept on. "The Pope keeps his own porcelain shaving mug of the highest professional quality?"

Something passed over the guard's eyes that made them look even more lifeless, if that were possible.

"He keeps his own brush of the finest boar's hair?"

The guard looked dead. Furious, but dead.

"From China?"

The crocodile narrowed his eyes, took a deep breath, and prepared a speech that must have taxed him to no end: "What are you, Belzoni? A Protestant? His Holiness could *buy* all of China if it suited him."

He was correct, of course. And we saw the proof for ourselves as soon as we'd been escorted to the lavatory that occupied the uppermost floor of the Residence. The room was cramped in comparison with other chambers we'd passed, which is to say that it was only slightly larger than a royal ballroom. The ceiling must have been the height of ten men. Birds nested in the chandeliers, singing as we made our preparations.

"Where do you suppose they keep the coal?" I asked my father.

"Acquiring that information would be a task for the apprentice," he said. He was standing in the exact center of the room, thirty or forty feet below a crystal chandelier bedecked with sparrows. His eyes were half shut and he was breathing deeply of the mingled scents that filled the air: rosewater, oranges, floor wax, Egyptian spices, raw alcohol. It seemed to me that he was floating on a cushion of air.

I almost hated to interrupt his reverie, but circumstances demanded it. "Of course," I said. "I'll find the coal. But where, then, do you suppose they keep the *stove?*"

His eyes snapped open, and he spun to take in the entire room in a single pass. There were mirrors everywhere, a gilded wooden throne on a high pedestal, tall chests of drawers, a pair of golden basins, rank after rank of glass-fronted cabinets, and shelves stacked with enough pure white cotton towels to swaddle every babe in Jerusalem—but not the slightest indication of a stove. He charged from one corner to another, frantic as one of the rats in the basement of San Clemente. He flung back thick tapestries to reveal frustratingly blank plaster; he pushed at mirrored walls in case one might open onto a secret niche. I followed behind, wiping away his fingerprints as he went, and together we found nothing.

"Go ask the guard on the balcony," he said when we were done. There was a look of desperation in his eyes, for he would not have dared shave the humblest beggar without gallons upon gallons of boiling water. "Go!"

So I went. And before I'd even reached the guard's station I could see the answer coming up the stairs: an army of children, the tallest hardly reaching to my waist. Each wore an immaculate white linen robe tied with a thick velvet cord. Their faces were hidden in voluminous hoods, and in their hands they clutched rude wooden buckets filled to the brim with steaming water. Now and then a little would splash out and spill onto a bare foot, but the children knew better than to cry out. Silently as ghosts they labored up the stairs, half-concealed in a cloud of their own making. They looked for all the world like a band of imprisoned angels.

My father was behind me, standing on tiptoe in the doorway so as to see over my shoulder, watching the children troop up the stairs as if they were intended as his own personal salvation.

The angels knew their routine by heart. The first pair set down their buckets, businesslike as lawyers, and scampered over to a low cabinet. They pressed some hidden catches and the entire front fell away into a slot in the floor, revealing a gigantic golden tank that gleamed like pirate treasure. The two angels produced a small ladder from another cabinet, unscrewed a heavy gold cap from the top of the tank, darted back, recovered their buckets, and climbed back up one by one to empty their contents into the gurgling belly of that golden whale. After which they were off down the stairs for more hot water. Judging by the way they ran, there was not a moment to lose.

By and by the tank was filled to the brim, and the last pair of angels screwed the cap on tight. They returned the ladder to its hiding place and vanished down the stairs, but the room still echoed with the diminishing patter of their little feet and the air in the hallway was still hung with tatters of steam when the great man himself—his Holiness, Pope Pius VI—stepped through the door. He was all alone, a smallish peasant in an oversized costume that might have been a much larger man's pajamas, and he looked more or less like any of a thousand other men I'd seen shuffle into my father's shop. He was wearing a plain skullcap instead of his mitre, and so it was only by his cruciform staff that I recognized him. That, and the fact that upon his entrance my father dropped to his knees as if he'd been shot. I did the same, and we stayed that way until the pontiff urged us to our feet with a cough and little flutter of his wrinkled hand.

"Up, up," he said, poking at us with his staff. "I don't have all day." He shuffled toward the chair, and my lips nearly had time to graze his brocade slipper as it scuffed past my nose. But not quite! Father Mullooly had said the Pope would be offhand about the foot-kissing business, and he was certainly making a good job of it. I reminded myself that he'd had lots of practice, and I vowed to act more decisively when the opportunity next presented itself.

We followed him to the massive chair—it had a little catwalk built up all the way around, where we could do our work—and we draped him in billows of cloth as white as new-fallen snow. Between the drapery and his gigantic pajamas, he could have been the victim of an avalanche. He could have been an Alp. "Too tight?" my father asked as he pulled the drapery snug around the Holiest of Necks.

The Pope ran a finger around it in answer. "Is the water hot?" he asked.

"It should be. The children just brought it up."

"I hate to see them do that. Don't you?"

My father nodded and made a humming sound between his lips. He bent to assess the scissors arrayed on a little floating tray hung by the Pope's elbow.

"Such a waste."

I was bursting to agree—What a humanitarian this Pope was! What a gentleman! It was just as Father Mullooly had promised!—but my father only hummed some more and shot me a withering look over his shoulder.

"Honestly," the Pope went on. "By the time those little urchins have finally gotten it all the way up here, half of the heat has dissipated." He waggled his fingers ceilingward, as if he were casting a spell.

"Hmmmm," said my father, stretching the syllable out and hitting three or four different notes before he was done. He had apparently decided that this was the best way to deal with Popes.

"And no power on earth can speed them up. No power in Heaven can speed them up, for that matter. And I should know, shouldn't I?" He turned his head to give my father a wink, only to get a comb jabbed into his Holy Cheek.

My father steadied himself by pressing his fingertips against the tank. "I'm certain that the water will be quite hot enough," he said.

The Pope went on. "Not that I resent their being given meaningful work to perform, you understand."

My father added a little cluck to his repertoire, and then resumed his humming.

"They're *orphans,* you know." He rearranged himself under the mountain of snowy fabric, apparently hunting for signs of his slippers. "Did you know that they're orphans?"

My father selected a pair of scissors with handles of garnet and blades as thin as rapiers. "I am but a simple barber. I would not know the specifics of your Holiness's generosity toward orphans. But I must confess that I am not surprised by it."

Pius VI swiveled his neck and broke out into a grin. "You confess, you say? You're confessing? You're making your confession to the Pope himself? Not everyone has that opportunity!" He could still show the common touch, he still had a sense of humor, you had to grant him that.

But my father, bless his heart, didn't know what to make of it. So in desperation he pocketed the scissors, fell to his knees, rummaged under the sheets, and pressed his lips to the toe of the first slipper he found. The Pope held still for a second, the way I'd once seen my brother Lorenzo do when my father had bled his arm to cure a fever, until at length he could take no more. "That will do, that will do. I was only making a little joke, Signor Belzoni."

From my position on the catwalk, my father looked very small. He tilted his head up with an expression that was somehow both grateful and abashed at the same time. I vowed then and there—the Devil take my heathen soul if I was wrong—never to kiss that brocade slipper. Or any other, for that matter. And as a kind of corollary, I promised myself that I would one day free those imprisoned angels.

My father could tell that something was bubbling up inside me, for even then I possessed a face completely without guile. He stifled me with a glare, and once or twice shot his eyes toward the Holiest of Feet for my benefit, but I didn't budge. I merely held my ground on the catwalk, holding a soft little brush at the ready.

Three snips with the scissors, and the Pope's tonsure was restored. "Excellent!" he cried, although it could not have been more than twenty-four hours since his last haircut. My father promenaded around the catwalk holding up a mirror so that the Vicar of Christ could see himself from every angle, and with each step he beamed as if he'd just learned that today was his birthday.

"Monsignor O'Toole promised that you would do a fine job," admitted the Pope, "and he was correct."

My father fanned himself with the mirror. "Monsignor O'Toole? Really? I honestly don't know him. Not well, I mean. I don't know him all that terribly well."

The Pope nodded.

"Who does? There is his elevated position to consider, not to mention his age. Certain handicaps to intimacy."

The Pope nodded again.

My father bent a long finger backwards against his cheekbone and lifted an eyebrow. "Yet," he sighed, "One must assume that in the church—as elsewhere in the world—there are those who broadcast one's reputation. Whether one happens to overhear them or not."

The Pope nodded one last time, and rubbed his fingers indicatively over the stubble on his cheek. "He tells me that your wife's family has attended San Clemente for generations."

"Giovanni! The lavabo!" My father shook himself out of his reverie and thrust a finger toward the basin, where it lay beneath a gleaming gold spigot on the side of the tank. It was half-covered by a linen cloth that gave the entire affair an ecclesiastical aspect. Were we about to partake of Holy Communion, or to depilate the chin of an egomaniacal peasant? Was there any difference?

While my father got the shaving mug ready and laid out his tools, I folded the cloth and set it aside. Then I bent to address the spigot.

"Go easy, Giovanni! Just a little bit at first. Barely enough to moisten the soap."

His warning was less than necessary., for no matter how I turned the spigot—tentatively at first and then with mounting speed and desperation—the golden tank gave forth nothing. Not a gurgle. Not a wheeze. Certainly not a drop of hot water.

"Hurry, Giovanni. His Holiness cannot devote his entire morning to your incompetence."

Around the other side, out of sight of my father and the Pope, I struck the tank with my knuckles. I suppose that I was hoping to shake something loose inside it, but I got no response beyond a dull reverberation that quickly lost itself, thank God, in that big echoing room full of birdsong.

"Giovanni? Quit wasting time."

I rose up to my full height. "There seems to be something wrong with the tank, Father."

"Father?" repeated the Pope. "Father?" He spoke as if he'd finally seen something in this life that he didn't quite comprehend, which is an unusual experience for a Pope. He looked from my father to me and back again. "This individual, Signor Belzoni, is your *son?*"

"With apologies, I confess it."

"How is it possible?"

"God works in mysterious ways, as you know. Each of us has a cross to bear."

I was sweating furiously from beneath my upswept hair. The golden tank, for all its recalcitrance when it came to parting with water, gave off heat like a furnace.

"No, no, no," said the Pope. "I'm not questioning the boy's wit or ability. Not by any means. He seems capable enough."

Which I suspect may have disappointed my father at precisely that moment. If the two of them had united against me, perhaps then I would have had sufficient motivation to work the spigot.

"It's just that he's a giant!" said the Pope. "The son of a colossus, I should think. Not of a barber."

My father hung his head in a sheepish sort of way and then looked up from under his eyebrows. "Perhaps his father is a colossus among barbers."

The Pope spent some time searching for a knee to slap underneath those piles of white linen. "Excellent!" he cried. "Excellent, Signor Belzoni!" His little Alp shuddered around him. "With confidence like that, I fear you have the makings of a Cardinal!"

My father was too busy to misinterpret his remarks. He and I had fallen to our knees alongside the golden tank, and we were frantically studying its surface for a sign of some hidden mechanism that would send forth hot water from the spigot. We hissed at each other like conspirators. My father's forehead pressed against the tank for the briefest instant, and he came away with a gleaming red mark in the shape of a coin.

"Loosen the cap," the Pope advised when my father had regained his feet. He pointed at the tank with a hand that was cripplingly encrusted with gemstones. "That will release the water."

Embarrassment and frustration reddened my father's face until the burned spot blended right in. He hated not knowing everything in the world. "But of course, your Holiness. We must loosen the cap!" He turned away, struck himself in the forehead, and winced. "Giovanni! The cap!"

"But first make certain you close the spigot—to avoid a deluge."

I was well ahead of the Pope, however, because his initial mention of the cap had set off a series of reverberations in my young mind. Of course! Water could never escape from the bottom of the tank if air could not displace it from the top! So I had already fallen to my knees—the last time I would do so in front of him, I can assure you of that—and was closing the thing off as rapidly as my fingers would go. The science of hydrodynamics had unfolded before me. It had leapt whole from the convoluted crevices of my own mind, where it must have lain buried since the moment of my birth, hidden like the treasure of some lost civilization.

I leapt to my feet, loosened the cap, and bent again quick as a flash to open the spigot. Just as expected: hot water, and plenty of it.

"Careful, Giovanni. Not too much!"

But rather than dutifully closing the spigot, I drew myself to my full height, watching my father's face grow redder and redder as I rose.

"No more than half full!"

I crossed my arms across my chest and gave him a steady look.

"Giovanni!"

My disobedience was about to blow him to pieces, so as the water in the basin neared the midpoint I shot out one arm and screwed the cap down tight once more. The stream from the spigot trickled to a stop. My father's jaw fell open.

"That boy," cried the Pope, "if a boy he is, will be going places in this world!"

About that, he was correct.

*

THE WORLD BUZZED WITH POTENTIAL on my walk to San Clemente that evening. I could feel energy coursing everywhere, in the aqueducts ranged overhead, in the ruins hidden beneath the street, in the complex and unknowable design of Rome itself. I detected power in the way that the cosmopolitan city and the Arcadian hills upon which it floated had accommodated one another over the years. It seemed to me that they were doing one another's bidding, or that they were somehow in silent collusion, or that the pair had taken their eternal shapes in response to some force even greater than either one of them. It was a dark night in Rome—the red-roofed city lay huddled beneath an impenetrable canopy of cloud—and I have remarked already on the power that Roman darkness had over me. Yet on this night I felt something greater and more peculiar still, for my sense of the magical and the incipient had grown a hundredfold—thanks to my experience with the Pope's hot water tank.

Never mind whether or not God works in mysterious ways. I'd discovered that the entire world works under those terms—and the revelation had set me afire. It was all I wanted to talk about with Father Mullooly. I suppose that my juvenile single-mindedness was a blessing, after a fashion, for it prevented me from giving him the unvarnished truth about the pontiff as I'd encountered him in the disappointing flesh. I didn't even mention the squadron of children who labored up the stairs on his behalf every morning. I was all water and pressure and confinement and release. The stuff of magic.

Despite my talk, it wasn't long before we had descended the stairs and leapt over a river or two of scuttling rats and made our way to the crumbling arch where we'd left off digging. If ever there were a night for a breakthrough, this was it. And it wouldn't be long in coming. I bent to my work while Father Mullooly positioned the candles and laid out our bread and cheese. I thrust the point of my shovel between two likely-looking stones and applied my weight to the long handle, only to watch wide-eyed as—wonder of wonders!—the upper stone toppled backwards and vanished with a *thunk*. We fell to our knees and took turns jamming our hands into the opening, laughing like a pair of madmen while the candlelight danced on our faces and the square black hole yawned before us as unknowable as the future. Going backward and forward in time are alike, after all, except that charging into the past requires an act of will that is absent from the lazy drift of today into tomorrow.

Imagine how Father Mullooly and I would have looked from the other side, had there been living eyes to witness. One moment, nothing but utter blackness accompanied by distant footfalls, low talk, and a muffled scraping. The next, a burst of light from which a grasping arm thrusts out like the reanimated dead. Of all the terrors I have imagined or beheld in the subterranean world, I have never seen the like of it. I pray that I never shall.

Our arms were in up to our shoulders, and we could feel back there nothing other than bits of rubble, a stone floor exactly like the one we crouched upon, and the edges of the fallen block. We held up our noses to the opening, but the air of the past smelled no different from the air we knew: dust, antiquity, rat droppings. We reached a candle through the hole and peeped in after it, but it illuminated nothing beyond itself.

"As yet we see through a glass darkly," said Father Mullooly. That's the way it is with the Dominicans, even the best of them. Nothing in the world is sufficiently interesting—sufficiently its own wondrous and irreducible self—that it can't be made over into a metaphor for the Kingdom of Heaven.

As for me, I just wanted to break down the wall.

Father Mullooly had no time for my impatience. He was perfectly content to spend the rest of the evening tap-tap-tapping at the interlocking stones, studying the potential movements of their various seams and joints, watching while rivulets of liberated dust ran down cracks and leapt gaps and piled up at terminal points to form little deltas and stalagmites. Just now, he said, caution was to be our watchword. Having battered our way this far, having come within spitting distance of the Promised Land by sheer brute force, we'd now alter our tactics and move ahead by only the tiniest of increments. And he actually seemed to be taking a kind of hesitant, philosophical pleasure in it.

I stood in the dark, slapping the handle of a pick against my hand, wanting only to begin dismantling something. As messily as possible. There was rock dust on what remained of my pompadour, and there was yearning in my heart.

Father Mullooly removed his attention from the stacked stones, took the pick, and led me to a seat by the candelabrum. "What if you were to bring down the whole inner wall, John the Baptist? We'd be in a worse position than when we started."

A pile of rocks was a pile of rocks to me, orderly or not. I couldn't see the value in being careful with this one.

"What if so much of it crumbles away that we weaken the support for the church above?" He cast an appraising look into the darkness, counted off columns on his bony fingers, and did some mathematics in his head. "Unless I miscalculate, we're very near to the spot where your family sits for Sunday Mass. You wouldn't want your poor mother to go tumbling down into the abyss, would you?"

I had to admit that I would not.

"Very well then. Easy does it."

Easy did it for what felt to me like the next ten thousand years, while Father Mullooly calculated and paced and took measurements. He studied the wall from every angle: crouching in the center of the room, standing atop the big rock pile alongside a candle set in a puddle of wax, lying on the floor with his nose in rat droppings. He sized it up from the left and from the right, his frame sealed as tightly against the wall as a fresco. At one point he lighted another candle and held it near opening we'd made, holding his breath and turning his head away and advising me to do the same, while from the corner of his eye he studied its sensitive flame for telltale movement. There was none that I could see. Finally, he invited me to take up a trowel and strike the butt of its handle just so, at a joint among the stacked stones where there was something that was either a slight depression or a smear from his dirty fingers.

I did as I was told.

Nothing.

"Harder this time, but not too hard."

Nothing.

"Again. Harder."

Still nothing.

Father Mullooly stopped me with a look. He stroked his chin with his filthy right hand, giving himself a sudden and devilish goatee. "That does it. Our next step is to wait and reflect. Tomorrow is another day."

"Just one more tap?"

"No."

"Why not?"

"Because I've obviously chosen the wrong pressure point."

I held the butt of the trowel at the ready.

"We've made great progress." He grinned with a mouthful of teeth that were as wooden and ill-assembled as the rest of him. "More than enough for one night."

"But if you've chosen the wrong place, what could possibly be the harm if I tap it again?"

In this moment lies a profound argument against the Vow of Celibacy. Any man who had fathered children—the illustrious Giacomo Lorenzo Belzoni, for example—would have seen my argument for what it was and snatched the trowel from my hand. Not Father Mullooly. Father Mullooly didn't know the first thing about children and their wiles. So he took me seriously, decided I had a point, and told me yes, I could strike the wall just one more time if it would make me happy.

I drew back my strong right arm and let fly. Where I found such power I shall never know, but I do know this: from that moment forward, it has ever abandoned me. Something erupted in my arm, my shoulder, my back and my legs, and I struck that inner wall a blow sufficient to have thrilled Hercules himself. It came down with a roar and a mighty cloud of dust that set Father Mullooly to sneezing without letup—which was all to the good, may God forgive my insensitivity, because if he hadn't been making noise I never would have been able to locate him. We locked arms and plotted a course for the exit, and by the time we made the top of the stairs we were so exhausted—our tongues thick with dust, our noses caked and clogged, our breath coming in ragged bursts—that Father Mullooly put off criticizing me for another day. He didn't have the heart for it, and he surely didn't have the wind.

*

AFTER THE COLLAPSE OF THE WALL, the excavated room was so still that it might have been located at the stationary center of the earth. *How do I know this,* you ask? I know it because I returned four or five hours later in the company of my brother, Lorenzo—the second of us, known far and wide as *the tall one* even though he was at least a head shorter than I—and barely a particle of dust had altered its location. Lorenzo and I crept through the rear entrance of the church and down the stairs, hiding our mouths behind handkerchiefs like a pair of bandits, to discover that the room was precisely as Father Mullooly and I had left it. *Precisely.* The dust still hung like curtains, and it parted almost palpably at our touch. The light from our torches traveled not at all.

Exactly how we would clear the remainder of that collapsed wall under these conditions was a mystery to me, but I was young and I had not yet met a challenge that could not be overcome by will power and physical strength. I would make Father Mullooly proud of me. I would take up the work that he and I had left unfinished, and complete it to our mutual glory. And I would share at least a little bit of the latter with Lorenzo, too—or so I had whispered in his ear, encouraging him to climb out of bed and follow me through the black streets to San Clemente.

The two of us shuffled our way through the static dust, holding our torches before us as much to ward off colliding with some wall as to provide light, and as we inched forward something else in that caliginous chamber finally did stir. A rat—at least one, and where there is one there are always two, and where there are two there are always a thousand—scurrying over Lorenzo's feet on its way to God knows where. My brother gasped and froze as if he meant to become a part of that immutable scene for ever and ever.

"Come on," said I. "It's only rats. I'm surprised they haven't choked to death by now." I waved my torch in his direction and dimly illuminated him where he stood, grim and gray as a Pompeiian relic. "Let's go. We have work to do."

But I must confess that his alarm—and the rats' impossible persistence in the face of the choking atmosphere we shared—had set my mind working. The rats. Father Mullooly and I were forever working over and around and among them. But where had they been going all this time? And where were they going still? There must have been generations of them, more generations of rats than there had been generations of Irish Dominicans, all traveling the same unmarked trails down here in the sub-basement. I dropped to my knees and vowed that I would learn their secrets.

Their footprints were easy to track in the layers of dust, and I scurried along the floor as if I desired to become a rat myself. My brother, fearful of being left alone in darkness that closed in faster than you might imagine possible, followed right behind. The tracks kept near to the wall, and so did we. I was certain that at any second we'd blunder straight into an appalling nest constructed from rags and straw and bits of bone and furnished with several thousand years' worth of droppings. A piled-high rat metropolis built stratum upon stratum by generation after generation of industrious beasts. But no. We found nothing but more tracks along the base of the wall, winding deeper and deeper into parts of the sub-basement that I kept telling myself Father Mullooly must surely have explored long ago. Soon I was thoroughly disoriented, reassured only by the thought that we were leaving behind us a trail in the dust that would have pleased Theseus himself.

"Where are you taking me?" asked Lorenzo. His voice was thick, tentative, and muffled by the dusty handkerchief.

"We're exploring."

"You said we'd be digging. You didn't say anything about exploring."

"I changed my mind."

He was quiet for a while. We came upon a rat sitting idly in the path, frightened him away, and forged ahead.

"You have to follow your nose in these matters," I said over my shoulder. I was thinking of Father Mullooly, how he studied every crevice and blew air at traces of dust and sneezed himself silly when the past caught up with his lungs. But I was also thinking of the track before us, littered with desiccated scraps of fur and strewn with droppings old and new. If not for the handkerchief and its insulating layer of dust, I could have closed my eyes and followed that trail with my nose alone.

Until it stopped.

As abruptly as that, the tracks and their swirling accompaniment of fur and droppings simply ran out—or, more precisely, ran *down*. Down a hole in the rock floor, a hole as big around as my mannish fist, surrounded by clumps of nesting material and blackened around the edges by the repeated passage of the rats' greasy bodies. A bit of tail poked out still, but it vanished at my touch. Precisely where its owner had gone, I could hardly begin to say.

But this much I knew: he had gone *down*. Precipitously, irreversibly, astonishingly, inarguably, enchantingly down. No other direction could have captivated me so. Breaking through walls was one thing, but even at my tender age I knew that horizontal movement generally takes place within a fixed, if sometimes admittedly remote, present. Vertical movement, on the other hand—passage downward through the ages—was the thrilling stuff of dreams.

I stayed on my knees and sought out the joints in the floor with a finger. Working outward from the rat's greasy crevice, I soon traced clear the outline of an octagonal slab about three feet across. The other stones in the floor were rectangular for the most part, so this one was begging to be pried up and cast aside for the impediment to discovery that it was.

There were some markings on its top—a cross, I think, and maybe a circle with some radial lines emanating from it—but I have never had patience for decorative details. I stood, set the tip of my shovel into the rathole, and pried until the slab rose up with a harsh groan. I don't know what Lorenzo was thinking—I suppose he was just as thrilled as I was, and equally overcome—but as I strained away he gave a little exultant cry and dropped to his knees, jamming his fingertips into the opening as if they could possibly have supported even the hundredth part of that precarious slab. His movement startled me and I eased back on the handle for the tiniest fraction of an instant—just long enough for the slab to slip back down perhaps an eighth of an inch, putting Lorenzo's reflexes to a test that neither one of us would soon forget.

We took a moment to strategize. Then together we levered the slab upward again—this time by an inch or two—and stood there sweating, straining on our handles, our eyes fixed on that evocative black sliver of the past that yawned at our feet and sucked in our torchlight. The slab was elevated for certain, but now what? Mad with frustration, still a child despite my size, I gave my shovel a petulant heave. But instead of popping the slab off like the lid of a jug and sending it careening across the room—a handy trick that I certainly could have accomplished later in life, once I'd gotten my growth and laid my hands on proper equipment—I only succeeded in snapping the shovel's handle off at its base. The blade clattered to the floor and the slab fell back down, but not before its downward course had levered Lorenzo's shovel up and over like the arm of a catapult, lifting him into the air and hurling him against the opposite wall with a crash.

"That's it!" I shouted at his fallen figure. "We've got it!"

He rubbed the top of his head.

I shook the handle, now a mere denuded pole, directly at him. Heaven knows I never should have expected Lorenzo to understand the revelation I'd had—it was an almost religious vision, and an instance of the gift that would make me great—but you cannot fault me for trying. "This pole," I pointed to it as if I'd invented it myself, "is precisely what we need." And before Lorenzo could drag himself to his feet, I'd gathered up his shovel, pried up the slab, and kicked the pole underneath it to act as a roller. Another minute and the pair of us were gazing downward into a black and mysterious pit.

I dropped my torch into it and watched as it fell.

May God forgive me. The floor at the bottom of the black well at our feet burst into flame and came instantly alive with the dying screams of half a hundred immolated rats. I had found their nest after all, their age-old desiccated tinderbox of a nest, and I had inadvertently set it ablaze. May God, as I say, forgive me.

A river of rats poured up a stairway revealed by the fire, their coats aflame and trailing smoke, while Lorenzo and I stood helpless at the top and minded our combustible pantlegs. The confusion dissipated soon enough, and the conflagration died back, and with our trusty handkerchiefs keeping out the smoke and the acrid smell of death we ventured down the narrow stairs. My torch had been consumed in the blaze, but Lorenzo's burned on.

What we found below, at the end of a long passageway haunted by the smoking corpses of rats that had fatally miscalculated their chances of escape, was a sight that I hope I shall never see again (although I have surely spent the remainder of my life risking precisely that, as I have gone about unsealing one underground chamber after another on continent after continent). How else to put it, but to say that Lorenzo and I learned in an instant that the curled and smoking entrails of rats were not the only sacrifices to have been made in that vile place. Nor were they by any means the largest.

A vast hall with an arched ceiling opened at the end of the passageway, its walls ringed about with windows that in some remote time must have given upon daylight. A ledge ran along the margin of the room, supporting a few bowls and amphorae, and a set of stone benches described an aisle down the middle. The walls, which seeped water like the tears of the ages, were decorated round about with decayed and uninterpretable frescoes depicting scenes long lost to mankind's memory.

And in the center of it all stood an altar stained red.

Time and filth and rats had done their best, but the ghost of blood by the gallon was there all the same, streaming in frozen torrents over the rim and down the sides. The stained altar was cut from white marble, pure as snow, and one face showed a carving of some primitive god—surrounded by a dog, a raven, a scorpion, and a snake—frozen in the act of murdering an ox. He had thrust the fingers of his left hand into the poor beast's nostrils, and he bent its neck backward to plunge an enormous blade into its breast. Yet it was not oxen that had been sacrificed here—not upon an altar of that size and shape. Here, in the broad unforgiving daylight of a time long gone, men had sacrificed men to a terrible god whose name I'd heard only in rumors and ghost stories: Mithras, the ancient God of the Sun.

Lorenzo turned and ran, more frightened of an altar bespeaking the grisly past than he'd been of a cataract of burning rats in the present. Under other circumstances I might have let him go and lingered behind to pursue my business. But as you may recall, he was holding our only torch.

*

AT CONFESSION THE NEXT MORNING, Father Mullooly forgave me everything. The midnight trespass, the collapsed wall, the broken shovel, everything—right down to the slaughter of the poor blameless rats. For that, in fact, he thanked me again and again. And then he began to slide shut the panel between us, inviting me in a few words to accompany him down below.

"I don't believe I can," I said.

The panel snapped open again, and the silence behind it asked its own question as clearly as could be.

I gathered my courage for the space of a heartbeat. "I'm *afraid*, Father Mullooly." This was a confessional, wasn't it? What worse could one such as I confess than fear?

"You're afraid?" He let the word hang between us for a moment, and then gave a bitter bark of a laugh. He probably meant it to be encourag-

ing, but in the absence of eye contact it fell far short of the mark. "Our great big John the Baptist is afraid?"

"Yes, Father. I am."

"Of what?"

I didn't answer. I couldn't.

"Surely not of rats?"

"No. Not of rats." I cast my eyes about in the darkness, assessing the dimensions of the little chamber where I sat. The confessional fit me like a coffin. Beyond its walls, thundering out in every direction, lay the unknown. Discovering that your church was built on top of another church was one thing, but learning that that lower structure had an abattoir for its foundation was something else altogether—something shattering in the extreme. Today, I would say that in discovering that Mithraic temple I had brought myself to the very fountainhead of *mystery* itself, Christianity's ultimate terror and delight. An insight that cool and sage, however, is suited to an adult Giovanni Battista Belzoni, the reformed carnival giant and celebrated Egyptologist for whom death is no more than a familiar companion. But remember that I was a mere boy then, huddling alone in a confessional booth with the unknowable expanse of the sky arching overhead and the terrifying abyss of the past yawning below.

"I just don't like it down there." Could any answer have been less satisfactory? "I'm not even entirely comfortable up *here*," I went on, "now that I know what's underneath our feet."

Father Mullooly missed his opportunity to investigate the chill that had laid itself upon my childish heart, a lapse that confirms much about his character—chiefly that his interest lay more in the excavation of relics than in the cultivation of souls. What brothers he and I would make, were he still alive! "But Giovanni," he said, missing the point, "you've made an enormous advance. Our work has just begun."

I would need to grow up a little before I could see that he was right. In the meantime I remained adamant. I vacated the confessional, returned myself for the time being to the ordinary daylit world, and turned my attention from history to hydraulics. Father Mullooly couldn't very well complain, for I had been inspired by the Pope himself.

*

YEARS WENT BY, and each of my older brothers—Mario, Francesco, and Lorenzo—went off to study in one monastic school or another until I alone remained to assist in my father's shop. Thus did my childhood end as it had begun. And thus, drawing near to early manhood and finding myself swayed by Father Mullooly's never-ending entreaties, did I resume my dual daily routine—days in the shop near the Campo de Fiori, nights in the sub-basements of San Clemente. God bless him, Father Mullooly taught me not to fear the unknown but to drag it into the light and reveal it for what it was. The rushing of that invisible stream beneath the foundations of San Clemente—I swore that it was right there alongside me as I labored away amid the spent breaths and spilt blood of the Mithraists, that it was as close as my own shadow, just behind those weeping walls—the rushing of that stream reminded me of the upward-flowing river of captive angels in the Papal Residence, and together they set my mind working like a water pump.

PART TWO:

Water & Bone

"If the Capuchin brothers had had their way,
or if the armies of Napoleon had had theirs, vast portions of
ancient Egypt might rest undiscovered to this day."

— John Ray, Jr., *Unquiet Beneath the Sands*, Paris, 1955

*

THOSE WHO KNOW MY LIFE STORY better than I do would have me
arrive among the Capuchins with a dream of studying for the priesthood. This may have been my dear mother's plan, but I can assure you
that it was never mine. Oh, better to be a priest than a barber, that much
is certain. But better still to be a plundering hero—freeing captive children by means of cunning hydraulics, astonishing the masses with feats
of strength and daring, unearthing the treasures of the dead past by
sheer will and brute force. I realized even then, midway between twelve
years and twenty, that no school on earth would teach me these skills
and that I would therefore need to assemble them on my own—as I
have assembled myself, as I have indeed assembled this life of mine that
I spill out to you night after night upon the rocking deck of this warship
sailing beneath the Southern Cross —out of whole cloth. The Capuchin
monastery, that little cluster of low buildings just off the Piazza Barbieri,
seemed as good a starting place as any.

Father Mullooly accompanied me there on my first day, each of us
carrying half of my meager belongings in a sack. The sack that he bore

would have looked to you much larger than mine, had you been there to watch us go, because at that point I was already a head taller than he was and at least twice as wide. "We'll miss you at San Clemente, John the Baptist," he said as we approached the Capuchins' gate.

"Keep your eyes open, Father, for I could appear behind you at any time. I might even have a shovel over my shoulder and be ready for work." I spoke in a voice that had dropped two or three octaves over the last year, but the words themselves still carried the exuberance of youth.

Father Mullooly stopped, studied me from head to toe, and laughed his rickety laugh. "If you think you'll be getting free of the brothers for even an hour, you'd better think again. They'll have you busy from the Matins to the Nocturns, either on your knees in the chapel or scratching your head in the library. And when your brain is worn out, they'll set you to work in the garden."

This prospect didn't trouble me, for I knew that I had an infinite capacity for work of all kinds. Time, however, would prove Father Mullooly correct: As long as I stayed among the Capuchins I would never get far from that walled compound, not even for a minute. But it wasn't prayer and study that would keep me imprisoned, and it wasn't even the oversight of Brother Silvestro, that black-eyed conundrum whose acquaintance I was about to make.

It was the captivating power of love.

*

BROTHER SILVESTRO APPEARED at the gate the very instant I pulled on the bell cord, his hands hidden deep within the folds of his cassock as if he were concealing something. He gave me an appraising look that I felt right down to my bones. For Father Mullooly, he had nothing—not even a look of contempt—and he took the sack from his shoulder as if he were removing it from a shelf.

"Follow me," he said. "Brother Tomaso has been expecting you." His voice sounded as if it were coming up from the bottom of a well. He turned his back on the pair of us and began walking away, but he must have detected our four separate footsteps even through the thick cloth of his hood, for he stopped, turned his upper body halfway around just as slowly as death, and growled to no one in particular: "The boy alone will suffice."

Father Mullooly shrugged, clapped me on the back as if he were patting the haunch of a draft horse, and went on his way. I knew little about the rivalries that had long tainted relations among the various orders. Further, and more to the point, I did not know then that Brother Silvestro in particular would have been abrupt with my escort had he been the Pope himself. Looking back over my shoulder I saw that Father Mullooly was careful to close and latch the gate once he'd passed through rather than risk a wrathful return visit from Silvestro. As for me, I followed that mysterious individual to the office of Brother Tomaso, where he presented me like a prize he'd won but could imagine no practical use for.

The two of them were a study in contrasts, even though their cassocks and their haircuts—those little circular tonsures that make the tops of the Capuchins' heads look like so many foamy cups of cappuccino when you look down upon them from a height, as I did—were identical. Silvestro was small and lean, as if made to slink down cramped passageways forbidden to the rest of us. He had a sunken chest and eyes to match, the hooded black pair of them glaring at me from beneath a single brow every bit as thick as a shaving brush. He looked wasted but vigorous, composed of nothing but bones and evil intent, and he sized me up with a look that I hope I never see again this side of the undertaker's slab. Tomaso, on the other hand, was an enormous jolly cherub with a face as round and open as a cup. His age was unguessable, his girth unimaginable, his enthusiasm uncontainable. He wore his cassock with no more formality than he would have worn a bathrobe, and he was forever making adjustments to the way it lay across the vast expanse of his belly. Even now, as he heaved himself up from behind his cluttered table and bustled around to show me to a chair, he was unconsciously tugging away at the rope around his middle. I thought I detected a veiled look of disgust from Brother Silvestro, but I was to learn that if you paid attention you were always detecting a veiled look of disgust from Brother Silvestro. So it was hard to say what it meant, if it meant anything at all.

"Welcome, my boy," said Brother Tomaso. He smelled of fresh-baked bread and ancient sweat, and his blunt fingers pressed into my arm like so many sausages. "My, my, my, Silvestro—our young Giovanni is a big one, isn't he?" Tomaso took a step away from my chair and stood stroking his many chins.

"He's a fair enough specimen, that I must confess." The admission seemed to give him pain.

Tomaso outlined my schedule and duties around the monastery while Silvestro leaned against the wall and looked out the window as if he'd heard it all a thousand times before, which I suppose he had. Somewhere in Tomaso's litany—he'd reached the middle of my well-regulated afternoon, when I was to be knee-deep in the Old Testament with Tomaso himself—something in the yard caught Silvestro's attention and he disappeared, silent as a snake. "Pay no mind to Brother Silvestro," Tomaso whispered when he was gone. "He has some rather *specialized* interests, and the Abbot has found a set of duties that fit them quite well."

"Interests?" I asked.

"You won't have much to do with him. No one does, really. Except for the Abbot, of course."

"Duties?" I asked.

"Brother Silvestro is an *artiste,* after a certain fashion." And that was all that I could get out of him on the subject.

*

MY DAYS IN THE MONASTERY were full, just as Father Mullooly had predicted. If study and prayer weren't enough to keep me busy, there was always an abundance of chores—a superabundance, in the case of a specimen as capable as I. When I wasn't in the laundry with waterlogged Brother Andrea, I was in the kitchen with Brother Ruggiero, a tiny tyrant whose temper flared with the alarming suddenness of a grease fire. Heaving my body into bed once Nocturns were finished, I would hardly know where to let my overwhelmed brain come to rest: on the bits of the Gospel I'd studied with Brother Tomaso? on Brother Ruggiero's latest recipe for calamari? on the scientific principles that the Abbot doled out so parsimoniously that you'd have thought they were more precious than Bible verses?

For yes indeed, it was the Abbot himself who instructed us in the natural sciences—although he seemed more interested in describing how Saint Francis spoke with the animals than in helping us plumb the mysteries of the physical world. Time and again I have thought that St. Francis could have made a fortune at Sadler's Wells, on the stage where I first made mine. That great theater was also the place where I was first called *The Patagonian Samson,* for however much that information may be worth to you. Either now or after I am gone.

Science has never gotten a fair hearing from the Holy Roman Catholic Church. It fared particularly poorly, I can tell you now, in the hands of our Abbot—who reduced its sturdiest principles to a sticky ragout of superstition and hysteria. Still, I was just a boy then, and an authority figure was an authority figure. So I sat in his stern presence more or less patiently, and made notes as to the various miracles and dispensations that he insisted made the world go around.

How shall I have you picture the Abbot? Take the master of this warship of ours, and double his every quality. Where Commander Black is decisive, make the Abbot arbitrary. Where Black is resolute, make the

Abbot inflexible. Where Black attends to detail, make the Abbot petty. Physically too, feel free to make the Abbot our master's doubled self. Hawk-nosed for Roman, black-eyed for gray, hump-backed for bent.

He held my life in his fist for the better part of five years. In the classroom, he proved himself again and again a master of misdirection. "Why does water flow downhill?" asked one of my fellow students on a rainy morning in May, when the gutters ran like sluices and the flagstone walks jumped with raindrops and the garden out behind the refectory was an angry torrent.

"Because God wills it so," was the Abbot's airy answer.

I cocked my head to look out the window. You didn't have to be Sir Isaac Newton to see gravity at work everywhere.

"Then what of Newton's Law?" I asked, all innocence.

"God makes the laws," said the Abbot. "The sooner Mr. Newton learns that, the better off he shall be."

"But he's dead, Father."

"Just so." He looked up from under his eyebrows. "As you can see, God's laws prevail in the end."

At which point the bells rang out and all of us, the Abbot included, scrambled to find our seats in the chapel.

That morning's rain was the last we'd see for a long while. I remember wondering day after day if perhaps God, thinking I'd pressed my case a little too intently, meant to punish me by withholding any further evidence with respect to gravity. Certainly, as the summer wore on and the earth in the garden grew hard as the Abbot's principles, it was clear that the late Sir Isaac could have lingered beneath our apple trees forever without having a single piece of ripe fruit come crashing down upon his head. He could have died out there waiting, and the earth was so hard that we'd have had a devil of a time burying him.

The garden withered before our eyes. The Abbot ordered all of us— boys and brothers alike—to spend every idle minute running huge buckets of water up and down the rows in order to save what bits of it we could. Although I have mentioned that we enjoyed little enough time away from study and prayer, there must have been more of it than I'd thought, given how my arms and legs throbbed when I fell into my bed each night. A stone fountain stood in the corner by the refectory door, nothing like the ornate one out beyond our walls in the Piazza Barbieri but still an oasis in our bleak little desert. Brother Andrea issued us buckets from his laundry, and we flew to the task. Poor frantic Brother Ruggiero, whose realm stretched outside the doors of the refectory to encompass the garden, ran among us like the ringmaster of some mad circus. He'd thrust a finger at a scrawny tomato plant, then at the pale rusty stalk of a pepper that had clearly given up the ghost, all the while shouting at the top of his lungs that we boys must *save them, save them, save them.* His voice was high-pitched, desperate, full of apocalyptic woe. And in the end, it didn't matter what he said or where we slopped the water, for there was plenty of desiccation and death to go around.

The devastation continued without letup for the better part of June, until I devised a plan that changed everything. Including my own life.

*

MY PLAN REQUIRED ONLY the simplest of components: a dozen buckets, an empty barrel, a length of rope, and Brother Andrea's old dog, Trumpeter. The dog was feeble and nearsighted and practically deaf, a charity case if ever there was one. He was some type of hound, I believe, with a coat that was mottled and matted and nearly worn through at the joints. His favorite haunt was a hollow beneath an apple tree in the garden, and whatever color he'd once been, the years and the drought had bleached him to a uniform pale brown. If you scratched him, he would release a cloud of dust.

I drew out my plans and I showed them to the Abbot, who approved my executing them during the hours when I should have been attending his tutorial. "Perhaps you'll learn more out there in the garden than you've been learning in here," he said, with no trace of irony whatsoever.

Little did he know how much I might learn. The day I left his study with that rolled-up paper in my fist should be marked on every calendar, for on that morning the world became my classroom—and my studies would carry me clear around its circumference many times over. The little giant who strode from the Abbot's dim study would one day build a machine capable of draining the Nile, and never again would he stoop to confining himself to the limits of what smaller men choose to call science.

Don't misunderstand me, though; I certainly kept up my reading. A circulating library in London would one day introduce me to both the love of my life and Jean d'Outremeuse's *The Voiage and Travaile of Sir John Mandeville, Knight,* and I can't say which of the two—the woman or the book—affected my fate more profoundly. But that's a question and a story for another day, provided I live long enough.

On my knees in the walled-in garden, my nose full of dust and my long legs constantly in the way of clumsy boys who ran up and down the rows bearing water according to Brother Ruggiero's furious instructions, I set about building the pump that would save us all from ruin.

It didn't take long. I could sprint between the fountain in the refectory dooryard to the big poplar tree at the upper end of the garden a thousand times without tiring. My hands were stronger than any man's but still as flexible and fast as a boy's. (I could have become a famous escape artist, I realize now, had I not preferred using my gifts to escape from the genuine perils of a life dynamically lived.) My mind boiled so furiously with ideas and improvements that I'd completely redesigned the pump three times before the first components were up and another four by the time it was finished. I kept the plans in my head, except when I thought that a sketch or two might help wrangle me free of lessons with the brothers. The Abbot seemed not to mind if I spent all the livelong day on my work, and I could count on him to nod his slow approval if someone dared to offer me so much as a lifted eyebrow. I believe he was learning that he could count upon me. I believe I was an answer to his prayers, whether he liked it or not.

Day by day the pump grew. It was like a thing alive, expanding as I strung rope and mounted buckets, contracting as I rethought its geometry and dismantled bits of it in order to streamline its operation. It became my textbook and my teacher, that first ungainly water pump of mine, and at the end of each day I would set old Trumpeter running inside its roller-mounted barrel to assess how much I'd learned. The rest of the boys came to my aid whenever they could, taking turns greasing pulleys and tarring ropes and laying the courses of tile and stone that would soon direct the flow of water through the garden. I must have looked like their ragged king as they milled around my feet, fighting one another for the opportunity to do my bidding. I remember standing there among them, scratching at the beard that was beginning to sprout from my jaw and contemplating my place in the world.

It was at one such moment, during a pause during my hectic and heroic act of creation, that I first noticed Serafina Randazzo. How could I have helped it?

Serafina was the girl next door. She leaned from her balcony with her hands entwined upon her breast and a look on her face that was yearning and furtive all at once. I clapped my eyes on hers, and the fireworks that erupted would have been sufficient to burn down the garden had there been plants within it robust enough to catch fire. I was suddenly thirsty—thirsty and lightheaded and confused and dizzy as a ninepin, too; all of that and more—and so I bent to take a long drink from the fountain. When I looked up, she was gone.

But what an impression she had made! That first appearance of hers is engraved upon the backs of my eyelids even now. May God and my sweet irreplaceable Sarah have mercy upon me, I shall take it with me to my grave. Her hair was black and gleaming—in the bright Roman sun of that June day, it glinted blue as a distant glacier—and she wore it swept back from her high forehead and gathered into a bun at the nape of her neck. Her face was heart-shaped, plump of cheek and narrow of chin, sweet as some delectable pastry waiting warm in a display case on a sunny piazza. Her wide blue eyes kept secrets, and the pink bow of her mouth promised to reveal them when the time was right.

I vowed then—vowed as if I were a tireless knight-errant of old—that to earn the favor of that dear sweet beauteous and as yet entirely unknown Serafina, I would reverse time within the Capuchins' walled garden. I would reverse time and restore Eden.

From that moment on I worked with the fury of twenty men. I barely slept, preferring to be out in the garden making refinements to my machinery. I wore Trumpeter out with my ceaseless demands, and I scoured the alleys for strays to take his place. (I built a pen for them in the corner of the garden, and I kept them hungry as lions to be sure they'd run when I put them in the barrel and tempted them with some morsel on a string.) At one point I tore the entire pump works to the ground and rebuilt everything with the addition of a second barrel—I now had a limitless supply of dogs, after all—so that it could carry twice as much water.

Brother Ruggiero asked me one morning: "Will I have a garden left when you're through, or do you plan to let the machinery push it out altogether?" He was growing desperate. The food he'd been reduced to setting before us was pale and thin and watery, so much so that even Brother Silvestro—already a skeleton—seemed to be losing weight. Each time a tomato or a pepper came even close to ripening, thanks to the boys who still ran to and fro with their buckets, Ruggiero would pluck it gingerly and tuck it deep inside his cassock like the rarest of gems, which I suppose in a way it was. Each of us would poke cautiously through his soup that night in the candlelit refectory, hoping to find a scrap of it lurking there among the soggy coils of pasta.

Serafina watched my work from her balcony, and I swear that she too was dwindling before my eyes. I dared not look too closely at her or risk making conversation, for fear that I might lose my compass altogether, abandoning my work to linger instead over the sight of her luminous face, the sound of her musical voice. Yet in such glimpses as I permitted myself, I grew certain that she was suffering from the very same hunger that we residents of the monastery endured. No doubt her family's garden was as unproductive as ours; no doubt her mother lacked Brother Ruggiero's genius for making do. But how could I help? How could I save her? Even if our garden leapt back to life under my hands, I could hardly picture her father, the stern Dr. Luigi Randazzo, accepting charity from the Capuchins.

The answer came to me in a dream, and I rushed outside in my nightgown to set it into motion. A culvert, hastily dug beneath the wall separating our gardens where the trees were sufficiently dense to hide my handiwork, would let me share the monastery's soon-to-be abundant water with my famished love. And if someone noticed, I could build my defense upon either charity or erosion.

Other lovers have no doubt scaled higher walls, but none has ever outdone the Great Belzoni in the plumbing department. I put on another barrel and a third dog, just for good measure, and had the whole works going by the end of that very week.

*

AT FIRST THERE WAS MORE water than necessary. The parched earth was impervious, and rather than risk flooding the monastery—and the Palazzo Randazzo in the bargain—I reduced the power by at least one dog, sometimes two. The distribution system of flagstones and tiles worked perfectly, and during the first day or two I improved upon it by adding some movable tiles to act as valves and diverters. I even took a chance and lined the culvert I'd dug beneath the wall with bricks—the

Aquedotto Serafina, I took to calling it in my overheated heart—when I was certain that nobody was looking.

Soon we were over our heads in abundance. The garden grew like a jungle, as if each tomato plant were desperate to make up for the time it had lost, as if the peppers were competing to see which of them could produce the most succulent and shapely fruit. On the other side of the wall, conditions were the same. From time to time I would climb the poplar tree and hide among its leaves to watch for Serafina, and often as not I'd catch her father standing on his flagstones scratching his bald head and puzzling over the source of his good fortune. He was a medical doctor, with an office on a prestigious street many blocks away, and the workings of the natural world were a mystery to him. When he wasn't busy with his patients, he was bent over his books. The sudden eruption of new life in his garden took place while his back was turned, and for him it had all the qualities of magic or religion.

Enough about him, though. For soon, and almost by accident, I was to come face to face with his daughter.

Overwhelmed by the bounty of our garden, we had begun placing its excess outside the gate for the benefit of Rome's hungry. Transporting it there was another task that fell to me—rightly so—and a duty that I accepted most gladly. It became a kind of complex game or puzzle, the practice of which would serve me well in my years at Sadler's Wells and elsewhere. I would report each morning to Brother Ruggiero's kitchen door, and there discover such foodstuffs as he believed we could spare that day—bright round tomatoes and sturdy green peppers and fat purple eggplants all heaped up like a range of mountains. Out of a nearby niche I would draw a rough plank table and a set of interlocking wooden boxes and any number of baskets made of wicker, and from these pieces I would assemble a display worthy of representation in an Flemish still life. More to the point, I would create my masterpiece right there by the kitchen door, in the contemplative quiet of the monastery grounds, and then I would flex my knees and hoist it all—table included—upon my shoulders for transport to the street. Between my muscled frame and the pyramids of fruit silhouetted against the rising sun, I must have looked like Atlas bearing all of ancient Egypt upon his back..

So I must have seemed to Serafina, on that day when I approached the gate from one side and she approached it from the other. She bore a wicker basket of her own, heaped with the bounty of the Randazzo garden (courtesy of no benefactor other than me, for the Almighty's contribution, as far as I could tell, had been only to subject us one and all to the longest drought that Rome had seen in generations).

"Oh!" she said with a little gasp as I unlocked the gate. One hand went to her sweet round mouth; her basket tipped, and an eggplant fell to the cobblestones.

I blushed, for I realized that despite my highest intentions I must have appeared to her like some kind of circus performer. "Miss Serafina," I said, bowing slightly, careful to keep my burden in perfect balance.

"How did you know my name?"

"Why, everyone in the monastery knows your name." I was lying, of course. Her name was known only to a few, and I had sought it out with an obsession that bordered on madness.

She gave a nervous laugh. I recall it as musical in the extreme, unless I am recalling the birdsong that shimmered from the plane trees all around. The two sounds are mingled together in my memory. "You must think me a poor neighbor indeed," she countered, "for I confess that your name is a mystery to me."

"Giovanni," I said. "Giovanni Battista Belzoni."

"A name to conjure with."

I was unsure just what she meant, so I accepted it as a compliment. All through my life I have learned that this is the best course. "You'll forgive me if I set down my burden." I bent my knees and, muscles bulging, lowered everything to the ground. Her eyes never left me.

"Here," she said when I was finished. "These are for you." She held out the basket.

"For me?" I admit that I was confused for a moment. It was possible, even likely, that she intended them as payment for bringing her family's garden back to life. But she clarified her intentions quickly enough.

"For your charity work," she said, nodding toward the table. "We have more than we could ever eat...Giovanni."

My heart stopped at the sound of my name upon her lips. A single beat, a single breath would have been enough to ruin everything. A single tick of the clock would have been sufficient to destroy the world.

Having reversed time, you see, I now desired to stop it altogether. But it was not to be so. Life moves forward, always forward, until you find yourself on the deck of a warship bound for Africa with a belly full of disease and hardly enough breath to tell your own story.

*

EACH MORNING FROM THEN ON, we met at the gate. And each afternoon, as I tinkered away in the garden, she scrutinized me from her balcony like some self-assured naturalist. Her shrinking violet days were over. I fascinated her, and eventually it came out that I'd hurt her feelings by committing at our first meeting a number of offenses so ephemeral that even now, as a mature and worldly gentleman uncommonly attuned to the sensibilities of others, I have trouble describing them with complete accuracy.

Her heart had leapt, for example, when I'd let slip that I knew her name. But an instant later I had crushed her by saying that the information was common knowledge around the monastery, suggesting that I knew her identity as I would have known the identity of a beggar in the alleys or a streetwalker in the piazza. She could not have guessed that a boy like me could always be counted upon to deliver a bashful lie in such a trying circumstance. An innocent herself, she'd been hoping for the unvarnished truth—a confession that I had indeed plotted like a Medici to learn her name, and that now that I had it I lay awake each night reciting its musical syllables like an incantation. But I had been too shy to reveal the truth. I had chosen to feign indifference, when nothing short of madness would have sufficed to achieve my aim. Such are the ways of young love.

Have I mentioned that Serafina was a tiny thing, even smaller and more delicate than she looked behind her balcony rail? The top of her head barely reached the center of my chest. I found myself hunching over a little each time we met, diminishing myself in her service.

"Stop doing that!" she said to me one day.

"Stop doing what?"

She pointed at my shoulders. "Hunching over like that. You look like a gorilla."

I squatted down next to the table instead, my back to the wall, and she took a seat beside me on an overturned basket. In this way we were leveled out, shoulder to shoulder, in an arrangement we came to adopt with the familiarity of an old married couple.

"My father's very interested in you," she said.

"Your father? What have you told him about me?"

"That you're one of the nice boys who study with the Capuchins next door. That you're a genius with machines and water. That the brothers don't seem capable of educating you."

All true, all true.

"He says you're a giant. Or if you're not a giant already, then you're fast on the way to becoming one."

My feelings were hurt. "So I'm a curiosity."

"In a way, I suppose."

"Hmmph." I chewed on my lower lip.

"Being a curiosity isn't so bad. I've been curious about you ever since the day you first arrived at the monastery."

"Really?"

"You weren't like the other boys, that's for certain." She drew the toe of her shoe across the dust in the walkway. Growing up alongside the monastery, Serafina hadn't had much else to keep her occupied. At first, too small to see over the garden wall and too young to care, she'd focused her attention on the natural world outside her door: the flowers, the vegetables, the bees, the birds. She became a little calendar and clock, tuned to nature's cycles of blossoming and dying. But the world grew larger as time passed, and soon her curiosity reached beyond her garden walls. The monastery, luckily for her, proved to have all the bustling and complex appeal of an apiary. There stood Brother Andrea, hanging out the wash. There went Brother Ruggiero, his arms laden. Here came Brother Tomaso, hot on his heels, angling for a treat before suppertime. And back there among the shadows slunk Brother Silvestro, up to no possible good.

Silvestro in particular fascinated her from the start. He was always lurking just at the edge of her vision, and spotting him soon became a game for her, as if he were a figure sewn so cunningly into a tapestry that his sandals were a bundle of sticks, his cassock a pile of fallen leaves, the hooked nose beneath his hood the beak of an owl within its rotten tree-trunk. Why was he always scrubbing his hands in the fountain? What was the white powder that coated his arms, making the narrow pair of them look like bones when he drew back his sleeves? He was a man of mystery, and there was no understanding him from externals.

In the end, it was I and not Serafina who learned first-hand the truth about Silvestro.

The opportunity came courtesy of our gray and hunch-backed Abbot, who approached me as I sat talking with Serafina one morning. He shuffled through the gate on sandaled feet in his cunning impersonation of piety, plotting all the while to change my life for the worse. He waggled a finger in my direction. "Do you know what they say about idle hands, Giovanni?"

"Yes, Father."

"Then come with me." He crooked the finger he'd pointed at me, let it quiver in the air for a second, and then drew it back into the folds of his cassock.

I was on my feet in an instant.

The Abbot nodded once toward Serafina, his hood barely moving. "Good day, my dear." Anyone with ears and eyes could have told you that he didn't mean to wish her anything even resembling a good day. He looked at her as if she were a fish gone belly up in the Tiber.

Serafina, to her credit, rose gracefully, bowed her head just the slightest, and bade the Abbot to go with God. She'd surely have preferred that to his leaving with her friend Giovanni. But things took their own course, and the two of us abandoned her there in the street, and within a few moments the Abbot had delivered me into the chalk-white hands of Brother Silvestro.

We located him by a route that took us into an alleyway at the little-visited rear of the monastery, through a stubborn and mossy door that shrieked as if it were being murdered, and down a tunnel that led, surprisingly enough (I'd thought I knew the premises by heart, for I had been living there for the better part of a year, but as we shall see, I still had plenty to learn) into a secret chamber behind the altarpiece. The room was high and cluttered and dusty, a disturbing sort of a trash heap littered all over with moldy books, the burnt misshapen ends of candles, and castoff robes and tapestries within the folds of which mice had made themselves at home. Almost out of sight in such dim light as filtered in from far overhead, fetched up in a corner like a discarded plaything, lay a battered censer. I had but an instant to take it all in, because the Abbot didn't pause for a moment. He tugged on a rope that dangled from the ceiling, put his hand into a little recess in the wall, and turned something that produced a muffled clanking in the distance. A door appeared before our eyes, its edges resolving from the wall like an apparition. One pull and it was open, two steps and we were past it, one last tug and we stood in absolute darkness. Or more precisely we walked in absolute darkness. And we walked briskly, for nothing slowed the Abbot.

The going was hard, and I stumbled over some piece of trash or wreckage with about every third step. As months went by I would learn to shuffle my feet through this passage as the Abbot did, a technique that I would call upon more than once in the strewn tombs of the pharaohs, but on this first journey I careened through the mess like some ungainly force of nature—until all at once I lost my footing and tumbled head-first into a pile of something that crashed about me like shattering crockery.

"Now you've done it," said the Abbot.

Before I could even come to a sitting position and commence to rub my throbbing head, a light sprang upon us from out of the darkness. It was another door, appearing from nowhere just as the first had, a sharp angular gleam of light defining its edges for a second and then leaping out everywhere. Along with the light came a sound like savage thunder, the offended voice of Brother Silvestro.

"Good God!" his black silhouette shouted at me, at the Abbot, at the world. "You'll wake the dead!"

In this assessment he was more correct than I should have liked to believe.

*

I FOUND MYSELF INTERRED beneath a cataract of skulls.

Hundreds of them, thousands of them, they had conspired to bury me and make me one of their own. Their crumbling teeth slid down the pile in streams; their dreadful jawbones, irrevocably separated, clattered and mingled and lay still wherever gravity let them rest. And their surging, billowing dust—the living particles of centuries gone—caught in my throat and filled up my nose and threatened to choke me to death.

"Cheer up, Belzoni!" you say. "It was high time you got accustomed to that kind of thing, given the course that your career would take." Probably so. But it was a rude introduction all the same.

The Abbot rolled his eyes at Silvestro and lifted his shoulders in an apologetic shrug. "I've brought your new assistant, such as he is." He then turned his attention to me, compressing his features into a look that was far less companionable. "On your feet, boy. Don't let your precious *gravity* get the best of you."

Did I argue? Did I observe that in the world as he understood it I had plunged into that mountain of skulls as the direct and unmediated result of God's will? No, I did not. Instead I coughed into my fist, regained my feet, and began slapping the dust of the ages from my trousers.

"Don't bother," said Silvestro, his eyes shining under his single black brow. "It'll get worse before you're through."

"Your first chore," said the Abbot, "will be to re-stack those poor old bones." He looked over my shoulder, the expression on his face growing tender.

I turned to look behind me, and I saw that the entire wall—rising all the way to the twelve-foot ceiling, stretching as far into the darkness as I could see in either direction, and layered five or six deep or more—was nothing but stacked skull after skull after skull. Each was different from the others. Each had its own peculiarities, almost its own character. In fact I would have very nearly said that each of those fleshless visages had a personality, even those that had tumbled down from the wall and nearly buried me. I dreaded picking them up. I dreaded thrusting my hands into their empty eye sockets. I dreaded coming to *know* them so intimately.

"There'll be time for cleaning up," said Silvestro. He stood before me stroking his chin as if it were a cat, narrowing his eyes at the stacks of skulls I had freshly revealed. "Right now," he said, "I do believe that this young miscreant has done us all a favor."

The Abbot cocked his head.

Silvestro grew animated. He lifted the hem of his cassock and shot toward a wall of raw bones that had not been exposed in years, in decades, in lifetimes. He went straight to one skull in particular that had claimed his attention, a huge misshapen and sideways-leaning monstrosity with a gaping hole in its syphilitic brow. Without hesitation he thrust out his hand and grabbed the thing's jawbone, wrenching it loose with a clatter of falling teeth.

"Perfect!" he shouted, raising the jawbone like a prize. "Come with me, boy." He flew past as if his cassock were on fire, and the Abbot and I chased him through the doorway.

The low room beyond was nearly as wide as it was long, and the scene within it was apocalyptic. Bones perched on tables and chairs, bones sloped on the floor in great precarious piles, bones lay in ragged heaps upon tables and shelves. A tall basket held a bouquet of leg bones arrayed like so many umbrellas in a stand. Bucket after bucket of castoff bits stood here and there, some tipped over and spilling out their contents like treasure. And over everything lay a thick dusty blanket of pulverized bone, ground tufa, and fine sand. Silvestro's cassock threw up a storm of it as he dashed across the room to a workbench lighted by candelabra.

"Behold!" He indicated an object that consisted of a half-dozen stacks of vertebrae arranged on a flat square of stone. He studied it from every angle, squinting and pursing his lips, sighting down his long nose and angling the jawbone this way and that against the array of bones already in position. Finally he found the spot he'd had in mind, and he pressed it into place with a precise and satisfying snap. "Exactly what I was looking for, Belzoni! None of these *others* would do." He gave a dismissive wave of his hand, and I saw that scattered all around his feet were so many discarded jawbones that it looked as if the floor meant to gobble him where he stood.

A few quick turns with some cord, a knot in a long rope, and Brother Silvestro was dangling his handiwork in the air before me. He grinned. "What's the matter, boy? Haven't you seen a lantern before? Use your eyes!"

Use my eyes I did, and I saw that the workshop—for a workshop it clearly was—was even more dense with bones than I had noticed at first. The sconces on the walls were skulls whose eyes flickered. The candelabra were stacked ulnae. Upon the workbench Brother Silvestro's various tools leaned as orderly as you please against a pair of pelvises, and long sturdy femurs supported both the worktable and the stools.

This would require some accommodation on my part.

But even stranger than my surroundings, even farther beyond the pale, was the complete shift in Brother Silvestro's demeanor. Irritable and furtive above ground, down here he was content, happy, even playful. I had never seen the like of it. He danced away with the lantern and hung it in a corner. "You, my boy, are my lucky charm." He said it over his shoulder, but I could imagine the look in his eye.

"Careful now, Silvestro," said the Abbot. "Don't blaspheme."

"Then he's a gift from God. And it's about time. That last boy you brought down here was worthless."

"Who was assigned here before me?" I couldn't imagine. I'd seen no one but Silvestro wandering the grounds dusted all over with powdered bone and ground lime.

"This was a very long time ago," the Abbot put in. "Many, many years. Brother Silvestro has a long memory."

"That's all in the past," Silvestro reassured me. "And you can be certain that I've repaired the damage, good as new." He paused and measured me with his little black eyes. It was the very same look he'd given me in Brother Tomaso's office so long ago, and it gave me the very same shiver. "I can see that you have quite a reach, eh? That will prove most useful."

I couldn't tell if he were picturing me fetching bones and hanging lamps, or if he were anticipating the day when he could make a hatrack out of my component parts. As long as I was down there in his employ I would never learn what had become of my predecessor, but there was sufficient evidence that some of the bones lying about were fresher than others to keep me on my guard. From that day forward I had no higher aim than to keep Brother Silvestro happy.

"Come," he said to me. "I will show you marvels."

Tapers burning in our fists, the two of us ducked through a doorway. Silvestro capered ahead, lighting candles as he went, and as the room slowly bloomed with light it was as if he were drawing back a curtain. We were in a disturbed graveyard, with skeleton after skeleton arrayed on the floor amid piles of dirt as if they had been surprised in the act of climbing up from their graves. Their disarticulated bones swirled and danced across the floor in artful arabesques, attenuating and merging until you couldn't tell where one skeleton left off and the next began. The walls themselves pulsed with eddying, hypnotic patterns composed of digits, kneecaps, socketed joints, and teeth, all of them cemented there with mortar concocted in Brother Silvestro's workshop. Around the corner at the far end of the room, down a little passageway where you least expected it, was the most unsettling display of all: a pair of skeletons laid out wearing cassocks and clutching rosaries in their bony fists, surrounded and supported and surmounted by an architectural arrangement of skulls, thousands of them, intricately stacked, peering at us from the emptiness of their ancient implacable eye sockets.

These bones spoke to Silvestro, you see, because what Brother Tomaso had said was true: Silvestro was an artist of sorts. He was an artist of death. And I had yet to see his masterpiece.

"Oh, that's nothing," he said as he caught me gaping, and then he vanished down a little corridor and through a slit in the wall. I tumbled after him—the crack was a tight fit for me, but I didn't care to be left alone with all of those fleshless faces—and staggered out into a nightmare of the highest order. Where the resurrection scene in the first room had been disconcerting and the tableau in the passageway had been unsettling, the scene in this room was absolutely appalling. Arches made of ribs and long leg bones ran from floor to ceiling, buttressing the roof with the stuff of death itself. A handful of those now-familiar chandeliers—cobbled together of vertebrae and jawbones—dispelled the gloom and replaced it with something far worse. And above it all, cemented into the middle of the ceiling where the sweep of the arches instantly drew the eye, was Silvestro's most astonishing creation: a likeness of the Grim Reaper, his face a human skull and his bones the bones of a hundred unlucky Capuchins (one leg was longer than the other, I noticed, and the ribs were clearly of differing vintages). In his hands he wielded a scythe made of tapering tailbones, sharpened one by one to razor thinness.

"It isn't quite finished," said Silvestro. "But you get the idea."

*

FOR THIS I HAD TRADED AWAY SERAFINA—but not entirely.

The summer soon began to wane, and there were still some apples left on the trees, and each afternoon when I emerged from Silvestro's chambers of horror—painted to my elbows and knees with white powder, white powder streaked across my face and clumped in my hair—I looked through their branches to catch Serafina looking my way from her balcony. She'd lift herself up on tiptoe and lean out over the railing, and I'd raise my dripping hands from the fountain, shake my wet head like a dog, and grin back.

Oh, the life embodied by that girl! It thrilled me more than ever, now that my mind held the vistas of Brother Silvestro's mad cemetery for contrast.

For that was what he was building, after all: a miraculous and mad cemetery, where the bones of the monastery's dead—thousands upon thousands of them, given up over centuries—were disarticulated and remade into a single great seamless sweeping testament to death. What exactly was in his mind? We can never know, and Brother Silvestro is not alone among men in withholding that power from us. Suffice it to say that he awoke every morning thinking of death and how he might immortalize it, and that he began each day in his workshop with a gleam in his eye and a song in his heart. Often I found him whistling over his worktable when I arrived, his exhalations stirring up little eddies of dust.

"Not a word about this to a soul," he'd told me, and he meant it. He wasn't entirely comfortable with the Abbot's occasional visits, much less with the idea that I might leak some of his secrets to the outside world. "Others must know of our work only when we have completed it," he said. "Even if it takes all of my lifetime. Even if it takes all of yours."

So what did I tell Serafina when she asked? I lied, and fell back on the familiar routine from my days at San Clemente. "We're excavating," I said. I told her the story of my boyhood days underground just as I have told it to you, except with Brother Silvestro playing the role of Father Mullooly. It explained my exhaustion (more spiritual than physical these days—so many twisted backbones, so many empty skulls), along with the dust that covered me from head to toe.

We'd meet out by the gate when we could, and I'd squat as I always had alongside the table where a few apples and a handful of late tomatoes would remain from the day's bounty. One evening, as we were watching the light die in the west, a youth came strutting by—I say a youth because I was a youth, and he was about my age—a certain youth came by, as I was saying, an arrogant and haughty youth by the look of him, and although he was dressed in the manner of a gentleman he helped himself to an apple.

"Those are intended for the poor," I said.

"I can assure you that I am poor in spirit," he answered. "Does that qualify?" He kept right on walking, and as he did he took a great juicy bite clearly meant to render our disagreement moot.

I unfolded myself behind him like a pale shadow, and caught up to him in two of my oversized paces.

"Giovanni..." Serafina warned from her seat on the basket. She thought I meant the youth harm.

"Excuse me, friend." I tapped him on the shoulder hard enough to make him flinch.

"Don't be presumptuous." He kept walking and took another bite, his cheeks ballooning out like a rodent's. "I'm no friend of yours."

I was undeterred. "Judging from your fine clothes," I said, "I'd say that there are many in Rome who have more need of charity than you." I held out a hand, a hand so large that he could have put three or four apples into it, indicating my desire to have that particular apple back regardless of its condition.

"I don't accept charity," he said, still chewing. "I do, however, take what I desire." I could swear that just then he cast an ominous glance at Serafina.

"Sir," I said, "you truly *are* poor in spirit."

"Then I shall see God."

"Perhaps you shall see him sooner than you'd like." I loomed over him.

"Fine," he said with a sneer, turning theatrically on a polished heel and depositing the apple core into my hand. "Have it your way." He strode back to the table and spilled out upon its surface a handful of coins. "Incidentally," he said as he turned to go, this youth whose spittle was even then pooling in my palm, "your hands are positively filthy. I really don't think you should be handling food. Not even for the poor."

Thus ended my first encounter with Bernardino Drovetti. I regret to say that it was not to be my last.

*

BROTHER SILVESTRO HAD ONE LAST THING to accomplish in that vaulted room before he moved on to the next empty chamber. He wanted to build an enormous clock face made of bones.

"Perhaps you might be overworking the point?" I was certain that any eventual visitor would take Silvestro's morbid meaning without the need for such reinforcement.

But once Silvestro got an idea in his head, he was unstoppable. "Hardly," he said. "In fact, I've been thinking about an hourglass, too. We could set some of this ground bone running between a pair of glass globes, suspend the whole of it within an armature of femurs…"

I must confess it: his mania had a way of igniting mine. "Perhaps you should consider an entire *room* of timepieces, then. I can see it. A Japanese water clock in one corner, a Greek stereographic mechanism in another. Your clock face and hourglass in the remaining two. And in the center…"

He leaned forward upon his stool, all ears and imagination.

"…in the center, in a place of honor lit by candles in mirrored holders, up on a high pedestal…"

"Yes, yes?" said Silvestro.

"…we'd stack a thousand vertebrae into a single giant gnomon."

His look interrogated me.

"On a sundial. It's the part that stands up."

"You're a genius, boy." He clapped his hand upon his knee. Dust billowed.

"And how about a pocket watch? We could assemble it of inner ear bones, but we'd need a magnifying glass."

Silvestro sat back, dazzled. "I must say you've given me plenty to think about."

So what if he was a lunatic? So what if he was possessed by a weird and unwholesome obsession? Every time I entered his magnificent cemetery I gained new appreciation for his devotion and his energy. And

I could tell, especially after I dreamed up the Room of the Passing Hours, that he was beginning to favor me too.

We set to work on the clock face right away. Silvestro had long since decided that too much advance planning was a liability in his line of work. He made everything up as he went along, acting as the spirit inspired him, using such raw materials as presented themselves. "Not that you couldn't do things differently when I'm gone," he said ominously. "You and your grand ideas."

I imagined myself carrying on his work down here in the catacombs, like some mythical ferryman unable to escape once he'd laid his hand upon the tiller.

We crawled around the workroom on our hands and knees, trying out various combinations of bones for shaping the clock. From time to time Silvestro would recall a particular ribcage or knucklebone he'd seen that was perfectly suited to fashioning this strut or that bit of ornamentation, and he'd send me off to fetch it armed with a candle and some alarmingly precise directions. "Old Brother Paulo has a shoulder blade that'll be just the ticket!" he'd say, a gleam in his eye, and off I'd go. I never asked whether he'd learned the skeletons' names or just invented them to suit his own purposes. I didn't want to know.

*

WHEN I EMERGED FROM THE WORKSHOP at the end of each day, I took note of how quickly the seasons were changing. Brother Ruggiero had stripped the garden and raked it clean. The last leaves had fallen from the apple trees. And Serafina was no longer so reliably at her post on the balcony. The blame for her absence lay not with the turning of the earth, however, but with that vile young sophisticate, Bernardino Drovetti.

One day I found the two of them, Drovetti and Serafina, on a stone bench on her parents' sun-washed patio, absorbed but not entirely by the

view of the bustling Piazza Barbieri. I did not appreciate that tableau
one bit, as you can imagine. I shambled toward them like a whitened
ghost, assessing how far apart the two of them were seated. It was not by
any means far enough. You could barely have thrust a straw between
them.

"Giovanni!" She spoke my name warmly and with her customary
delight, which suggested a wide range of possibilities. Either she was a
cool individual indeed, or else she was so naive that she didn't guess
what mischief Drovetti was most certainly up to. Or perhaps she knew
exactly what he was up to, and wanted rescuing from it. Unless, on the
other hand, it was she who was courting Drovetti (perish the thought!)
and she hoped that by feigning affection for me she could drive him to
new heights of jealous desire.

Ah, youth!

I helped myself to a seat on an iron chair opposite them. Serafina
rose and touched my hand for just a moment and settled again on the
bench, a book at her side and more room between herself and Drovetti
this time, and thus the three of us made a hopeful triangle. Perhaps he'd
disturbed her at her reading. Who could say?

"You've met Sr. Drovetti, I believe."

I nodded.

"Bernardino, this is my friend, Giovanni. Giovanni Belzoni."

She had called me her friend. How was I to understand that? How
was Drovetti to understand it?

Fixed in his chair, the interloper gave me the long slow cool appraising blink of a hungry wolf. He was a small individual, compactly and
lightly built, with a sleek head of pale hair brushed forward and a tiny
clipped mustache. His nose was so delicate and narrow that I wonder to
this day how he managed to breathe air. I decided that he looked like
money.

"Giovanni is originally from Padua."

Drovetti showed me his excellent teeth. "So, how do you like the big city?"

Before I could explain that I was no bumpkin, that I'd lived in Rome for more than half of my life, Serafina went on.

"And believe it or not," she said to me this time, "Bernardino grew up practically right next door to you—in Barbaria."

So! We were again on equal footing!

"Yes," he allowed, "Barbaria." He followed the word with a disdainful little sniffle. "My family *owns* the greater part of it." He spoke as if everything that a man loves and possesses is meant only to be used up and thrown away. I looked at Serafina with panic. She seemed not to have noticed a thing.

At once I was conscious of the ground bone caked beneath my fingernails. I drew my hands back into my filthy sleeves, which did not improve my appearance much. "Tell me, Drovetti—what brings you to Rome?"

"I'm waiting for Napoleon Bonaparte," he said.

I had no idea what he was talking about. As I may have mentioned, I'd been spending most of my time beyond the reach of mankind. So I concealed my ignorance by remarking on the little emperor's heritage. "Ah yes," I sighed, "Bonaparte. Another displaced Italian."

"Corsican, you mean."

"And Corsica was once part of Italy."

"Until just before Bonaparte's birth, that is."

He had bested me. "Yet he's a displaced person all the same, just like you and me."

Drovetti had tired of the discussion and tired of me as well. His gaze drifted toward the piazza, where the cafes were coming alive with candlelight. Both he and Serafina were disappearing into the gathering dark on their bench by the wall, while my bone-white cassock and I glowed in the last rays of the sunset. Drovetti rose to his feet like a puppet yanked upward, throwing me into sudden shadow. I could see that his light jacket and soft trousers fit his slender frame perfectly, but all that I could think of—blame it on the influence of Brother Silvestro—was the value of the bones beneath his skin. It wasn't much.

He turned and spoke to Serafina as if I were the one who'd gone invisible: "I believe that our table is ready." He tilted his head imperiously toward the piazza, and she stood, and then they left me all alone on her family's empty patio with its luminous sad romantic view of the Piazza Barbieri.

*

THAT NIGHT IN THE REFECTORY, I kept my ears open and my mouth shut. What choice did I have? The two subjects nearest to my heart—Drovetti's successful courtship of Serafina, and Brother Silvestro's mad cemetery—were strictly off limits. All around the table, the talk was of Napoleon. His army was marching toward Rome, the boys all said, and Rome seemed as was its custom ill-suited to put up much of a fight.

"I'm thinking of joining up," said Pietro, an older boy from Tuscany. He was lanky as a farmhand, and rough around the edges even after his years in the monastery. Anger pulsed in his temple and made his jaw jut.

Crooked little Carmine, a sophisticated and cynical Roman through and through, took a more philosophical point of view: "If you join the Italian army today, you'll be scrubbing dishes for the French army within a month. That's the way it works, in case you haven't read your history books."

Pietro looked daggers at him.

Carmine went on. "I'm thinking of taking my vows before that cocky little Corsican walks in and conscripts the whole lot of us. The rest of you fellows might want to start considering your alternatives." He bent and blew on his soup.

Lying on my hard bed after vespers, listening to the wind sigh in the bare branches of the apple trees, I took stock of myself and my future.

Anyone could see what a desirable acquisition I would make for the French army. My budding skills in hydraulics alone would have made me worth my weight in gold. Not to mention my size, my brute strength, and my skill with a shovel and a pick. I was certain to have a difficult time concealing myself and my many powers from the eyes of the invading Frenchmen, unless I took up permanent residence—one way or another, alive or dead—in Brother Silvestro's cemetery workshop.

I was beginning to suspect that Carmine was right: taking my vows was the only way to escape the indignity and disloyalty of conscription into an occupying army.

But circumstances would prove more complex than that. And there would prove to be other ways out, too, ways that Carmine hadn't considered. If a lifetime of narrow escapes and close brushes with mortality has taught me anything, it's that circumstances are always more complex than they seem, and that there is always more than one escape route open to a man of courage and imagination—although some of them may be a bit more difficult to negotiate than the rest.

*

IN THE MEANTIME, to assess my fitness for a future devoted entirely to monastic life, I threw myself into my studies. I composed extra exercises for my Latin class with Brother Elmo, I surprised Brother Tomaso with ever more sophisticated readings of scripture, and I even went so far as to enroll myself in the Abbot's science class all over again, vowing as I did so to keep my heretical opinions to myself.

Study wasn't the only way that I thrust myself back into the life of the monastery. I arrived early for every Mass. I volunteered to ring the steeple bells when it wasn't my turn, even if it meant going without sleep for half the night like a sailor on the last watch. I tried joining the monks' choir, but was turned away on account of my inability to carry a tune—along with my thunderous rumble of a voice (in those days I could strike notes audible only to bog turtles and bullfrogs).

I stoked the fires for Brother Ruggiero in the kitchen, I stirred boiling pots of lye-soaked linens for Brother Andrea in the laundry, and I never missed a moment of my long underground workday with Brother Silvestro.

Above all else, I prayed like a condemned man. I prayed for guidance and I prayed for illumination. I prayed for Bernardino Drovetti to fall off a cliff or to take a dagger to the chest and thus leave the field open for me, since what I really desired even more than my liberty—more than my life—was a chance at regaining the attentions of the lovely Serafina Randazzo. Just seeing the two of them together on that patio had lit a flame in my heart that I should have guessed religion could never extinguish. But as I have said, I was yet a child.

Time passed. I measured it by Brother Silvestro's clock. Constructing its frame was my responsibility—I chose bones and mixed mortar and mounted the thing to the wall in bits and pieces—while Silvestro worked out the finer details of the numbers and the hands. And as time passed and the autumn came on in full, I rarely found Serafina on her balcony at day's end. My knocks at her door were answered only by her mother, who looked at me as if I possessed a curious yet not altogether unpleasant smell. Serafina was out, she would say, out with Sr. Drovetti visiting a museum or a café or a gallery. Would I care to come in and wait for her? Her invitations seemed sincere, but I always had my chores and my studies and my prayers to think about instead.

One day, though, my knock drew Signor Drovetti. *Lieutenant* Drovetti, I should say in the interest of accuracy, Lieutenant Drovetti, strutting like a peacock in the gaudy plumage of the French military. I hadn't realized that Napoleon had gotten this far. I said as much, and Drovetti set me straight—ignorant bumpkin that I was. The main body of the French army was yet hundreds of miles away, he explained. He was its vanguard, he whose family and wealth had facilitated this high commission in an occupying force. His papers had come through only days before, and his uniform had arrived from the tailor's that very morning. It was of satin and silk—the first-class materials of leadership at second hand.

"You're a turncoat," I said to him, loudly enough that Serafina, who was emerging from the parlor, would be certain to hear.

"A turncoat?" said Drovetti. "You would do better to think of me as a pragmatist."

I ignored him and addressed myself instead to Serafina: "Your new doorman, despite his elegant uniform, is a traitor to his country."

She concealed her quick smile beneath a hand. The newly hatched lieutenant wouldn't have noticed her reaction anyhow, for he was staring at me and steaming like a prawn in the kitchen of some overpriced French café. "This uniform cost more than you'll earn in a lifetime," he sputtered.

"Then keep it away from flying bullets."

"I mean to."

"So I thought. More's the pity."

He thrust a finger at me. "On the other hand, my dear Belzoni, it will take more than those rags to protect you from danger. You'd require the cassock of a real Capuchin. And I don't suppose that you're quite prepared to take so drastic a step, given your fondness for beautiful young ladies."

At that moment I discovered that it's possible to learn from anyone, even an individual as ignorant as Drovetti. For that little uniformed serpent was correct about one thing: I was not prepared to take the Capuchin vows and forever give up hope of visiting a girl like Serafina in any capacity other than, shall we say, the strictly pastoral.

"Papa!" said the girl, breaking off the conversation between myself and Drovetti, as up the walk behind me came her father, headed for his own front door.

The doctor thrust out his arms to her as I longed to do myself—as I feared Drovetti probably did when no one was around—and Serafina rushed headlong into them. "My child," he muttered into her hair, "I see you've drawn a crowd again."

I tipped my head forward and Drovetti bowed at the waist. "Doctor Randazzo," we said.

"Gentlemen."

"Lieutenant," corrected Drovetti. But Dr. Randazzo wasn't interested in him or in his dearly purchased rank. He was interested in me.

"Has Serafina mentioned that I'd like to examine you one day, Belzoni?"

"Yes sir, she has."

"You're a busy young fellow, I'm sure."

"Yes sir."

"Healthy as a horse too, I'll bet."

"Never sick a day in my life." This was not one hundred percent true—as an infant I'd once suffered a fever high enough to vaporize ice with a touch of my little hand—but it was a useful fiction and one that would to serve me well in my early career as a mystery and a wonder. Even then Serafina blinked at me in admiration.

"So I suppose there'll never be a reason for you to come visit poor old lonely Dr. Randazzo." He made himself look sorrowful.

"There'll be reason enough before long," interjected Drovetti. "If this fellow keeps to his present course, you can expect to be bandaging up a bullet hole in the near future. Mark my words."

I bristled, imagining myself challenged to a duel, but it was the doctor who took his meaning more accurately. "If Giovanni should be wounded in the interest of his country and mine, I shall be honored to serve him in any way I can. On the other hand, Lieutenant Turncoat, there is not enough gold in all of Napoleon's treasury to make me pull a sword from your dishonorable chest."

Drovetti looked to Serafina, who looked away. He got her attention by taking her hand and placing a kiss upon it, and then he spun on a shiny heel and strode off toward the piazza.

Randazzo swung wide his door. "Come with me, Belzoni, and we shall get to know one another."

In I went, leaving Serafina alone with her better judgment.

*

"SAY AHH."

I did.

"Take a deep breath."

I did.

"And another."

I did.

"You have the lung capacity of three men, Belzoni. And the pulse of a sleeping lion."

"Is that good?"

"Absolutely. You'll live to be a hundred, God and Napoleon willing. How much do you weigh?"

"I don't know exactly."

He took his chin in his hand and sized me up, and then scribbled something into a little book placed upon his knee. "Height?"

"I have no idea."

"Go and stand under that archway, if you please."

I went and stood, eyeing him as carefully as he eyed me.

He counted bricks, did some figures in his head, and scribbled in his notebook again. I had achieved most of my growth by then, at least vertically, so the answer must have been something close to seven feet.

"Are your parents remarkable too?"

"Oh, yes, sir—in many ways. My father is the finest barber in all of Italy. He once gave me the honor of assisting him in shaving the neck of no less an eminence than Pope Pius VI. My mother, for her part, is a woman of extraordinary piety. Her goodness and faith are revered by authorities as high as Monsignor O'Toole himself."

"But neither one of them—your parents, I mean—is oversized?"

"No."

"Have you any brothers or sisters?"

"Three brothers. I am the youngest."

"All normal?"

"Yes," I said. "All normal." I gave him a grin as big as I was, revealing a set of teeth which, as you can see for yourself even in the shadow of these starlit riggings, might have been the bones of some prehistoric creature. The thought of which—the thought of the bones, I mean—brings me back to Brother Silvestro.

I was carrying a pail of mortar and a wicker basket of finger joints from the workroom out to the high vaulted hall, part of my latest experiment in delineating the clock's face. "So, Giovanni," he said as I passed him, "where are you headed?"

I stopped and tilted my head as he eyed me from over his shoulder. There was no question as to where I was headed. I shook my pail and my basket and I lifted my eyebrows toward the vaulted room.

"No, no, no. I can see where you're going *right now!* I have eyes! What interests me, Giovanni—and what ought to interest *you*—is where you're headed in this life of yours." Silvestro rotated on his stool and gazed hungrily upon me. His eyes were sunken, nearly invisible in the flickering glow of the bone lanterns, and they lay in their sockets like pools of the blackest oil. It struck me then that for all his inscrutability and obsession, Silvestro was a mortal like the rest of us.

"You have a gift for this work," he said a little ominously.

"Thank you."

"But it's just one gift among many. Anyone can see that. Things were different for me when I was your age. God provided me from the beginning with just one gift—a single great vision that belonged to me and no one else. It made things easier."

It didn't seem to me that there was anything easy about Silvestro's life. He worked like a draft horse, he communicated with next to no one, and he lived year after year in a sort of self-induced solitary confinement with nothing but his dream and his skeletons for companionship. His dream and his skeletons and, lately, me.

"Do you know what comes next for me, Giovanni?"

I did not.

"An entire chapel. A chapel constructed entirely of bones. It's the achievement that I've been working toward for my entire life." His lower lip quivered, and he clamped it down under a determined grimace.

I shook my head. "It will be magnificent."

He just sat there with his severe look, that gaze of his fastened upon me like a noose.

"I can picture it."

He brightened. "You can?"

"Oh, absolutely." I could indeed, and I must say that the vision horrified me to no end.

"I knew that you could, my boy. I *knew* that you could. You and no one else." There was a strange kind of lust in his eyes—something composed of obsession and faith and terror and doom and love all mixed up together. "You haven't disappointed me yet, Giovanni."

"I appreciate that. I do my best." I rattled my little basket of bones, a vain pantomime demonstrating my urge to be going about my business. *His* business.

"So have you thought about where you're headed in this life?"

"I think of nothing else."

"Good boy. And tell me: have you felt a calling?"

"The whole world calls to me, I'm afraid."

His face fell, but after an instant he recovered. "But what of this place, eh? What of this work? What of this monument to God and our forebears and the fate that binds us?" He lifted his white hands to take in the workroom, the mad cemetery, the potential chapel. "Does this not call out most loudly of all?"

"It's a magnificent work. An important work. But it's yours."

"Bah. It belongs to the ages. And besides, I won't live forever."

"Considering what you've accomplished," I said, "you'll come as close to immortality as any man."

That seemed to satisfy him a little. He sat for a minute composing himself, deciding if I were being one hundred percent sincere. "It's the girl, isn't it?" he said.

A girl, I suppose, was the only thing he could possibly imagine being capable of seducing me more completely than a chamber crammed with skeletons.

"No. Not really. I mean, she's fine and all, but I think she has a suitor."

Silvestro clucked.

"He's an Italian—from Barbaria—but these days he's a lieutenant in the French army."

He clucked again. "So the armed service is calling you."

"It's not as if I want to join up so that I can run him through with a sword or anything."

"No?"

"Although someone really ought to."

"Hmm."

"I don't want to join up at all."

"I can't say that I blame you."

"Carmine says that we'll all be conscripted before long, whether we like it or not."

"He may be right. And what then?"

I shook my head.

"I'll tell you what then. With any luck, you'll have the good fortune to report to someone other than that turncoat lieutenant. That, as you can imagine, would be uncomfortable."

I almost dropped the basket of bones.

"If I were you, and my motivation weren't the girl, and I desired to stay clear of the army, then I believe I would prepare to take my vows." He focused those sad passionate eyes on me and did not look away.

I said that I appreciated his advice. I told him that I'd consider all he'd said very carefully. I finished up my day's work on the clock. And by nightfall I was below decks on a cargo ship bound for the coast of England.

*

I SET OUT WITH BARELY A GOODBYE. There was no one in the monastery for whom I felt an attachment, no one to whom I could give up the secret of my escape. Had I told Silvestro, it would have broken his poor cracked heart. Had I told one of the other boys, it would have incited a revolt. So after supper I crept into the secret room behind the altarpiece, shook the mice out of one of the castoff robes I'd spied there, and took the moth-eaten thing as my disguise. I had to crouch to lower the skirts to a position somewhere near the ground, but as I emerged from the mouth of one of Silvestro's tunnels I discovered that it concealed me well enough, given that the sun was down and the moon was new. I bent over and slipped through the gate, hardly casting more than a single glance back at the Palazzo Randazzo as I crept away. Out in the piazza, in the deep shade of the fountain, sat a figure I was quite certain was Drovetti—waiting for Serafina, perhaps, or keeping an eye out for an escapee such as I. Half a dozen shuffling steps more and I was around the corner, down a lane, and pelting toward home.

It was my father who answered the door, but it was my mother who flew to me and wrapped her arms about me and would not let me go.

He retreated to his chair and his newspaper and his cigar, just as if my arrival on their doorstep were a thing that occurred every day.

"What's happened?" asked my mother.

"What did you do?" asked my father.

In their questions lay the difference between the two of them.

"Nothing," I said first to one and then to other. "All is well."

"The Abbot didn't toss you out on your ear?"

"Giacomo," said my mother. "He's not like his brother."

Whatever incident she was referring to was news to me. "Which brother? What happened?"

"Francesco," said my father, giving his newspaper a shake. "The Jesuits threw him back. He's helping me in the shop these days." The illustrious barber slid his glasses down his nose and studied me gravely. "There's not enough room for two of you. Not while I remain on this earth."

"I shouldn't think there would be."

My mother pushed me toward the couch. "That father of yours. Always assuming the worst." She settled me among pillows and cushions. The place had a familiar smell that tugged at my heart, something composed of cooking and woodsmoke and soap and the bodies of the two people who had given me life. "So tell me: how are things with the Capuchins? Do you have news for your poor old mother and father?"

"I'm going to England," I said, and with those four words I began to dismantle her dream.

"I didn't know the Capuchins had established a monastery in England."

"They might have. I wouldn't know."

Her face collapsed.

My father folded his newspaper. "Then you're leaving them after all. So what happened?"

"Nothing, really." I took my mother's small hands in mine. "There's a big world out there, that's all."

"It's not so big as that," said my father.

"It's bigger than any monastery."

"And it has girls in it too, I suppose, eh?" He'd been riding herd on my eldest brother, Mario, for long enough to remember how boys' minds worked. (By this time Mario had managed to get himself in trouble with a nun from somewhere in Tuscany, although I wouldn't find out about it for years and years. It involved his cell in the little monastery at San Pietro a Marcigliano, a bottle of young Chianti, and a vast quantity of purloined votive candles.)

He took up his newspaper again. "At least you're not joining the army. Francesco talks of nothing else."

"They'll conscript him sooner or later. The French, I mean. He'd better watch out."

"So you're running from that as well?" He was a man of little worldly experience, but he knew a thing or two about human nature.

"I guess you could put it that way."

"It's hard to put it any other."

"I'll try." I leveled my eyes at him. "I'd happily fight *against* the French," I said, "but I shall never fight *for* them." My testament didn't sound half so poetic as I'd hoped it would, but it was accurate.

"And how do you plan to do that in England? Fight the French, I mean." He was a bulldog, that father of mine. He'd learned all about argument in the toughest school there is—a barber shop near the Campo de Fiori.

"Honestly, I don't plan to fight the French for a minute. I plan only to live my life as I see fit—unhampered and unconscripted."

"Oh, Giovanni," said my mother, "I had such hopes for you."

"Then it's time to raise them," I advised her in all sincerity. I kissed her on the cheek and embraced my father and went on my way, vowing in my heart that I would never disappoint her again."

PART THREE:

London

"How Giovanni Battista Belzoni came to be known as
The Patagonian Samson is but one mystery—in a life
as crowded with them as the Valley of the Kings."

— Sir Charles Walpole, *Samson At The Circus*, London, 1862

*

FOR THE PURPOSES OF THIS STORY, let us agree that the ship upon
which I arranged my passage was exactly like this one. In truth it was
entirely different—three times the size, twenty times the age, and a
clumsy wallowing pig of an overladen freighter instead of a fleet warship—but to a boy laboring below decks, one ship is much like another.
Especially if that boy has to bend himself double to pass through the
low openings between one cabin and the next.

Either way, I emerged on the docks at London a little paler, a little
stronger, and armed with a handful of pounds sterling that I'd earned
along the way. My stake would not last me long, this I knew. What I did
not know, and could not have known, was that I'd arrived a good deal
poorer than I should have. Our irascible Scottish captain, one Cyrus J.
MacLeod, had a slippery way with figures and an opportunistic eye for
naïve foreign labor. Regardless, I was happy. So I did as all young sailors
do upon making landfall—I set out to find the liveliest part of town, the
place where my meager pay would most easily vanish without a trace.

I found St. Bartholomew's Fair. And there James Curtin found me.

St. Bartholomew's Fair was a smorgasbord of wickedness. It was a
place where a man could get his fortune told, his pocket picked, his liver
ruined, and his sexual apparatus exercised—if you will excuse my blunt

language—all without taking more than twenty paces in any direction. Yet it wasn't all merriment. Brutality was in the very air, and vicious fights erupted on every hand with the speed and regularity of gunfire in a pitched battle. The ground beneath my feet ran with urine, cheap whiskey, cheaper beer, and spilled blood. To a young man just done with a channel crossing and only recently escaped from the Capuchins, St. Bartholomew's Fair was the wide world itself.

My instincts took me straight to the sideshows. I paid up, lowered my head, and ducked beneath a canvas flap painted with garish images of bearded women, monkey-faced men, and little boys with the shells of tortoises. The first booth, dimly lit if lit at all, contained a headless body that seemed strangely genderless and looked as if it had been hastily lumped together out of paraffin. The second booth contained that body's missing head, a garrulous thing with a salt-and-pepper beard and a top hat, lodged in a dented tin tub that had served in better days as a trough for watering livestock. He called out to each of us as we passed, lamenting his sad fate and pleading to be reunited with his body. If his condition weren't enough to terrify the impressionable in the crowd, I can assure you that his language surely was. I have spent many a month in the company of sailors, and believe me: there is no sailor on earth who can curse with the vigor and invention exhibited by that beheaded man. He was profanity personified, if only from the neck up.

Encouraged by the nastiness of the beheaded individual to waste no time in moving along, we shuffled past a woman wearing a cotton wool beard, a snake charmer seated before a dusty basket overhung by plainly visible wires, and an alleged human giant who was no taller than I and far narrower in every other dimension. I permitted myself to drift into the middle of the crowd as I realized that I'd been gulled. There was nothing here for me to see.

But then something did catch my attention. Something caught my attention and would not let it go. In the deepest part of the tent, where daylight from the ragged flaps at each end could never penetrate, sat a glass tank illuminated by a much-abused oil lamp nailed to a post. The glass was unclean, greasy, smeared outside and in, and the flickering of the lamp made it hard to see exactly what it might contain. I moved close enough to read the sign: *Victor,* it said, *The Human Snail.* I moved closer still so as to peer over the open top, and sure enough—the tank held a babyish slug of a creature, pale as death. Lacking arms and legs, it lay on its belly and humped itself about the perimeter by means of great effort, progressing around and around the tank with a kind of angry determination.

"You must be Victor," I said without even meaning to speak.

"No time to talk, genius," said the figure in the tank, his voice at least twice as big as he was. "I'm in the middle of my constitutional." Victor, wonder of wonders, would turn out to be something of an exercise enthusiast. Right now, though, he looked past me with a penetrating glance and then fixed me hard with one knowing eye. "Don't look now, Samson, but your pocket's just been picked."

And thus did I become triply indebted to Victor the Human Snail—not only for the recovery of my seaman's pay, not only for half of the stage name that would one day serve me so well, but for the friendship of the most patient and loyal creature I would ever know in this life, the thieving Irish orphan named James Curtin.

*

YOU MIGHT SAY THAT JAMES CURTIN did not only pick my pocket—he picked *me.* For as useful as a bundle of cash is to a boy in his state, a protector and guide is a prize far greater.

I suspect that somewhere in his heart he understood this, for as I spun away from the glass case he looked at me and hesitated for a single unprofessional second—exactly time enough for me to memorize his face. Then his felonious reflexes took over and he was off, fast as any wild young creature, expertly playing his small size against my bulk as the two of us wound and battered our way through the crowded tent. An ordinary man would never have caught him, but my strength and my height served me well. I managed to emerge from the shelter of the canvas just an instant after he did—leaving a string of fallen men and a litany of apologies in my wake—and although the boy scrambled across the open ground like a squirrel, his little legs were no match for mine.

In moments he was hanging from my fist by the collar of his ragged coat. *"Put me down, ye great bully, or I'll be calling for the constable."* He had a banshee's screech and the unrelenting fury of a storm over the North Sea.

James Curtin looked just the way you imagine him. Small for his ten years thanks to lineage and malnutrition, barefoot and filthy and barely clothed, crowned with a thick shock of red hair and a broad face across which freckles bloomed like poppies. He swiveled and squirmed and flung his little fists every which way, until I was positively terrified of putting him down.

Young James Curtin was, in other words, a fierce little leprechaun. Alas, the pot of gold he was guarding at the moment happened to belong to me.

I let him hang there until he was worn out, which took a good deal longer than I'd have liked, and finally I set him down on the broad marble stair where we stood. I crouched alongside him, keeping my right hand on his neck to encourage good behavior.

"Hand it over," I said. I resisted giving his little neck a squeeze. It was so thin that I feared I'd crush it.

"So ye'll be robbing little b'ys now, is that it?" He squirmed and filled his lungs to start shouting again, and I clamped my free hand over his mouth.

"Just give me back what you took from my pocket."

He struggled like a fish on a line.

"Give it back and I'll let you go. No questions asked. No harm done."

I'd just finished making that kindly promise when the ungrateful creature gave his head a little snap and nearly bit off my index finger. I attempted an appeal to his humanity. "I've just gotten off the boat," I said. "Beyond what you've stolen, I don't have a penny to my name."

"Oh, and I'm a rich man indeed. I'm one of the Medicis, I am. Ye'd know all about us, there's no doubt of it."

First he'd stolen my savings, and now he had the cheek to point out my accent. "What would you know about the Medicis, anyway?"

"Only what I read in books."

"You look like a highly educated individual," I lied. "I'm sure you've collected quite a few."

"Not so many. I used to borrow 'em right here, though, once or twice a week." He craned his neck to point his nose toward the plinth above the door at the top of the marble staircase. *Wycombe's Circulating Library*, it said. "And a fine arrangement it was, 'til they caught me."

"You've been apprehended before, then?"

He nodded, all regret.

"Although I'd wager you were never caught *returning* anything."

"Not so," he said, a little indignantly. And then, as if to prove me wrong, he reached into his pocket and fished out my pay. "If ye'll be maligning a poor orphan b'y all up and down the block, ye might as well have yer filthy money back. And let that be an end to it."

I took the money, but I didn't let go of him as I'd promised I would. For the next few years, I would try my best never to let go of him at all.

*

AS WE SAT THERE SIDE BY SIDE on the library steps, James Curtin explained that he'd wanted the money to acquire a volume he'd been admiring at a stall in Spitalfields.

"You're not kidding me?"

"Certainly not." Although he allowed that he might have spent whatever was left over on a paper cone of fish and chips.

He explained to me that his dear sainted father, may the Blessed Queen of the Universe have mercy upon his soul, had been a scholar. He'd taught the classics at Saint Somebody's in Limerick until his wife's death in childbirth broke his spirit and sent him and his newborn son— none other than our James—wandering footloose toward the streets and workhouses of London. There he'd read the poor child to sleep every night from tattered volumes of Shakespeare and Cervantes, until that dismal dawn when James woke up alone upon their shared cot. He was never to see to his father again, but he still kept the old man's *Macbeth* and *Don Quixote.*

Two or three times during the boy's story, the big oaken door at the top of the stairs slid open a crack and a tiny woman thrust out her beaked face to study the two of us. She radiated disdain. If she'd had a broom big enough, I think she'd have come down and swept the pair of us into the gutter.

"That's the witch herself," said James. "That's old Mrs. Gherkin. She don't trust nobody."

"Not everyone's trustworthy. Consider yourself, for example." I patted the money in my pocket.

"Ye'd think the books belonged to her, and not to Mr. Wycombe. Him with his name on the library and all."

"Be a little more understanding," I suggested. "No doubt she has a job to do. It could be that Wycombe's dead and she's his last living descendant, guarding his legacy the way you guard your father's *Don Quixote.*"

His bluster failed him a little at the thought, and to distract him I spoke about my own father and mother, about my two brothers away in monasteries, and about the prodigal Francesco returned home to work in the barber shop. James couldn't understand how I could have chosen to leave such a family behind—and at that point, neither could I.

He said, "Ye'll be needing a place to live then, won't ye?"

I admitted that I would.

"Me too," he said.

*

JAMES CURTIN CLAIMED TO KNOW of a boarding house on the far side of St. Bartholomew's, a disreputable place where my pay might last us a month or better. (He knew my net worth right down to the halfpence, although exactly when he'd found the time to count it I shall never know.)

I was reluctant to set foot in St. Bartholomew's again, and suggested that we walk around the perimeter instead of plunging right back into the thick of it, but James would have none of my timidity. He knew a short cut, he said, and before I knew it he'd lifted some flap or other and we were right back in the middle of bedlam. "Through here," he said as he vanished into a passageway that was only slightly higher than my waist. That boy was as cunning a disappearing artist as I'd ever see, but nonetheless I managed to keep pace.

We stopped for breath in the wings of a stage show employing a troop of inadequately house-trained monkeys, a grubby acrobat no more than two feet tall, an endless procession of young ladies in costumes of decreasing modesty, and a lightly clad gentleman who identified himself as The French Hercules. Sadly, his performance lacked anything in the way of a Continental flavor—unless you counted the accent that the announcer put on during his introduction. "Lahdees and Jhentelmehn," he brayed, "Mahdahms and Mohnswahs." Etcetera, etcetera. To tell the truth, I could see by his profile that The French Hercules was almost certainly a Greek. Yet even with that natural advantage, he fell a good distance short of being even faintly Herculean. In those days I was sufficiently naïve to think that a fellow billed as Hercules not only had an obligation to be potent beyond the dreams of ordinary men—which he wasn't—but that he should make at least a nod or two in the direction of the classics—which he didn't. A toga would have been nice, for example, instead of short pants of apparent Naval issue and a shirt so full of holes that Napoleon's armies might have once used it for target practice.

Nor were his feats in any way evocative of his namesake's labors. Instead, the French Hercules lifted a variety of weights prominently labeled with implausible numbers, carried a pair of scantily-attired young ladies seated on opposite ends of a long wooden pole, and walked the length of the stage on his hands. For his grand finale he climbed upon a cannonball and balanced the filthy acrobatic midget on the tip of his chin—an act that combined the unlikely with the unwholesome.

James Curtin glanced from the French Hercules to me and back again. "Ye could do that," he said. He was a mind-reader.

So half as an experiment and half for sheer joy, I hoisted James onto my shoulder and paraded with him through the lanes of London. We drew plenty of stares, even among crowds well accustomed to marvels of every kind. It was just after the dawn of a new century, and something unexpected was popping up on every streetcorner. James and I, the domesticated leprechaun and the friendly giant, may have been taken for signs of a new order in the world. The lamb and the lion, making our foreordained peace.

The boarding house, when we found it, proved disreputable indeed. A narrow brick pile held together by creeping yellow ivy and flocked all over with some kind of psoriatic moss, it listed to one side like a sinking ship. Its tilt was in fact so precarious that the chimney pot lay aground in the tiny side yard, smashed to a thousand pieces, while the chimney smoked away at an alarming angle directly overhead. One or two of the windows opened upon gray curtains as threadbare and despondent as ghosts. The shutters were cockeyed and rotten where they weren't missing, and a forlorn seagull flapped in and out through a hole in the roof.

The proprietor, one Mr. Jaundyce, slumped in the doorway and coughed at us as we approached. He had the sharp eye of an attorney and the florid snout of a wild boar, and his respiration was labored in a way that foretold an early death. "Get that boy as far from these premises as possible," he wheezed at me. "He ain't welcome here."

James, brave by nature and emboldened further by his elevated perch upon my shoulder, directed my attention to a broken window and remarked that Mr. Jaundyce really ought to be letting bygones be bygones.

"A good Christian would, I reckon. But ain't nobody ever accused me of that particular offense."

I addressed my little Irish burden. "There must be places in town where you haven't made enemies."

Jaundyce narrowed his eyes into a piggy squint. "Don't count on it, big feller. He's notorious, that one."

"There must at least be some house where we wouldn't have to make restitution for damages before we even started paying rent."

"Not bloody likely." Jaundyce hacked something up from the depths of his chest, spat it onto the step, and rubbed it in with the toe of his boot. And then he brightened up, like a sickly sunrise. "Excuse me, but did you just happen to mention *paying rent?*"

At length he forgave James the shattered window—it wasn't the only one broken in the place, as it turned out, and his plans for repairing them were indefinite at best—and demanded from us two weeks' rent in advance. Breakfast and supper were included, provided we could tolerate his cooking, which I didn't suppose we could for very long. But I was certain that I'd have a little income by and by, upon which we could dine wherever we pleased.

A sailor's duffel held the few belongings I'd brought from Italy, but moving my pint-sized partner into Jaundyce's turned out to be a good deal more complicated. He'd scattered the meager stuff of his short life over half of London. We found spare socks hidden within a mattress in the bowels of the poorhouse. We unearthed a sentimentally meaningful button or two from beneath a pyramid of trash in a dustman's yard. We prized back a loose board in the jakes behind a public house, freeing Macbeth and Don Quixote to breathe the fresh air again.

"I haven't had a proper room since me father passed on," said James when we were done. He'd removed his shoes, such as they were, and was bouncing on and off the cot. A little too confidently, I thought.

"You have a proper one now." I might have added that he'd apparently acquired a pet of some sort in the bargain, since there was a furtive rustling in the mattress that kept up whether James was bouncing or not. A mouse, judging from the droppings that sifted to the floor.

The light in the sky was dwindling, and Mr. Jaundyce hadn't provided us with so much as a candle. James hopped off the cot and ran to the window—a broken one, as luck would have it, but not the one he'd been responsible for—snatching up his father's Cervantes along the way. "I always like to get in a few pages before bedtime," he said. And then he turned and cast his eyes back over the room. "Ye'll be having the cot, I suppose. I'll take the rug."

In the end, of course, I did not deprive James of his bed. Whether from kindly paternal feeling or from the foreknowledge that the sway-backed cot would surely collapse under my great weight, it made no difference. The ratty little rug suited me just fine, I told him, I'd slept on a worse pallet in the monastery. And that was close enough to the truth.

*

JAMES READ ALOUD TO ME that night and every other, expanding upon the English I'd picked up from Father Mullooly. When he came to something I didn't understand he'd rush to enact the scene, making our little room over into one of the country inns or taverns where those hapless Spaniards underwent their never-ending humiliation. He'd direct me to the bed and attack me with a stick. He'd splash water from the basin to represent the red wine that Quixote was forever mistaking for blood. He'd place the chamber pot upon my head as if it were a helmet, and beat on it with his little ringing fists. And so on, and so on, until the mouse in the mattress was terrified and the catatonic law copyist in the next room was hysterical and Mr. Jaundyce was banging on our floor from below with the handle of a broom. And then I'd douse the candle and James would fall asleep like the veriest baby.

Each day I looked for work and struggled to reform my larcenous orphaned Irishman. It wasn't easy, for he was born to thievery through and through, gifted in the art and much-practiced in its application. Old habits, particularly if they've kept a body fed for the better part of its time on earth, die hard. Little James Curtin never met a pocket he couldn't pick or a purse he couldn't snatch. They hung all over London like so many Christmas stockings—right at his eye level, more often than not—placed there by some Nick more Old than Saint.

The boy's luck was poorest down by the docks. I went there seeking work as a longshoreman, a job I knew I could do with my eyes closed and at least one hand tied behind my back. But one fresh look at that tar-soaked, salt-caked littoral, where the seagulls flocked like rats and the rats swarmed like punters at St. Bartholomew's, and I knew that a life at the waterfront was not the life for me. I found it depressing. No doubt you are surprised that an individual of my vigor and zest for life could be depressed about anything—the venomous infection in my belly has not yet dulled my enthusiasm for this African adventure, or dimmed my hopes of finding Timbuctoo and the fabled source of the River Niger—but I must tell you the plain, unvarnished truth. The thought of spending my life unloading other men's goods from other men's boats sent me into a spiral of gloom. I was so despondent that I hardly noticed James slipping a fat roll of bills from the pocket of the only prosperous-looking gentleman in the vicinity, and it took every ounce of my will to convince him to slide it right back where he'd gotten it. "We'll have none of that," I reminded him with a sigh. "Not anymore. Not while I'm around."

"'Tis the only profit we'll see today, by the look of it. And now we've got Mr. Jaundyce on our backs, too." He stamped off in the direction of the prosperous-looking gentleman, throwing me a frustrated glare as he went. "Things were easier in the old days."

"Don't expect miracles," I said. But expect miracles he did, and I'd taken on the job of providing them.

I lingered there on the pier, tar sticking to the seat of my only pair of trousers, and I wondered what was wrong with me. Had my father ever thrown up his hands and refused to cut hair just because it didn't suit him? No. Had he balked when my mother insisted on moving back to Rome, saying that there was nothing proper for him to do there? No. (Well, perhaps for a while. But when we arrived in Rome he'd searched out that new location by the Campo de Fiore and gotten right down to business.) All my life, he had worked as if much more than our family's welfare depended upon his industry. He worked as if his dignity depended upon it. He worked as if the orbit of the planet depended upon it. He worked as if the very enactment of God's will for all mankind depended upon it.

He worked, I realized with a start, because he *loved* to work. He loved his customers—shopkeepers and bricklayers and priests alike. He loved the smell of talcum powder. He loved taking lavish care of his gleaming instruments. He loved smoking his big cigars and reading the paper all by himself in the most comfortable chair in the city of Rome. Above all, the illustrious barber Giacomo Lorenzo Belzoni loved the hope that someday one of his sons might follow along in his footsteps—even if that son was only poor Francesco, disgraced and turned out by the Jesuits.

What did I love? I couldn't say. Not boats, that was certain. Not barbering. And apparently not the pathetic half-starved little figure of my friend James Curtin stalking off to do his duty toward the prosperous-looking gentleman. (Or not enough, anyhow, to take on a job that I didn't fancy in order to save him.)

For all my size and vigor, for all my talent with a spade and a bucket, for all my study under Father Mullooly and the Capuchins, I was a pathetic case. How many years had passed since I'd sworn to free those tiny angels kept so cruelly in thrall to the Pope's toilette? Plenty, I'm ashamed to say. Yet there I slouched on a pier in London, feeling sorry for myself and worrying over my sticky trousers, not an inch closer to my aim. I hadn't gained so much as a single recovered child, not even poor fierce starving James Curtin who believed I had his best interests at heart. I hung my head, but only after I'd seen him slip our next month's rent back into the pocket of the prosperous-looking gentleman.

Then I stood up and shook myself, hoisted the boy up onto my shoulder, and strode off to discover my one true love.

*

WYCOMBE'S CIRCULATING LIBRARY was our first stop.

James had his heart set on a particular volume, and he promised that once we had obtained it he would sit on a park bench somewhere and read quietly while I looked for employment. He insisted on finding the book for himself, though—he couldn't recall the title, but he had seen it on a table in the public area, among some big leather chairs, near a fireplace—which meant I would have to smuggle him in under my long coat.

"When you say you mean to *borrow* a book, you understand that you'll be *returning* it as well—correct?"

He sighed his agreement.

"On time and in good condition."

"Yes." He kind of sang-hissed it. "On time and in good condition."

"Do you promise?"

"I promise," he said, and vanished under my coat.

We rounded the corner and headed up the marble steps with a halting gait that could only draw attention. By the time we'd reached the top, in fact, the door was already open sufficiently to let the inquisitive beak of Mrs. Gherkin protrude into the sunshine.

"Can I help you?"

James stiffened at the creak of her voice, and I very nearly fell back down the stairs. *"Signora,"* I said, recovering myself and bowing in the most continental of manners.

She softened immediately, of course.

The spell thus cast and the hook thus set, I forged ahead in my most enchanting broken English: "I desire to achieve for myself," I said, "the borrowing of a volume of the literature." Or words to that effect. The old bird's heart melted—as did whatever rules would have normally prevented an indigent stranger like me from even entering the place, much less touching the collection.

"Right this way," she said with a sweep of her scrawny arm. I was a foreigner, a giant, a cripple, and a speaker of the language of romance. How could she have refused me anything? So in we went.

She mounted a little step stool behind a high desk and tipped herself forward, eyeing me with a coquettish twinkle in her rheumy eye. As best as I dared, I made clear that I fancied a volume of adventure, a tale of exploration and invention, a story set in exotic locales and populated by brave men of purpose. Something nice and fat, too, if it weren't too much trouble. Her eyes popped, and she whispered to me like a conspirator: "I know just the thing." At such close range, she stank of tobacco and violets.

What made me specify such a book? Something in my nature, I suppose. That and an instinctive understanding that by requesting a tale of romance and adventure I might reinforce my own appeal.

The library was dead silent once she'd vanished into the stacks—silent as a pharaoh's tomb, take it from me—with the exception of a sharp impatient tap-tap-tapping of James Curtin's foot on the hardwood floor. I nudged him with my knee and he left off.

When she emerged once more, the little old librarian was singing to herself—actually *singing*, the many posted injunctions to the contrary notwithstanding. In her hands was a thick volume bound up in burgundy leather with hardware of tarnished brass: *The Voiage and Travaile of Sir John Mandeville, Knight*, by one Jean d'Outremeuse. She slid it in my direction.

I inclined my head toward the public area where James had seen the book that he desired. "Perhaps you would be agreeable to my adoption of a seat?"

Mrs. Gherkin invited me to be her guest, and I could feel her eyes burning into my back as I headed for a group of little tables and big leather chairs clustered around a cold fireplace. I made myself comfortable, choosing a chair that faced the desk so that I could keep an eye on her. I clutched my coat about me as I sat down, trusting that Mrs. Gherkin would take it for the uncomfortable self-consciousness of the recent immigrant, just another charming trait of mine. James twitched between my knees like a caged animal, but I clamped him tight, set the book upon his concealed head, and began turning pages.

Instantly, I was enraptured. *The Voiage*, despite Jean d'Outremeuse's florid language and love for the extraneous detail—nothing was too small to escape his obsessive attention, neither the fabric of a cloak nor the texture of a night sky—*The Voiage*, as I was saying, was an absolute catalog of high adventure. Its table of contents alone was sufficient to overwhelm a man, including as it did everything from the One True Cross (old news, as far as I was concerned) to Noah's wrecked ark, hinting at sights as perilous as the venom-bearing trees of Java and as miraculous as the twenty-two kings said to be entombed within the mountains beyond Cathay. I skipped ahead, I paged backward, I leapt among the pages of that great volume as if my attention were a waterbug. And only when James gave my shin a good solid kick did I look up and see that Mrs. Gherkin had, at least for the moment, vanished. I set him free with an admonitory hiss, and he disappeared among the tables and chairs. His little feet made no sound.

My attention snapped back to *The Voiage*. Sir John Mandeville was in the Valley of Peril on the Isle of Mistorak, quaking before the Devil's oversized head. I was in a comfortable leather chair in Wycombe's Circulating Library, utterly enthralled. As for where James Curtin might have gotten to, I'm sorry to confess that the details were at the moment of no particular interest to me. Until, that is, I heard footsteps from the direction of the librarian's desk.

I threw one ankle casually over the other knee as if to show Mrs. Gherkin that I had nothing—so to speak—up my sleeve. I hoped that James would have the good sense to keep himself out of sight until the danger was past. I stuck my thumb in *The Voiage* and held my breath. And I looked up.

Then, in the space between two heartbeats, I forgot all about James and his predicament. I forgot all about Sir John Mandeville and his adventures. I even forgot—for once—all about myself. Why? Because heading straight toward me was the most ferociously beautiful young woman I had seen in all my life.

Her walk was purposeful and confident, somehow easy and forceful and businesslike all at once, like the perfectly self-assured stride of a lioness. She was tall and slim and elegantly proportioned—not quite so tall as I, to be sure, but tall nonetheless—and she was gifted with the powerful shoulders and narrow waist of a lady pugilist. Her hair, lightly drawn away from her face and gathered loosely behind, was the color of honey mingled with chocolate. And her face—that face! its delicate shape! its clear-eyed expression!—her face was beyond improvement or description. As I watched her move toward me, I was possessed of a single thought: if the blind poet had known this woman, he'd have possessed his model for both the glorious Helen and the warlike Achilles in one matchless figure.

"How'd *he* get in here?" She nodded toward me and pointed her nose at a distant table, above which peeped the orange top of James Curtin's head.

Oh broken heart of broken hearts! That a creature of such unsurpassed beauty should, like that desiccated husk Mrs. Gherkin, be utterly uncaring toward the orphans of the world! Seeing the fair young woman for the stony-hearted beast that she most surely was—a sour acidic core buried inside the most tempting of confections—I set aside my manly instincts and rose in defense of my friend.

"I smuggled him in. Beneath my coat."

She looked at me as if I were a talking mummy.

"James may be a penniless orphan," I went on, setting down my d'Outremeuse and pointing with a trembling hand, "but he is nonetheless a great admirer of literature. His father, may God have mercy upon his heartbroken soul, was a professor of the classics. Thanks to the influence of that great man's mighty intellect, his spirit lives on through this innocent child. Yet you—you, my dear lady, and others like you—would persecute this boy! You would take from him his one and only birthright! You would deprive him of his patrimony! And you dare call yourself a librarian." I made various other chilling accusations on that order. My hope was that they would bring her low. My expectation, realist that I am, was that they would get the pair of us, James and me, thrown out on our ears.

She took not a second to compose her reply: "Thanks for the lecture, you big oaf."

My knees buckled.

"But trust me," the lioness went on. "I know *all* about this one." She brushed past me and made straight for James's little bobbing head.

"*Signorina,*" said I, lapsing back into my helpless native tongue, "have mercy."

117

"Go back to your fairytale," she said. "I'll help junior find himself a real book." Over her shoulder she gave me a look that was dismissive and disappointed all at once. It burned me to the core.

For as you have guessed by now, this astonishing woman was James Curtin's ally in his war with Mrs. Gherkin. She loved him. She understood him. And when the senior librarian's back was turned, she fed him on rough bread and ginger beer and poetry. Never mind that she had just dismissed *The Voiage and Travaile of Sir John Mandeville, Knight* as a fairy story. I cared not a whit for the reputation of Jean d'Outremeuse (who was a Frenchman, after all, and was thus linked in my overheated brain to both Napoleon Bonaparte and Bernardino Drovetti, my victorious but mainly forgotten rival). Let Napoleon have his way with Italy. Let Drovetti have his love affair with the French. Let that preening turncoat have his love affair with Serafina, come to that. I cared only for regaining my dignity in the eyes of a certain assistant librarian, a magnificent creature who even now strode away from me at speed, sweeping up little James Curtin in her skirts and whisking him off to some literary garden of unearthly delights.

I cleared my throat. I hummed. I made clicking noises with my tongue. I paced, rapping my knuckles on tables as I went, and I permitted myself to draw near to the huddled pair of them like an eccentric moon. And although James looked up, his native guide and protector did not. It was as if I did not exist.

"Pardon me," I said at last, completely exasperated and bursting with the kind of agony known only to the most deeply misunderstood.

She pressed a finger to those lips of hers and shushed me without looking up, condemning the innocent Belzoni with every librarian's impersonal and automatic response.

For his part, James gave me a terrified look. And in an instant I understood: my noise had attracted Mrs. Gherkin herself, back (judging by the smell) from a moment spent deep in the stacks with a forbidden cigarette.

"Can I help you?" she called in a hoarse whisper from behind the desk.

I spun. "Oh no, Signorina," I said, and that pleased her sufficiently that she offered up a hideously coy smile. "I am but stretching my legs."

Mrs. Gherkin craned her neck and blinked. "Sarah? Is that you, dear?"

Upon which words the astonishing young woman snatched open my coat and stuffed James between my legs, along with a thick volume or two and an accidental pencil that caught me just below the kneecap. Then she drew herself up to her full height—slowly, almost languorously—and smoothed the front of her dress with hands as strong and confident as any man's.

"Yes, Mrs. Gherkin. I'm right here." She fingered a lock of hair as golden as the irretrievable past.

"Why aren't you at your shelving?"

"Forgive me," she said, and I could tell by the little wince that passed over her features that she was thinking fast. "I was distracted by a rat."

Never mind what she may have been suggesting about me. She had a heart of gold, and I had her name. The rest could come later.

*

JEAN D'OUTREMEUSE WAS WRONG about many things, and he always preferred a whopper to a plain fact, but every word he wrote was gospel to me until the time when I was finally able to follow in Mandeville's footsteps. In the meantime I forgot all about my need to find work and lay instead on the rug in our squalid room, memorizing page after page of his astonishing book.

The third chapter—I remember it right down to the engravings, right down to the thumbprints of previous readers—was titled "Of The Country Of Egypt; Of The Bird Phoenix Of Arabia; Of The City Of

Cairo; Of The Cunning To Know Balm And To Prove It; And Of The Garners Of Joseph." No wonder it made me dizzy.

Here is Mandeville at a location you might recognize:

"Now also I shall speak of another thing that is beyond Babylon, above the flood of the Nile, toward the desert between Africa and Egypt; that is to say, of the garners of Joseph, that he let make for to keep the grains for the peril of the dear years. And they be made of stone, full well made of masons' craft; of the which two be marvellously great and high, and the tother one be not so great. And every garner hath a gate for to enter within, a little high from the earth; for the land is wasted and fallen since the garners were made. And within they be all full of serpents. And above the garners without be many scriptures of diverse languages. And some men say, that they be sepultures of great lords, that were sometime, but that is not true, for all the common rumour and speech is of all the people there, both far and near, that they be the garners of Joseph; and so find they in their scriptures, and in their chronicles. On the other part, if they were sepultures, they should not be void within, nor they should have no gates for to enter within; for ye may well know, that tombs and sepultures be not made of such greatness, nor of such highness; wherefore it is not to believe, that they be tombs or sepultures."

And you thought I was merely some illiterate tomb-robber. My head is packed full of that stuff. I have a dog-eared copy of *The Voiage* in my sea chest even now, and although it no longer serves as my Bible, in the fullness of time it has become my Shakespeare.

That particular volume is inscribed to me by none other than my dearest Sarah herself, Sarah whom I despair of ever seeing again unless my own troubled *voiage* takes a turn for the better. How it came to have her writing upon its pages is an adventure greater than any other in my life—greater by far than the day I first set foot inside one of d'Outremeuse's Garners of Joseph and found it to be the very thing that he and his pawn Mandeville had concluded it was not: a pharaoh's pyramidal tomb. The Frenchman, as you have seen, was fooled by appearances. He was a slave to convention and a victim of rumor. Above all, he lacked imagination—by which I don't mean mere invention, for he was bursting with that, but instead the true open-hearted spirit that permits a man to perceive the truth no matter how fantastic and impossible it may seem.

(Much as I loved him, d'Outremeuse was fixated upon building up his stories out of needless details and wearisome minutiae. He gloried in describing Mandeville's performance of the most ludicrous treasure-hunting techniques, many of which were based more on superstition than on science. Something called "fumigation," for example, whereby the burning of incense was supposed to reveal hidden passageways. Fairy stories like those were strictly for the most credulous, I thought then.)

Evening after evening I lay on the carpet and gorged myself upon adventure, while James mooned over William Blake and complained about his empty stomach. Only when I could not bear one more of Mr. Jaundyce's revolting suppers—and when both James and I were finished with our books and wanting more—did we set out again in search of employment and illumination. Our footsteps led us first to the library, of course. I had our volumes tucked into the lining of my coat, and I was busy pushing James in after them, when the young librarian came tearing down the marble stairs as if the building behind her were on fire. No, no. Not that. Permit me to correct myself, for in truth she ran as if the fish and chips shop across the street were on fire and she meant to rescue a loved one from its flaming environs. She did not—on that day or any other—look like a woman inclined to run *away* from anything.

She stopped directly in front of us.

"I'll take the books, Jimmy," she said to the space between my knees. It was as if I weren't there at all.

"Jimmy?" I repeated. For I had always called him James.

He rummaged around in the darkness and produced all three books, one after another. His small hand poked out and handed them over to her, just like that.

"Thanks. Mrs. Gorgon is on one of her rampages today. You'd better make yourself scarce."

"Jimmy?"

She gave me an airy look, suggesting that once she decided to call a person something, that was the end of it. I wondered what she'd call me, given the chance.

She was studying the three books, holding them in front of her and shuffling them like cards, her posture thrust forward just enough that I had to shuffle backwards a step or two in order to keep a respectful distance between us. "Didn't you just love the Blake?"

"I did, miss." His voice piped up from inside my coat. Somehow, speaking to her, he sounded more like Jimmy than like James.

She stepped forward, I shuffled back. "And the Wordsworth?"

"I loved that too, miss. I surely did."

Another step. Another shuffle. "And how about you, Atlas? Wasn't it a struggle to get through such a *big long book?*" Her eyes shone when she finally looked up and let them fall upon my face. She had enjoyed saving me up for last, and I suspected that she didn't mind my knowing it.

I gasped like a blowfish. "I'll have you know," I began, regretting it already, "I'll have you know that I was educated by the Capuchins. In Rome." As if she couldn't have guessed.

"That would explain a lot."

"I beg your pardon?"

She ignored me and knelt down on the stones. With one hand she drew open the skirts of my coat and tugged James out into the daylight. "You're not going in today. May as well get some fresh air."

I looked down and studied the part in her hair. "The Capuchins may not be the Jesuits," I said, "but their standards are high enough. I assure you of that." The less said about the Jesuits the better, after Francesco's disgrace among them. In my heart I was sorry I'd brought them up.

"Oh," she said, rising again. "Then no wonder you felt like giving me a lecture about charity the first time we met. I knew plenty about Jimmy—trust me on this; I know more than you—without being treated like some kind of harpy."

"I was just defending the boy. I had no idea."

"You had no idea. I'll say you didn't. You assumed that I was just another Mrs. Gherkin."

"I confess it. I did."

"The Capuchins aren't exactly the world's leading experts on women, are they?"

"I suppose not."

"Neither are the Italians as a whole, do you think?"

May my dear mother forgive me, I did not grasp the opportunity to lift up my love for that sainted woman in self-defense. She would have made a fine exhibit, but I was pliable and weak. "I suppose not," was all I said. "Not the Italians. Not as a rule."

"Then I guess you couldn't help yourself, Atlas." Her eyes brightened, and I believe that mine did as well. "It was your cultural prerogative. And besides, you were only thinking of Jimmy."

I hung my head. "Forgive me, *Sarah.*" I used her name so she'd know I'd been paying attention during our last visit, conclude from that fact what she might. She leapt upon the bait and took it.

"The two of you have been talking about me, is that it?"

"Who would ye be kidding?" said James. At his age, he was inclined to discuss a woman only if she presented an opportunity or a threat.

Sarah lifted an eyebrow.

"Ye know I'm not one to gossip about me friends. And Mr. Atlas here—Signor Giovanni Battista Belzoni, if ye care to get it proper—he's had his nose stuck in that Outraymoose all week long. We ain't done much talking. Nor much eating, neither."

"So, *Signor Belzoni,*" she addressed me with a kind of playful intensity, a finger on the dimple in her right cheek. There was no matching dimple on the left, which instead of making her look lopsided had precisely the opposite effect. "Exactly what is it that you do, when you're not up to your neck in great literature or busy smuggling children into libraries?"

"I look for employment, mainly."

"A big boy like you shouldn't have any trouble."

"Alas, I have standards. They limit my opportunities, Miss..." I cocked my head to ask the question.

"Banne." She freed up her right hand and thrust it toward me. "Call me Sarah."

"Sarah. That much of your name, as you have seen, was already known to me." My inclination as a gentleman was to take her hand and raise it gallantly to my lips, but I could see just how much trouble that would have gotten me into. So I took hold and shook it instead, just as she'd intended. The girl had the grip of an animal trainer.

"So you have standards," she resumed. "I suppose you got those from the Capuchins, too."

"I'm not at all sure."

"Standards?" James put in from below: "It'll be standards now, will it? Can we be eating your standards, then?"

Sarah looked pained. "How on earth did the two of you fall in together?"

"He picked my pocket, and then he adopted me."

"It doesn't seem to have done either of you a lot of good."

"He has a roof over his head."

"Until the money runs out," said James.

I reminded him—I reminded them both—that I was earnestly looking for suitable employment.

"But you have *standards.*"

"It's not what you think." She had made it sound as if I were looking for a position grading diamonds. I'd have been content to dig for them with a shovel and a pickaxe, half a mile beneath the surface of the earth, if only the activity had given me some kind of satisfaction. "Oh, I'm no stranger to hard work. I've done lots of it. Excavating, barbering, gardening..." As I ticked them off on my fingers I was careful not to overstate my case. I made no mention of discovering a Mithraic temple, of seeing the exposed neck of the Pope, or of creating my very own Eden in drought-wracked Rome.

"For a while he was going to be a strongman at St. Bartholomew's," said James. "But he lost interest."

That wasn't precisely true. "How many strong men do they need, boy? They already have their French Hercules, and I should think that's all they have room for."

"Have you tried Sadler's Wells?" she asked.

Tried it? I'd never heard of it. She could tell by the look on my face.

"It's a better class of place than St. Bartholomew's."

What wasn't? I've since been in opium dens that were better classes of place than St. Bartholomew's.

*

JAMES KNEW EXACTLY WHERE to find Sadler's Wells, of course—he knew exactly where to find everything, including the love of my life—and in comparison to St. Bartholomew's the place proved to be less carnival, more public garden. I felt out of my depth immediately, out of my depth and a good deal poorer, since management had taken measures to keep our sort from slipping in without proper tickets. Once inside, though, we took our time and wandered the grounds, relaxing under the sycamores and strolling down walkways refreshingly free of cutpurses and camp followers. We salivated over mugs of lemonade offered at stall after stall by costumed concessionaires, and we settled for a free taste of the allegedly miraculous waters produced by the medieval wells themselves. It was cold as a glacier, and it tasted like chalk.

Aside from the ticket-takers and the concessionaires—the paid professionals, that is—no one took note of us. Imagine that! A giant of my height and span, wandering about holding the little paw of a child so wasted of frame and jaded of visage that he might have been a thousand-year-old midget, and the two of us not getting a second glance from a crowd of gawkers packed as tightly as olives in a tub. They had witnessed other wonders, you see. Wonders as varied, according to the banners that hung all about, as the Magnetic Madame Minsk, Omar the Whirling Dervish, and the Three Flying Schmidtka Brothers.

James and I, though, were seeking a different and more subtle wonder altogether: a certain door, bound to be the least prominent and promising entranceway in the entire complex. We found it hidden behind the main stage, a forbidding thing cocked on its hinges and hastily lettered with black paint: Charles Dibdin, Manager—Keep Out.

I knocked. A bark from within advised me to go away, so I tried the knob, ducked my head, and admitted myself.

Dibdin sat at his desk in a thick cloud of smoke. Visibility in that cramped office was so poor that never once while we were in his presence did the man take note of little James—although he did hear the boy cough painfully once, which in the absence of visual confirmation he seemed to take as a sign of demonic or ghostly visitation. Luckily for me and my prospects of employment, I was large enough to resolve out of the miasma.

"You're a big fellow," said Dibdin, who knew talent when he saw it.

I agreed wholeheartedly, commending him on his acute perceptions. Then, with a bow that nearly scraped the floor, I introduced myself and offered my services as giant in residence.

"Bah," he spat, releasing a great lungful of smoke. "Giants are as common as bricks."

"I, sir, am an educated giant."

"Bosh. There's an educated giant on every street corner."

"I am an educated giant from Italy."

"Humbug. There are two of those on every street corner, and another one in the billiard parlor down the block."

"I am educated, I am from Italy, and I am strong as a pair of oxen."

"That's what they all say, friend." Dibdin's pipe had gone out, but the smoke in the room hadn't diminished by so much as a single atom.

Invisible James, ever the diplomat, ended our standoff with a simple question. "Then what class of giant would ye have him be, sir?"

Dibdin flinched and pawed at the air to reveal whatever spirit had made itself heard. No luck. But the mystery of his interlocutor's identity caused him to take the question seriously. "A Patagonian," he said. Heaven knows how he came up with that.

"Fine!" I said. "A Patagonian I shall be!"

Lacking any and all reservations about deceiving the public, Dibdin reached across the desk and shook my hand. "Will it be just 'The Patagonian,' then? That has a kind of stark quality to it. Sounds, though, as if you Patagonians might be an entire race of giants, which rather diminishes your individual import."

I chewed my lip. The name seemed altogether too unadorned. "I don't know. How about 'The Patagonian Atlas'?" James gave me a kick in the shins to show he knew where I'd gotten that idea.

"Nah. Sounds like a big book with a lot of maps. That sort of thing will never draw a crowd."

If Dibdin were no student of mythology, then perhaps he knew his Old Testament. Victor the Human Snail had called me Samson, hadn't he? Perhaps that would do. "Then I shall be 'The Patagonian Samson,'" I said.

"That's it!" Dibdin swept open a drawer and began hunting for matches. "Beautiful!"

It was.

"Now," he said, as he sucked at his pipestem and a flame lit up his features, "you'll be responsible for your own costume, but you can work with the crew on props. I believe we have some pasteboard weights left over from the last strongman. Check with Frankie Malone."

"Pasteboard?"

"Pasteboard."

"That's fraud."

"That's show business."

"I won't have it."

"Real weights cost money. Buy your own, if you insist. Your salary might cover them, provided you don't eat for a year or two."

"I'll find a way."

"Besides, the last strongman could barely lift a pint."

"I'm not the last strongman."

"Lucky for for you," he said. "Welcome to Sadler's Wells, Samson. You start a week from Wednesday."

*

THANK GOD FOR JAMES CURTIN. Not only had he pried an answer out of Dibdin and thus gotten me a job, but he soon became my sole aid in cobbling together a credible performance. He'd sneaked into every unsavory show in town, so he was bursting with theatrical ideas both original and secondhand. We sat in our room and scribbled notes, stealing a little something from every tramp player who'd ever pranced through London and making up bits of our own to tie it all together.

One afternoon my enthusiasm got the better of me, and I leapt upon the cot to declaim my lines.

At the sound of my voice, James struck his forehead with his little hand. "Jesus, Mary and Holy Saint Joseph," he shouted. "Ye won't be passing fer a proper Patagonian if ye'll be talking that way."

I slumped. "How does a proper Patagonian sound, do you suppose?"

"I don't know. But not like he just got off the boat from Sicily, ye can count on that."

So James became not just my collaborator but my Master of Ceremonies. He would handle the talking, while I took care of the feats of strength and balance. It was his best possible role in our theatrical alliance, given that if I had desired to make a show of lifting him—even in the palm of one hand, or on the tip of one finger—nobody in the world would have been impressed in the slightest.

The more we rehearsed, the more distant seemed the limits of my strength. I stamped around our room with the bed frame on my shoulders, the rickety thing piled high with every object we could lay our hands on. The contents of my sailor's duffel and the duffel itself, books both borrowed and owned, our washstand and chamber pot, a chair from the parlor, the tattered rug where I slept, James himself, and, on one memorable occasion, old Mr. Jaundyce, our reluctant host. I spun and I danced. I did deep-knee bends and I raised myself up on one toe like a ballerina. And all the while James lifted his voice to inflame the imaginary crowds by exaggerating each and every movement.

We drew my costume from the rags in Jaundyce's linen closet: a ratty bedsheet, which James folded into a passable toga. And we located the other essential, at least for an old-fashioned literalist like me, in a dustbin down the lane: a long black wig, symbol of Samson's uncompromised might. The thing smelled disconcertingly of mouse droppings and sandalwood no matter how thoroughly I washed it, and I resolved to grow out my own hair as soon as possible.

Frankie Malone, prop-master at Sadler's Wells, gave us as little help as he could. With his cigar as a pointer, he aimed us toward an attic full of junk above a series of catwalks obstructed by tangled ropes and rusty chains, torn canvas and leaky sandbags. From its contents, and such other castoffs as we could find in the streets and the dustbins, we were to assemble the tools of our magic.

Dibdin had been correct about the pasteboard weights. We found them in a corner of the attic, and I had to admit that even in disrepair they were impressive. I reinforced them with salvaged lumber and filled them up with sand just to mollify my guilty soul, and James repainted them a glistening black with white digits.

The finest artifact of all, retrieved from high above the main stage where it hung on a rotten rope, preparing like rain to fall on the just and the unjust alike, was a lion's cage. It was rough and rectangular and forged of black iron, and little tufts of tawny fur still clung to it. Its floor was fiercely scratched, and in the deepest of these scratches it gleamed dark umber with the blood of meals long past. Just the thing, I realized, to replace that poor old cot we'd piled so high in our room at Jaundyce's.

I hoisted it to my shoulders as easily as I had once hoisted Brother Ruggiero's table and its great piles of produce. James climbed up my leg and hopped aboard, pulling the door shut behind him. I ambled around backstage for a while, getting my sea legs—the thing was turning out to be a little heavier than I'd imagined, and James wouldn't sit still—and then I angled my way through the stage door and into the alleyway behind the theater. Dibdin was just coming out of his office, locking the door behind him.

I hailed him with absolute nonchalance. "Mr. Dibdin, of all people! Where might you be headed?"

He flattened himself against the door. "Ah! Belzoni! You took me by surprise!"

This was an understatement. I'd barreled down upon him like a steam engine. He was pressed flat, with only his little round belly and his bowl of his pipe poking out beyond the doorframe. Dibdin was a narrow man to begin with, slim as a shadow but for that potbelly. He possessed a Capuchin fringe of silvery hair, augmented by six or eight long strands that he greased and pressed over the top in sad homage to his younger self. He kept his pipe stoked with Old Beauregard tobacco, which imparted to him a characteristic scent of rotted pumpkins, household rubbish, filthy laundry, boiling sulfur, and a horsehair sofa set ablaze. I could have identified him blindfolded. At a distance of fifty paces. Underwater.

"Good sir," I continued, "wherever you're going, permit me to give you a lift." I extended a courtly leg, and indicated that he should climb aboard. "Unlatch the door and shove over, James."

"Don't mind if I do," said Dibdin. And once he was inside, he thrust out a hand and shouted, "To the jakes!"

It wasn't far, not even with a lion's cage balanced upon my shoulders. Along the way I discovered why Dibdin had been so amenable to my request to climb aboard, for we quickly became our own best advertisement, calling forth hoots and whistles from the people queued in the sunshine for whatever performances were on that day. After I dropped Dibdin at his destination I took the long way back, slightly more erect for his absence, and smiled for the enthusiastic crowds. Over my head, in his great black cage, James thrust out his hand and waved like royalty.

*

WE OPENED THE FOLLOWING Wednesday afternoon, and we rapidly became a huge success, and I rapidly grew miserable.

It wasn't the conditions. The audiences were enthusiastic and more or less civilized, the theater was well-lighted and clean, and Dibdin had ordered up a flying scrim that pictured me as a demigod of mythic proportions. Its imagery—which was duplicated on a set of outdoor advertising banners—was spectacular, romantic, and disorienting to anyone with any common sense or knowledge of geography. It showed me in my toga and wig, manacled to a pair of toppling pillars, surrounded by panicking Philistines and bounding kangaroos. The kangaroos were quite fine, actually. It seems that during the prior season Sadler's Wells had exhibited one trained in boxing, and our painter had made quite a study of him. My christening as a foreigner from the Southern Hemisphere was all the encouragement he needed to dash off a few highly realistic marsupials.

It wasn't the pay that troubled me, either. For although I have no doubt that I was receiving perhaps a quarter of the salary of the more established acts, I was a naïf whose needs were few. And it certainly wasn't lack of adulation, for we were playing to packed houses before I knew it. I was so much in demand that Dibdin had me written into a dozen of the little comic plays and charades that came between the major acts—among which "The Patagonian Samson" was well on the way to taking its place.

Nonetheless, my life lacked two things. And luckily for me, I knew how to obtain at least one of them.

With Dibdin's approval—I see now that I must have been making him money hand over fist—Frankie Malone put down his cigar and picked up his tools to construct an array of props and devices I'd sketched out. There were levers, ramps, and rollers. There were flags and spirit lamps and a handful of explosive charges. There were stairs that led nowhere and that seemed from the gallery at least three times higher than they were. Best of all there was a massive framework, far more presentable than my old lion cage and infinitely less chafing upon my shoulders, with seating for eighteen adult volunteers.

As time went by I grew famous for trooping from one end of the stage to the other with members of my audience—young and old, big and small—balanced atop my back. Ridiculous as it sounds now, it was the high point of the performance. I would take on all comers, and they began lining up for the privilege long before the show began. Compared against the French Hercules of St. Bartholomew's, that Greek *poseur* with his pair of barely clad damsels and his disgusting acrobatic midget, I gained a reputation as fearless, as a taker of great risks.

All of which would one day serve me well in the eyes of Captain Ismael Gibraltar and the British Consul Henry Salt. But I am getting ahead of myself.

*

I RECEIVED A RAISE OR TWO and was making enough money to buy James an occasional volume from the stalls at Spitalfields, but he was still slipping off to Wycombe's Circulating Library at every opportunity. I couldn't blame him. If books were rotten eggs, I'd have moved heaven and earth to obtain one from the hands of the enchanting Sarah Banne. For now, though, that pleasure was to be mine only at second hand. Which was particularly painful, since it so happened that I really and truly needed a book at that very moment—a volume very different from the books of romance and poetry that flooded the stalls at Spitalfields.

I persuaded James to obtain it.

"A textbook on hydraulics," I said. "Something thorough, covering the concentration and manipulation of water, the design of fountains, the construction and operation of high-pressure rams, and so forth."

James scratched his head. "*Water?* Where's the poetry in that?"

"Complex hydraulic devices possess a beauty that you have yet to imagine," I said, and left it at that.

He and Sarah tracked down a folio copy of Eduardo Escobar's famous *Treatise on the Most Malleable of Elements,* and with the esteemed Dr. Escobar as my guide I went straight to work. On what? Not on fulfilling my vow to free the Pope's imprisoned angels, alas, although I had not forgotten about it. For the moment I could only trust that my promise would work itself out in the fullness of time. My concerns on this occasion, quite the contrary, were immediate and concrete: I desired to harness the waters of Sadler's Wells for theatrical purposes.

Needless to say, I took to the *Treatise* like a duck. I set up my own laboratory in a corner of the prop department, where James and I studied and ran our experiments. The work had about it a sense of mingled invention and camaraderie; it was like the old days underground with Brother Silvestro, only cleaner and better lit. Frankie Malone requisitioned whatever we needed—planks of oak, piles of forged hinges and valves, buckets of tar and India rubber and gutta percha, a forest of bamboo, half a ton of lead—and Dibdin picked up the tab without too much in the way of complaint.

It was all worthwhile, he said, when for the first glorious time our fountains erupted from behind the footlights on the great outdoor stage.

He was just being polite, of course, for as far as he was concerned the real value wasn't in the startling beauty of our waterworks, but in the doubling and tripling of the queues at his ticket window. This gratified me too, I must admit, and in turn it funded further research.

We were the toast of London—a mere sideshow act, by nature the lowliest of the low, but baptized in fire and transmuted by water into something far greater—when Sarah Banne finally appeared in the crowd. She sat near the stage with an older couple, her parents, as I was to learn, and she hung on every one of James Curtin's piping words. He gave a compelling performance. We had him dressed in a tiny swallow-tail coat, and he stood atop a six-foot platform from where, as occasion demanded, he could leap onto my passing shoulders. There he'd balance in his shiny little shoes, clutching my wig with one hand and indicating the finer points of the performance with the other.

For James himself—he was just a boy, after all—the most thrilling moments were those when he could leap down from his high perch and swarm about the stage, dodging fountains and fireworks and even demonstrating at one point how the powers of science and geometry could make him my equal. This last involved a ladder, a fulcrum, and a lever nearly as long as the stage was wide; its climax was a shockingly (although briefly) airborne Patagonian. Archimedes would have given us a standing ovation.

During the performance on this particular night, Sarah's attention never wavered or wandered—although that distinguished her in no way from the rest of the crowd. I could feel her eyes upon me, this I swear. And as I flicked mine in her direction, I saw hers dart from me to my little assistant as if he were the one she had been watching all along.

Naturally, when the time came for my grand finale—the padded iron framework, the eighteen volunteers, and now a dazzling display of pyrotechnics and waterworks—I indicated to James that he must be certain to enlist her.

In case you haven't imagined it yet, permit me to inform you that Sarah was a natural. Agile as an acrobat. Gorgeous as an Amazon. Light as a feather. When she climbed up to the second-highest spot and reached down to give James a hand, I swear I could not feel a single added ounce. On the contrary, it was as if a great weight had actually been lifted from my shoulders.

Go ahead and call it love. I surely did.

We met backstage, but only after much cautious circling on my part. She was huddled on a bench with James, no doubt discussing poetry. I'd been self-consciously storing away my weights, sweeping up after the Roman candles, and tinkering with the pumps. She'd never been out of my vision for a moment, but I had been careful not to let on.

"Why so quiet?" she asked when we came face to face at last. "On stage, I mean. I have to tell you, Atlas, half the crowd thinks you're a mute—my parents included."

James began to answer on my behalf, the story about how little we believed I sounded like a Patagonian—whatever it was that a Patagonian might sound like—and while Sarah sat listening it was clear that her mind was working steadily. I could see it whirling away behind her gray eyes.

She lifted an eyebrow at me when he was done, clearly ready to hear my version of the story. "So, Belzoni? Speak for yourself."

I shrugged. "I would love to. If only I could manage it without being ridiculous."

"I could help."

"You've been to Patagonia?"

"No, but I've been almost everywhere else, and I have a good ear. I'm sure we could concoct something."

And thus began my elocution lessons. We settled on an elevated British diction from a century or so past, gilded it over with a handful of rolling French *R's*, and then plugged everything up with some glottal stranglings taken straight from the lowest of Low German. I sounded like an alley cat with a head cold, attempting to recite Wordsworth.

Sarah loved it. Each time I mastered a new phrase she would throw back her head and let out a howl, as undignified and unself-conscious as she could be. Once or twice, fierce precious creature that she was, she snorted through her nose like a racehorse.

Soon she was leaving the library early most afternoons and watching with us as the other performers went through their acts.

"And who would this be?" Dibdin inquired as he found me opening the door for her. He'd seen his fill of stage-door Johnnies and Janes, most of them as bent and broken as the curiosities who earned their wages beneath his spotlights. The middle-aged triplets who dressed identically and pursued the Three Flying Schmidtka Brothers like a pack of wolverines, the itinerant blacksmith who swallowed a spoonful of rivets each morning in the doomed hope of increasing his attractiveness to the Magnetic Madame Minsk. They were an odd lot, by and large. I could see in the manager's eyes that he thought I'd struck gold.

Sarah thrust out her hand, forward and plain as any man. "I'm a friend of James's," she said, and I desired her all the more for it. "Sarah Banne."

Dibdin thought he saw right through her, and at the moment I could only dream that he had. He moved his pipe to his left hand and took hold of her right as if he were wrapping up a particularly fine piece of horse trading. "Welcome, Miss Banne," he said, giving her an oily smile that revealed a caravan of teeth the color of dromedaries. "May you continue to enjoy my performers. And vice versa!"

She dropped his hand as if it were an asp.

James piped up. "Actually, sir, Miss Banne is our technical consultant on all things hydraulic and linguistic."

"But she's *not* on the payroll," Dibdin clucked, playful as a school-marm with a ruler lifted behind her back.

"Nor am I," said James. "In case ye ain't noticed."

*

DIBDIN WAS FOREVER TINKERING with the money-making engine that was Sadler's Wells, and I was forever improving my part in it as well. He hired a Swede who did card tricks. I decorated my iron frame with bright flags and bunting. He persuaded the Swede to begin sawing his wife, a substantial blonde, in half. I enlarged my hydraulic rams and adjusted their nozzles until they sent jets of water fifty or more feet into the air. He hired freaks of every sort and then fired them just as quickly, giving the place a reputation as a revolving door for the misbegotten. I added (at long last) the astonishment of speech to my act.

And thus went the escalation of our efforts. Always some new marvel to enchant the fickle London crowd. Always some new challenge to keep me interested.

One damp raw February afternoon the three of us—Sarah, James, and I—returned from our supper to see the entire family of Sadler's Wells' pinheads go scuttling downcast from Dibdin's door. They were lovely people, really, the whole lot of them, and in their hats and scarves they could have been anyone at all. That was the difficulty, as it turned out. Dibdin had decided that the pinheads were an old-fashioned kind of attraction, tired and shopworn and dull as dishwater. Worst of all, as a family of five (not counting little Oswald, the baby, who was as heartbreakingly perfect as a teardrop) they were a disproportionate drag on his profits.

There'd be no changing his mind, this I knew. But if I couldn't save the pinheads, then perhaps I could help elevate someone else instead, someone to whom I owed a great debt. I was thinking of Victor the Human Snail, the underrated wonder of St. Bartholomew's Fair. You've not forgotten Victor, have you? Who could? I pictured him heaving himself around and around that horrid glass tank in the darkest corner of St. Bartholomew's, subservient to the outlandish fakery of lesser curiosities: the evil-tongued beheaded man, the snake charmer beneath his tangle of wires.

"Bring him in," Dibdin said when I asked. "He can't be any worse than a useless family of pinheads. At least he's got just the one mouth to feed."

As if I weren't selling enough tickets to give half of the freaks in Europe a Christmas goose every day of the year. As if he didn't know that I knew. Why else would he have made an offer to Victor the very instant I returned with him squirming in my arms like a worm on a hook? (He was a tough one, that Victor; he was a fighter. Nothing came easy to him. Not even salvation.)

I'd found his tent nearly empty. The whole of St. Bartholomew's was a ghost town in fact, an abandoned necropolis blooming with faded banners and useless creaking turnstiles. It was dried up, depleted, as if the competition posed by Sadler's Wells were a hydraulic ram capable of draining the place entirely. The decapitated man snored in his tub, his ear resting on a bundle of rags and his neck wrenched uncomfortably to one side. His collar had fallen away and the ragged tin of his tub's false bottom was biting into his flesh, but he seemed not to mind. He drooled into his top hat and I could smell his breath from ten feet away. At least he wasn't peppering me with obscenities.

There was no sleeping for Victor, though. He was hurling himself about his tank like an agitated inchworm. At my approach he stopped and threw himself against the wall, panting. "Hey, pal, would you mind filling up my water bucket? I'm dying of thirst here. There's a pump out back."

Once he was sated, I set forth my proposition. He knew Sadler's Wells, naturally enough, and he'd heard of me—who in London hadn't?—although he didn't remember my face or recall the day when he'd alerted me to James Curtin's thievery. "I have to tell you: around here, getting dipped ain't no distinction. You're just another victim. No offense intended."

Victor's language was as plain and unadorned as his limbless self. Born into this world absolutely without defense, he had decided long ago that plainspokenness bordering on aggression was generally the best conversational course.

"So you think this Dibdin might have a spot for me?"

"It won't hurt to ask. There's an opening."

"Somebody get canned?" His eyebrows went up "Somebody *die?*"

For this was every carnival freak's worst nightmare: death, alone and unmourned, followed by the hasty dismantling of everything he'd ever held dear—his sets struck by the prop men, his possessions distributed among strangers, his body dissected by surgeons in what would amount to one final and alarming public appearance.

"No. Nobody died. There was some attrition, that's all." I was trying to put a pleasant face on things.

"Aha! So somebody *did* get canned! I knew it!"

"Yes. You're right. Pinheads."

"Pinheads? Plural?"

I nodded. "A whole family. Five of them, plus the baby."

"Ouch. That's a tough break." Victor knitted and unknitted his brow. "So how's the pay?"

"Better than it is here, I'd wager."

"How's the food?"

"Tolerable. There's a satisfactory pub or two in the neighborhood."

"I eat in the commissary. Or else I order in."

"You'll do fine."

Victor was convinced. "I come with my own tank and everything, just the way you see it. Home, sweet home, eh?" He banged the glass wall with the back of his head and it rang out, very nearly waking his decapitated neighbor.

"I don't know about the tank." I tapped it with a knuckle that came away greasy. "It's seen better days, don't you think?"

"In case you haven't noticed, Sammy, I'm a little handicapped in the housekeeping department." He was defiantly unapologetic. "But that doesn't mean that I don't care about the place."

I thought I saw the tiniest hint of a tear gathering in the corner of his eye, but he heaved himself over onto his belly—Victor could have been a gymnast, if only he'd had arms and legs—and shook it off with a brisk lap around the tank.

"Still," I said, "maybe we ought to leave it here by way of paying off your contract."

"I don't have a contract," said Victor. "Believe it or not, everything at St. Bartholomew's is done on a handshake."

*

VICTOR HAD A BIT OF MONEY, it turned out, kept by the snake charmer in the sham safety of his dusty old lopsided wicker basket. He handed it over and the two of them said their gruff goodbyes. *All of this stoicism is for me,* I thought, *all of this is for my benefit.* Left to their own devices they'd have surely dropped their guards and let loose the sorrow that burned in their lonely freakish hearts. Or perhaps not.

Once we were on our way, I fanned through the envelope of cash on Victor's behalf. He jumped in my arms with such power that it took all my strength to hold him steady. "Holy mackerel!" he shouted. "I'm rich!"

Relatively speaking, it was true.

"What do you say we stop off for a drink? Celebrate my liberation."

"Sure. Where?"

"How should I know? I don't get out much."

I swiveled my head, spied a place right down the block—in London, there's always a place right down the block—and set out for it.

"Wait wait wait wait wait," Victor shouted at the last second, throwing his head over my shoulder and twisting himself into a knot. Something else had caught his attention.

"I thought you wanted a drink."

"Yeah, yeah, sure. But I want one of *those* even more."

I followed his line of vision and spied what had captivated him. Gleaming in the sun outside a shop was a row of wicker perambulators, each one shiny and black as a hearse. Ashes to ashes, I thought as I walked toward them, and dust to dust. Enter life in one of these things, and leave in another.

"Now *that's* traveling in style," said Victor. "I'll take the most expensive one they've got, but only if I can get a deal."

Once inside he bargained like a mad gypsy, indignant one instant and pathetic the next, and before I knew it I was parading him along the street in a carriage fit for a baby king.

Dibdin was waiting for us in the depths of his smoky office. Victor was seized by a coughing fit as we stepped over the threshold, and he buried his face in my sleeve.

"Does he eat much?" Dibdin said, as if Victor were lacking ears and a tongue.

"Not half as much as a family of pinheads," said Victor, with a smile that said "Put 'er there."

*

SOON THE FOUR OF US—James, Victor, Sarah and I—had become quite the happy family, We had our difficulties, of course, as all families do. Now that I was making a little money, James wanted fish and chips from a different shop every night, which meant careening back to Sadler's Wells with takeaway for Victor (who liked his food served hot as embers, and though happy enough traveling about town in his perambulator was understandably self-conscious about dining in public). For her commitment to me, Sarah suffered daily at the hands of Mrs. Gherkin, who watched her comings and goings as if she were a prisoner and timed her work as if the shelving of books had become an athletic competition.

As a compromise, James and I spent many an afternoon camped out in the fish and chips place across the street from Wycombe's. The proprietor was a pious and shadow-thin Persian whose true name I never knew. He'd won the business from an unlucky Scotsman in a card game, and to remind himself of the transience of good fortune he'd left everything exactly as he'd found it on that fateful night—including the sign out front, which spelled out the proprietor's name in gilded letters three inches high. Thus everyone, even those who should have known better, came to understand that the nearly-invisible Persian was named Angus McPhee.

We'd huddle over a table, scribbling notes from Eduardo Escobar's *Treatise on the Most Malleable of Elements* and other volumes that Sarah would smuggle out to us during her free moments and sketching huge apparatus and outlandish effects on the newspapers that the fastidious Angus McPhee spread on every horizontal surface. What teamwork! James had an imagination joyously uninhibited by physics; I was blessed with an intuitive grasp of hydrodynamics and geometry; and Sarah's mind operated with the speed and agility of a cheetah. And at the end of the day, if the three of us could not invent a solution to some problem, she would dredge one up from the depths of Wycombe's.

One evening I sent James running to Sadler's Wells with a steaming basket for himself and Victor so that Sarah and I might linger alone over supper. With an idle finger she traced a device we'd almost finished designing. It consisted of a waterwheel as large as a man, two hundred yards of bamboo pipe joined with lead and wrapped with miles of reinforcing jute and waterproofed with tar, a half-dozen hydraulic rams fed by a nightmarish branching manifold of pipe, and a single cast-iron nozzle out of which the chalky water of Sadler's Wells would soar a hundred feet or more. "This should be something they'll never forget," she said.

"Thanks to you."

"Thanks to *James*, I should think." For sure enough the little figure drawn striding away within the waterwheel that powered the rams bore the boy's clear likeness. How far I'd come from my days with the Capuchins, from Trumpeter and his band of strays!

"He inspired the thing, after all. It's only right that he should provide the generative power, don't you think?"

"Absolutely." She paused, her finger where his heart would be. "He won't be in any danger, will he?"

She was always such a tender creature, at least where James was concerned. "Not for a moment," I said. And I reviewed with her the various devices that would insulate the wheel from anything that might go wrong down the line. Even if all six of the rams seized up and sent their mighty burdens of water backward in a single surge, the wheel and the boy within it would never feel the slightest tremor.

"Do you see these?" I took her hand in mine and pointed with her finger to a bank of one-way valves.

"I know, I know." She knew at least as well as I did. But—and this I took for a sign—she made nonetheless no attempt to withdraw her hand.

"And this?" The pair of axle-mounted ratchets that would prevent the wheel from turning backwards.

"Yes. I know, Atlas. You've thought of everything."

"No, no, no," I admonished her as tenderly as a mother. *"We've* thought of everything." I gave her hand a gentle squeeze in my overwhelming paw. How I yearned to lift that delicate thing to my breast! How I yearned to discover if she had such feelings for me as she had for James!

*

LONDONERS WERE QUEUED UP night and day to see the Patagonian Samson, and the receipts poured in like water down a sluice. I began to wonder what, if anything, I could do to embellish my performance once we had the new fountain in place, and in my heart I began to fear that I had gone as far as I could go. To test my limits I asked Dibdin for a handsome raise, and I received it without argument—another previously impossible hurdle that now came easily.

I very nearly despaired at his acquiescing, for I have always loved a challenge.

Dibdin had raised ticket prices three times, and the crowds continued to build. To further boost his profits, he secretly hired some of the scalpers who worked outside the gates to double and redouble the face value of even the most expensive tickets and funnel most of it back into the till. The resulting surge in income meant that when he instructed Frankie Malone to create a new display case for Victor, cost was for once no consideration.

The result would have made Kubla Kahn gasp.

It was a crystal palace three stories high. (Three truncated stories, to be sure, Victor's height being what it was, but three stories nonetheless.) The three levels, linked by a system of shallow ramps, were walled with glass and partitioned off into various chambers and hallways—some of which were provided with curtains behind which Victor could enjoy his privacy. Paintings hung here and there, and potted plants abounded. The roofline was castellated and crenellated and topped with a delightful weathervane forged into a shape meant to suggest Victor himself. And on each floor was a balcony, outfitted with cushions suitable for a harem, where Victor could emerge and make conversation with the paying customers. The Pope never held an audience in a setting more splendid.

After hours, before James and I headed home to Jaundyce's, I liked to knock on the wall of Victor's glass house and wait for him to emerge from one of the curtained areas where he did his stretching exercises. I could usually hear him groaning away back there as I walked up, although sometimes he was out in plain sight heaving himself up and down the ramps. "You really ought to try this for yourself sometime," he'd say, and then he'd hurl himself panting onto a satin pillow for our little talk.

One particular evening he was bursting with curiosity about Sarah and me. "So where are you two headed, Sammy?" He sounded like Brother Silvestro. And like Brother Silvestro, he clearly had a destination chosen in advance.

"We'll see."

"*We'll see.*' That's no answer."

"Sorry."

"You should be. No—you *will* be, unless you make some overtures before long."

Ow! A shot to the heart. "Have you heard something that I haven't?"

Victor shook his head. "Nah. But I know how things go in this world. I've kept my ear to the ground for a long time, if you know what I mean."

"So I see." Please understand that I would never have dared to make such a joke at his expense.

He narrowed his eyes. "Women, they don't like to wait."

"Things will happen when the time's right."

"But Sammaroo—you're a man of action! You've got to take steps!" He'd have pounded his fist, if he'd had a fist. "Take me, for example. I've had my eye on that Madame Minsk for a good long time now—but she doesn't know I exist."

"Imagine that. With this palace of yours and everything."

"I know! Can you believe it? At any rate, I've worked something out with Omar—you know Omar, the Whirling Dervish?—I've got it all worked out with him, and tonight after dinner he's going to steer her past on the way back to her room. I'll be lounging here in my smoking jacket, I'll strike up a conversation, and we'll see what develops."

"What if Omar has other ideas?"

"He's a married man. Besides, she doesn't wear enough clothes to suit a religious fanatic like him." Victor cocked his head to one side and his look grew dreamy. "You know that chain mail corset of hers? It fits her like a second skin, don't you think?"

"It ought to. Considering that she's magnetic."

"I see what you mean," said Victor.

And I saw what he'd meant, too, regarding Sarah. So after I got James home and bundled up in his cot, I set out for the Banne residence. Need I tell you how your friend the fanatical Belzoni knew the address?

The place was modest, a little threadbare, tucked away down an un-prepossessing lane. Her father answered the door. A round little wood-chuck of a man with white mustaches and a fistful of whiskey, he glanced from me to the hall clock and then back to me again before ask-ing—with more sincerity than you might suppose possible—"To what do we owe this honor, Mr. Belzoni?"

I bent myself double and held out my hand. "Your daughter, Mr. Banne. I was in the neighborhood, and it occurred to me that she might be at home."

"*Most* decent people are home at this hour," he said, taking a half step back and beginning to turn away. Then he spun back to face me with an impish smile. "Present company excepted."

What did he mean to suggest about me? I couldn't quite tell.

"Sarah!" he called up the stairs. "Sarah Banne! A visitor awaits you in the library, my dear!" And then, quick as a wink, he lit out for that distant room and beckoned me to follow: "Hurry! She'll be downstairs before you know it."

But she didn't appear. Mr. Banne introduced me to his wife, a sweet little silent hedgehog all bedecked in lace and ribbons, and the three of us sat in a circle by the fire, drinking whiskey and awaiting developments upstairs.

"So..." Mr. Banne began. And stopped.

I sighed. There was a splashing of water from above.

"Sarah's at her evening toilette," her mother confided, so softly that I had to bend toward her to hear.

I nodded sagely, as if I'd known her schedule all along and had come just to keep them company while their daughter was occupied.

"So how goes the gianting business?" Mr. Banne asked.

"Splendidly, splendidly."

"Excellent."

"In all candor, though—and thank you for asking—I'm afraid that I may soon reach its limits."

"Is that so?"

"Yes. I may not be cut out for it. Not over the long term."

"Really?"

"Really and truly."

"Bigger ideas, eh?"

"You could say that."

"What a happy coincidence," Mother Banne put in. "Sarah has some bigger ideas too. But you probably knew that, Mr. Belzoni."

"We didn't raise her to be shelving books her whole life long."

"Hardly," I said. "She'd be better off writing them."

"You may be correct. I suppose she must have read them all by now."

Mother Banne just shook her head.

"So what options are you considering, Mr. Belzoni?"

I rubbed my jaw and chewed on the inside of my cheek, realizing all at once that I was completely without alternative plans. "Hard to say." I prayed to every saint in heaven for deliverance, and my salvation arrived before long—in the form of a vision worthy of any hallucinating martyr: Sarah, fresh from her bath and radiant as the moon and scented ever so faintly with the warm spices of an Arabian idyll. I stumbled to my feet, knocking over my chair and nearly shattering the glass in my hand with my powerful grip.

Sarah spoke. "I see you've met."

"Met?" said her father. "I feel, my dear, as if we and Mr. Belzoni are old friends—considering how much we've heard about him..."

"From the newspapers, yes. His reputation..."

"His reputation quite *precedes* him, as they say." He sipped his whiskey and pursed his lips and let the rest of us think whatever we might.

Somehow Sarah and I escaped.

"Your parents seem very charming."

"Oh, very charming. Everyone loves them," she said.

"I can see why."

"Mmmhmm."

"They've a comfortable little house, as well."

"Oh, very comfortable."

"Charming too, in its way."

"And it's a charming and comfortable life we have there, the three of us. We're just a charming and comfortable old married couple—plus one."

We turned the corner and emerged into the lamplit street. "Is that the kind of life you see for yourself?"

"That would depend on whether you mean *with* my parents, or *like* my parents."

"Like them."

"In that case—no."

"Then how about with them?"

"In that case—no. Emphatically and a thousand times over."

"I see."

We walked in silence for a while.

"Your father mentioned that you have some big ideas."

"He did? How did that come up?"

"He'd asked me how the gianting business was going..."

She stopped cold. "He said that?"

"Yes."

"He actually said that?"

I shrugged, and we began walking again.

"And what did you say?"

"I changed the subject. We moved on to your big ideas."

"I may have to kill him."

"Please," I said. "Not on my account."

We walked in the direction of the Thames, although it was unwise then as now to linger in the presence of that pestilential thing, especially after dark. Sarah clutched her collar to her throat against the night air that crept through the streets like a vile rumor.

"So what did they tell you about my big plans?"

"Nothing, really."

She paused at a corner and looked down an alleyway as if she were readying herself for something that might emerge from it and try to eat us up.

"By any chance," she started up again, "did they mention that I am able to speak of nothing but you?"

What was I to say?

"They tease me about it mercilessly."

"Now..."

"They really can be quite cruel about it."

"Now why would you..."

"I'm positively mad on the subject, they say."

"On the subject of...."

"The subject of you, Atlas." She let go of her collar and looked up at me under the lamplight. *"You."*

I gathered her up in my arms and, there by the sickly mud flats and rickety wharves of the Thames, with the little lights of ships flickering across the water and a sea chantey in the air, we embraced for the first time.

"I had no idea," I said into her soft ear, still warm beneath her hair. "I'd hoped, but..."

Sarah withdrew to show me her astonished face. "You had? You did?"

"I did. I do." And I embraced her once again, more tightly this time, as if I should never ever let her go.

But let her go I did, of course, and after I'd said my goodbyes at her doorstep—you should know that rather than wandering around all night like characters in some romance, we'd turned and headed back straightaway, too dizzy and disoriented to trust our instincts in the dark streets—after I'd left her at her doorstep, I set out for Jaundyce's by way of Sadler's Wells.

How proud of myself I was! Things had gone better than I'd dared imagine, and I'd hardly needed to do anything beyond rapping at the door and presenting myself. I was dying to tell Victor the entire story.

But alas, he wasn't at home.

I banged on the walls of his little glass palace, careful not to wake the other curiosities slumbering nearby in their shacks. When he didn't emerge I stuck my head inside each of his three balconies in turn and whispered his name, but to no avail. For a moment I considered taking a seat in the stands and waiting for his return, but I chased the idea from my mind when I realized that he probably wouldn't be coming back under his own power. Victor had made plenty of friends, make no mistake about that, and instead of fretting over the unlikely chance that he might have been kidnapped I told myself that he was no doubt socializing with the raucous group of carnies and curiosities whose company he enjoyed at least as much as he did mine.

My path homeward, though, took me past the row of shacks where most of them lived, and there wasn't a candle burning in the entire lane. Not a light anywhere, except for one—a lone candle flickering deep in the recesses of the exotically bedecked lean-to occupied by Madame Minsk. I instinctively slowed and searched the faint darkness with my eyes and ears, hoping for some sign of Victor. There was nothing. The only thing out of place was a surprising article of clothing, Madame Minsk's previously described chain mail corset, dangling from the doorknob as if flung there in a moment of surrender.

*

I CAN SEE BY THE NIGHT SKY that Commander Black has ordered our ship to tack eastward, owing no doubt to some caprice of weather or current. I have absolute confidence in Commander Black, for the Royal Navy has entrusted him with a ship whose fate is a thousand times more important than that of a mere carnival strongman and grave robber. How many times, I wonder at this late date, have I entrusted my life to the hands of seafaring individuals like Black? How often have I permitted my fate to be dashed upon the rocks of their suspect mercies? Often enough, I'd have to say. Perhaps more often than was entirely wise. For it seems now that ill-considered confidence in the gifts of such individuals has not only been my stock in trade, but may have been the reason I found my true destiny within a league or two of the Nile River, where I could toil untouchable in my ocean of sand while the grandest and most luminous of ships passed distantly, harmlessly by.

With that, permit me to introduce Captain Ismael Gibraltar. He found me on a shopping expedition he'd undertaken for the Pasha Mohammed 'Ali, and he plucked me from Sadler's Wells like a ripe pomegranate from a greengrocer's bin.

Gibraltar was tall, gray-bearded, thin, and possessed of a gaze as intense as a thunderstorm breaking over mountains. I felt his eyes upon me as I worked in the fenced yard behind the main building, smearing pitch onto the barrel that Frankie Malone's prop men had constructed for our waterwheel. The morning was hot—hot for late May in London, I mean, but not half so sizzling as certain other mornings I would spend in Gibraltar's company—and I had stripped to the waist. I have always been a fastidious workman, and there was not a speck of tar anywhere upon my white trousers or my massive body. I was as clean and imposing and lovely as Michelangelo's David, although not quite as tall. With my long hair pulled back into a severe ponytail, and with little James scurrying at my side for contrast, I must have presented quite an exotic picture.

Troubled by the pressure of Gibraltar's gaze upon my back, I turned just in time to see him whisper something to Charles Dibdin and then stride away. He was to return every morning for a month or more, admitted behind the scenes by Dibdin for who knows what reason and in return for who knows how much *baksheesh,* and as time passed he studied our progress with the air of a superintendent. Before long his presence began to trouble James.

"Let's go to Angus McPhee's early today," he'd say. "I'm starving." Or, "How about I make a run to the library? You need anything?"

But I couldn't trust the assembly of our new diversion to Malone's crew alone, and as long as the works remained incomplete I was obliged to oversee their every step. Only when they went on their protracted and unauthorized afternoon siesta was I free to let down my guard.

Sarah took notice of our observer one morning, when she stopped by Sadler's Wells on her way to the library. I was tightening some bolts and swabbing soapy water on a pressurized fitting in order to check for leaks. "So who's the Peeping Tom?" she asked, cocking her head in the stranger's direction.

"I can't say. Some friend of Dibdin's, I suppose."

"Dibdin doesn't have any friends."

"If you put money in his pocket," I said, "you get to be his friend."

Sarah snorted. "By that standard, he ought to make you the godfather of his children." She tossed James an apple from her bag, and wiggled her fingertips at the prop men. They studied her as if she were as remote and lovely as a constellation, which she was, as her attention returned to the watcher by the fence. "I don't like the way he's looking at you."

"Really?"

"I'm serious. He could be any kind of troublemaker. He could be a white slaver, for all you know."

I rubbed my chin and pretended to give the idea some thought. "Not likely," I decided. "Dibdin would never tolerate the competition."

"Keep an eye on him, that's all." She let it go at that, happy to have gotten the last word. But before she could swivel her gaze back in his direction, shielded beneath cautious lashes and the brim of her hat, he had vanished once more.

"Easier said than done," I said. "But I'll try." I had no fear of being abducted by the mysterious stranger, you see, for I had already been taken captive by Sarah.

*

AT LAST, THE DAY CAME for testing our waterworks. Sarah arrived first, and took a seat high in the stands with her breakfast, devouring a runny peach and mopping her chin with a pale kerchief. "I'll take no responsibility if anything goes wrong," she said, with a smile indicating her certainty that nothing possibly could. Whether because I'd built the thing or because she'd researched it, I couldn't say.

The prop crew filtered in like a school of lazy fish, took up their tools, and positioned themselves as required. They were there mainly for appearances, and I suspect they knew it. Certain tiny leakages and early breaks might be manageable during the test, but once the pressure began to build there would be no turning back. Every man had instructions to do his best with a rag and a wrench for as long as it took him to count to ten, and then to abandon hope and make for high ground.

James reported for duty in the wheel, and Frankie Malone took up his position at the main valve. It was where he'd stand during every performance, awaiting his cue to turn loose the torrent. But this time—just this once, since during the test I wasn't occupied with feats of strength and daring—I desired the position of honor for myself. As Sarah shielded her eyes with the sack she'd brought her breakfast in, and as a pair of familiar figures appeared behind the distant fence, I took Malone's place at the valve. I shall never forget the look of relief that passed across his face.

I nodded to James, and he took a tentative step within the barrel. At first it didn't look as if he had the weight necessary to set the thing in motion, but all of the counterweights and lubricants paid off and soon the wheel and its attached spiderweb of ropes, buckets, and supporting members lurched to life. The prop men eyed their fittings as if the whole contraption were one great writhing mass of poisonous snakes. James began to trot, light on his feet and happy as could be, and water began to gurgle through the bamboo.

Sarah leaned forward.

The hydraulic rams began to fill, all six of them at once, their indicators as coordinated as mechanical ballerinas pirouetting all in a row. James sailed effortlessly in the barrel, his legs churning and his eyes shut and a big merry grin on his little freckled face. He was probably dreaming of the old days, when his hapless victims would chase him for miles down the alleyways of London.

Once the rams were full I signaled James with a sharp whistle from between my teeth and watched while he slowed to a stop. The barrel gave a final creak, the ratchets and one-way valves held, and my accomplice stepped to the ground with a bow.

Sarah was on her feet, applauding.

I waited a moment or two, took a deep breath, pinned a couple of panicky prop men with a red-hot look, and noticed that Dibdin and his friend were climbing over the fence for a closer look. Then I opened the valve. Only a very small amount of water was pent up behind it—barely enough to float a paper sailboat—but when it flowed into the main it was precisely enough to overwhelm the rams' exit valves and set loose a six-fold torrent.

The device rumbled like a volcano, shaking the ground and giving birth to a column of water that rose far higher than I'd dared to calculate or even dream. Up and up it went, direct and unhesitating, slicing the morning sky in half until it finally burst in midair like a Roman candle.

The prop men let go their breath in a collective sigh that turned into a whoop. Frankie Malone appeared from nowhere, beaming as if he'd opened the valve himself. And down by the waterwheel the one and only James Curtin was dancing, positively dancing, jigging and slapping his heels in the mud that our man-made rainstorm had stirred up.

The rain kept falling while Sarah made a run for me from the stands, and it was falling still as she threw her ecstatic arms around my shoulders. I lifted her from the mud with no more effort than I'd have needed to raise a honeybee or the remnant of a dream, and together we spun until the storm exhausted itself.

I was light-headed when I put her down at last. No wonder I didn't know what to say when I found myself face to face with Dibdin's reedy, gray-bearded associate. He, on the other hand, wasted no time.

"My name is Captain Ismael Gibraltar," he said, thrusting forward a military hand, "and I am in the employ of His Majesty the Pasha of Egypt. How would you like to go to Cairo?"

Sarah, God bless her, spoke right up. "We'd love to," she said, and thus was my fate forever sealed.

PART FOUR:

Cairo

"In Egypt, Belzoni found his true calling—as surely as if his fate had been concealed there by the ancients."

— Jesus D'Peanut, *The Pillage of History*, Princeton, 2004

*

OUR WEDDING WAS THE AFFAIR of the season for a very small number of people, most of whom didn't get out much to begin with. For a setting, we had a storybook chapel in the countryside. For witnesses, we had a collection of individuals the like of which shall never again be gathered in this world or the next: James, our Irish orphan; Victor the Human Snail (in a top hat and tails, no less, acquired God knows how); the Three Flying Schmidtka Brothers; a modestly attired Madame Minsk (ravishing in red and carrying Victor like a prize); the perpetually beclouded Charles Dibdin; Omar the Whirling Dervish and his veiled wife; and our new benefactor, Captain Ismael Gibraltar. Mother and Father Banne sat in the first pew, and toward the end of the ceremony the outcast family of pinheads crept in from the narthex to glare at Dibdin and beam at Sarah and me.

The vicar had looked suspiciously at James when we three first approached, taking the boy as proof that Sarah and I had been up to no good for a very long time. Whatever his reservations, though, they crumbled at the sight of my purse, as did certain plans that a fine young churchgoing couple had made for a wedding at the very hour we required. We were in a hurry, we explained. We had to catch a ship bound for Egypt. And I promised, as a bonus, to consider eventual conversion from my boyhood Roman Catholicism.

After the ceremony we adjourned to a nearby tavern—the Sorry Sheep, I believe it was called, or something on that mournful and agrarian order—for food and drink and goodbyes. There were very few tears. Only Father Banne—who drank more whiskey than was good for him and began explaining to anyone who would listen that this was surely the worst day of his life, that he couldn't possibly face that shrew of a woman he'd married without Sarah for an intermediary, and that he'd have saved up money to attract a proper husband for the girl if he'd ever had any intention of her getting married in the first place—only he seemed to treat the affair as anything less than a grand celebration. For her part, the distinctly un-shrewish Mother Banne ate little and drank less, looked longingly out the window, and kept her own counsel.

"I've been meaning to have a talk with you, Sammy." It was Victor, back from dancing a reel with Madame Minsk as his partner and one of the Schmidtka Brothers as his legs. He tipped his head toward me and lowered his voice. "I don't exactly know how to put this."

Confidentiality being a rare thing for Victor, I leaned toward him in turn. "No need for embarrassment," I said to him with a brotherly pat on the shoulder. "These are emotional circumstances."

"Nah. I ain't going soft on you, Sammy. Besides—no offense to you and the missus—weddings always leave me a little cold."

"No offense taken."

"Good. So, here's what I've been thinking. Do you guess there's a market for my kind of act where you're headed?"

I glanced at Madame Minsk, who was on the dance floor with the selfsame Schmidtka Brother, or perhaps a different one. "I understood that things were just starting to get interesting for you."

"Please, Sammy. It's not like that. You know how she does her whole act in Russian?"

"I've heard. It's a fine gimmick." This, as you'll remember, from a man who for theatrical purposes had invented a language all his own.

"Bad news." He tipped his head toward me as far as it would go and knotted up his eyebrows. "It's not a gimmick."

I was surprised, but I shouldn't have been. A person can learn all there is to know in this world, and the smallest thing can still take him by surprise.

"I'm telling you, Sammy, she can't speak a word of English. And after you're past the get-acquainted period, where's the fun in that?"

I couldn't imagine.

"Like I was saying, do you think an act like mine could make it in Cairo?"

"I don't know why not."

"They don't have some kind of taboo or something about snails? Some kind of religious mumbo-jumbo?"

"I think that sort of thing has to do with cattle in those parts, but I could be wrong. You should check with Gibraltar."

"I mean, I can change my stage name if I need to. That's not a problem. Just so I don't offend anybody. They've got those big long knives over there, you know."

"*Scimitars*, they call them."

"Scimitars. Right. And I don't have a lot left for anybody to cut off."

When Victor presented Captain Gibraltar with the idea of coming along with us to Egypt, the old man received the idea like a long-delayed birthday present.

"I've got a little money," the Human Snail confessed with uncharacteristic candor. "I can pay my own way."

"God forbid!" Gibraltar laughed. "You keep that money right in your pocket, wherever it is that you keep your pockets." An uncertain cloud passed over his face, as if he were wondering whether he'd gone too far, but Victor had heard far worse and showed no sign of offense. Moreover, any offense he might have taken would have vaporized at the sound of Gibraltar's next words: "If you'd like, I can put you on the payroll right now."

*

GIBRALTAR'S SHIP, THE *CLEOPATRA*, made for Malta to take on cargo. "Anything you can get in London," Gibraltar told me, "you can get in Malta for half the price. And that's before you begin negotiating." By which he meant haggling, an art at which he would prove remarkably accomplished.

He gave me paper and pencil, and asked me to draw up a list of everything I'd need to reconstruct my Sadler's Wells miracle alongside the Nile. The plan, he had explained with all the evocative skills of the silver-tongued showman that Charles Dibdin had never been, was to take the scientific principles that we had used to construct theatrical trickery, and employ them instead to change the world. What could have appealed to me more?

"How about men?" I asked when I was done. "I shall need at least twenty-five."

"Make it a thousand," he said. "The Pasha likes people who think big."

*

VALLETTA, MALTA'S CAPITAL CITY, was no Rome, no London, and certainly no Cairo. I can hardly begin to picture it now, even though as you have seen I am gifted with a memory of superhuman clarity. Perhaps its role as an intermediate place, an interregnum, a low point slung between the thrill of London and the romance of Cairo, explains how the capital of Malta managed to vanish whole beneath the sands of my memory.

More likely, though, it's because I was a newlywed.

162

For when I picture Valletta, I see only my beloved Sarah Banne Belzoni. Sarah radiant against the azure sea, Sarah astonishingly splendid in the filth of the marketplace, Sarah fixed as a compass point before the rush of ships and the flapping of sail. I had dreamed of her before—my life, it seemed to me then as it seems to me now, had been little more than a dream of her, my boyish misfire with Serafina Randazzo notwithstanding—but during our month in Malta, that dream swallowed me whole.

It spat me out in Cairo, a place of slums and palaces, opium dens and minarets, water and sand. The city, to my surprise and disappointment, was empty. Abandoned. Vacant. And thus as quiet as a tomb, in my professional opinion, except for the eerie hiss of a million million grains of sand sifting through the streets and squares upon a wind that piled them before shuttered shops and at the mouths of dune-choked alleyways. To my ear it was as if a thousand asps had died at once and returned as sorrowful beseeching spirits, terrifyingly insistent and altogether unappeasable. To this day I hear those poor creatures in my sleep.

Gibraltar stormed down the *Cleopatra's* gangplank, and we were drawn along behind. We found the harbormaster's office as empty as everything else. Gibraltar put his hands to the shutters and peered through them. Then he cursed, sat down, and spat between his knees into the sand.

"So what now?"

"I don't know. Ordinarily, this place is an anthill."

I wetted my lips, and my traitorous tongue deposited sand between my teeth. Never once for the next seven years—*never once!*—would I be free of the stuff. Have you noticed how luminous my smile remains, even at my age and under these unsanitary shipboard conditions? Credit the abrasive qualities of those Egyptian sands.

"Does the Pasha have some representative around here? Some factotum or other?"

"You're looking at his office." I was, of course. And while I was looking at it, Captain Gibraltar was banging the back of his head against its wall of stone.

I may have been ignorant about the ways of the world, but I have never lacked initiative. "I suppose, then, that we'll just have to go see the Pasha ourselves."

"Hmpphh. We'd need horses."

"I'll take care of the transportation. You post a guard on the ship."

This last was probably a needless reflex on my part—the harbor was full of other freighters, ghost ships one and all, which we or anyone else could have sacked at our leisure—but my months with James Curtin and my experience at St. Bartholomew's Fair had made me cautious in such matters.

Some distance along the wharf we located a livery, unmanned and unlocked and filled with magnificent starving Arabian mares that leapt in their stalls at the sight of us. It took some time for the horses to restore their strength with sack after sack of long-delayed oats—at one point I had to defend Victor in his dangling pack against the attentions of a particularly spirited mare—but eventually we got them fed and watered, puzzled out the mysteries of foreign saddle and harness, and fastened ourselves aboard their backs. One after another we galloped through the gate and onto the wharf—Sarah first, James next, and finally myself, leading a spare mount for Gibraltar. That I was last in line was a fine piece of luck for my beloved and my companion, for as I ducked under the low gateway I heard the first sign of living human presence I'd heard all morning: The abrupt flinging open of a shutter overhead, followed by a guttural curse in fierce Arabic. Followed further by gunfire aimed at the largest target available.

The shots went high, presumably because our liveryman was reluctant to risk killing his own livestock. "I've got good news," I told Gibraltar as we reined in by the gangplank of the *Cleopatra*. "There's someone around after all. They're shooting at us."

*

WE LEFT THE WHARF by another way, and wound through streets of slowly diminishing poverty until we came to the royal palace. "The Pasha pays the bills around here," Gibraltar said. "Just try not to get yourself shot by his employees."

A task as easily said as done, since the guardhouses at the perimeter were abandoned like everything else in the city. Only when we clopped up to the main gate—a massive thing of wrought iron, gleaming all over with gemstones and bristling with as many honed edges as an armory—did we encounter a single soul, and a poor forlorn soul he was at that. His face, wrapped in a gleaming blue turban and wearing a look that mingled resignation with terror, rose within the window of his chamber like Mr. Punch behind his proscenium—minus the ferocity. He'd wrapped one end of his turban over his mouth, and he held it up with his left hand while his right leveled a huge black pistol in our direction.

"Oh, put that silly thing down, Mustafa. These people are with me." Gibraltar's horse danced beneath him, eager to run.

"Go away, Captain, for your own sake. There is death here."

I was thinking that if Mustafa would only drop the gun, death might get bored and wander off. But Gibraltar had other ideas. A look of alarm passed across his face. "Has something happened to the Pasha?"

"No no no. No no no. Absolutely not, may Allah be praised. The Pasha is in his bed, his royal bed hung all about with curtains washed fresh every hour in a tub of boiling water and lye. By virgins! The Pasha is fine. Fear not." Then he remembered his pistol and tipped it toward us again. "Fear not, I say, but nonetheless go."

"I have to tell you, Mustafa: you and the Pasha seem to be the only living beings in the whole town—not counting somebody who tried to shoot us for borrowing his horses."

Mustafa nodded.

"And not counting the virgin laundresses."

Mustafa nodded again. "You must do as everyone else has done. You must abandon the city. You must leave Cairo altogether." He pointed his gun toward the horizon.

I must confess that I didn't like the sound of this. Had I given up a perfectly good job, carried an orphan away from the home he'd finally found, and dragged the woman of my dreams off to this godforsaken foreign city only to be told to leave? Only to be sent right back where I'd come from? By an angry puppet with a scarf around his chin and a gun in his hand?

Happily for me, Gibraltar was not to be deterred. "Absolutely not acceptable, Mustafa. Not in the least. We need to see the boss."

"What you ask is impossible."

Gibraltar leaned forward in his saddle and sighted down his nose at Mustafa. "Did you know," he swept his right hand in my direction, "that this man before you is here for no less majestic a project than the draining of the Nile? At the command of the Pasha himself?"

Mustafa gaped, and dropped the tail end of his turban onto his chest. "Then he is not merely summoned by the Pasha; he is sent by Allah. May the Pasha forgive me, of course." The guard remembered himself and yanked the fabric up again.

"Because?"

"Because the disease that plagues this city has arisen—some say— from the Nile herself."

"Disease?" said I.

"Plague?" said Sarah.

"Unlock the damned gate," said Gibraltar, "and let us into the palace before we die out here."

*

HOW SHALL I DESCRIBE THE PASHA? If I reported that he were anything short of magnificent and imposing, anything less than a warrior god transmuted by some arcane magic into a philosopher king, you would be disappointed. Worse than that, you might doubt my veracity not only on this subject but on others. So let it be said that his majesty Mohammed 'Ali, Pasha of Egypt in the year 1814, was everything that you can imagine and more. He was, in other words, a singularly worthy successor to the gods-made-flesh whose brittle bones I would soon be retrieving from grave after dust-choked grave in the Valley of the Kings.

However you choose to envision the Pasha's personal appearance, however, you must envision him shocked in turn by mine—although not half so much as he was by the plain fact of our presence in his bedchamber, given that the palace was under absolute quarantine.

The five of us made fine tableau as we gathered around his curtained bed, aping Mustafa by covering our mouths with whatever loose bits of fabric we could find about our persons—scarves, sleeves, James's cap. Victor, luckiest of us all, just kept his head down and breathed through the packcloth, pretending he wasn't there at all. The Pasha peered at us from behind the curtains, his eyes wide as serving dishes. "Gibraltar!" he gasped through a half-dozen layers of the finest Egyptian cotton. (I realize now that he looked a little like a mummy himself.) "What do you think you are doing? How did you get here? Are you mad?"

Gibraltar, ever the valuable employee, chose to ignore the Pasha's questions and answer instead the question that he should have asked. "These kind people, your highness—Signor and Signora Belzoni, along with their associates—are here to drain the Nile."

The Pasha's eyes rolled back into his head. "Praise Allah! The Nile is the source of the plague, you know."

"I do not doubt it."

"It is rife with evil vapors."

"I understand."

"The sooner it is drained, the better."

"Correct me if I'm wrong, sir—but eradicating the plague wasn't your original purpose in pumping water from the river, was it?"

"This is no time to argue specifics, Captain."

"You had smaller and more agricultural aims in mind, didn't you?"

The Pasha narrowed his eyes and hissed through the curtain. "Who's the Pasha around here?"

"Forgive me. I am only considering the increased scale of the project. I am only wondering how much work our guests—without the aid of your servants and your armies—can hope to accomplish on their own. And what might ensue, may Allah forbid it, should they fail."

The Pasha's eyes darted from one of us to another. He was stymied. Luckily, I had an idea. I bowed my great head and asked, "How long has Cairo been under quarantine?"

"Six weeks, perhaps eight."

I cogitated for a minute, just for show. "And how long since you've had word of the last death?"

"News does not travel well under these circumstances, so I can judge only by the passage of wagons beneath my window, bearing off the dead."

"Very resourceful of you. How long, then?"

"I should think that I have not heard one for—allow me to think," his eyes rolled back in his head, "not for two or three weeks, at least."

"That's fine." I almost dropped my scarf at the good news, but managed at the last minute to keep it in place. I had watched enough magicians in my day to have learned a trick or two.

The Pasha's eyes grew round. "You don't suppose that everyone is *dead*, do you?"

"Everyone except the liveryman with the gun? That would be just my luck, but I doubt it."

A smile of affection and good humor crept into his eyes, and I capitalized on it. I said we had arrived in the nick of time, and that contrary to Gibraltar's invocation of armies and servants, we would require no assistance whatsoever. The *Cleopatra's* crew would serve as our helpers, and we would live on provisions from her galley. The Pasha and his people were free to think of us as angels, sent from afar to risk everything—even our very lives!—in order to reverse their fate.

But how long, he asked, would it take to drain the river? Such things surely took time, didn't they? Already he was impatient, although I must say that I didn't blame him one bit. His bedchamber stank of sweat and lye despite a hot breeze from the window, and with every flutter of his draperies things grew worse.

I explained that he had been misinformed. Not only would draining the entire Nile be unnecessary, but it might actually worsen conditions by exposing the contaminated river-bottom. Instead, we would apply scientific methods to locate the most influential of the river's foul currents—and then, having found the root of his problems, we would undertake to purge them.

"And how do you propose to accomplish this?"

I strolled to the window and poked my head out, sniffing the breeze through my scarf and analyzing the view. It would do the Pasha good to study my back for a moment. The river was visible at a half-dozen spots from my vantage point. When I'd seen enough—and when I thought the Pasha had learned sufficient patience—I turned slowly and leaned back against the wall, blocking the window with my great shoulders.

"I don't *propose* to accomplish it, your majesty, any more than you *propose* to rule this plague-ridden desert."

Captain Gibraltar saw how the Pasha bunched the curtains in his fists, and he placed a cautious hand on my forearm. "Now now, Belzoni..."

I shook him off. "Please. The Pasha and I are men of the world. We don't *propose*. We act." I smiled into the eyes that peered at me from behind the curtains, and watched as the Pasha tried to make up his mind whether to embrace me or have me shot. At the moment, he was power-less to do either.

I went on to tell the Pasha how I would decontaminate his river, restore his city, and free his people. It was malarkey, of course, a theatrical mingling of philosophical mumbo-jumbo with a hint of actual hydraulic and physical science, all of it building to certain improvised but passable conclusions as to the cleansing action of air and sunlight upon atomized water. In other words, I said that I would construct a fountain that would restore to him his desert paradise. And then I bowed from the waist and strode from the room, followed at a trot by Sarah and James.

Captain Gibraltar emerged a moment later, having no doubt endured some formalized ritual of royal farewell. He caught up to us and whispered to me through his sleeve: "Good God, man—do you think it's possible?"

"Not at all," I said, dropping my scarf and taking a deep breath. "But I do think that every living thing wears itself out eventually. Even the plague."

*

I SUPPOSED WE COULD HAVE the fountain operational within a week, which would give the plague another seven days to exhaust itself. While Gibraltar mobilized his crew, I surveyed the riverside for a location with a clear line of sight from the Pasha's bedroom. Then we unloaded our works onto a number of light boats that we were able to commandeer without gunfire or even negotiation, set up shop on the riverbank, and went to work.

This would be my first experience toiling in the Egyptian heat, and before the week was out I'd boiled off sufficient flesh to have manufactured an additional man. I could have used that individual's help, for Gibraltar's sailors were as lazy as a pride of lions. They were skilled with ropes and tar, though—and one of them was a fair cooper—so I suppose that in the end I could have done worse.

Almost from the very beginning we had an audience, and why not? Between my barked orders, the grunting of the men, and the bright clang of metal on metal, we announced ourselves in bursts of sound that echoed down the empty streets and alleyways. Our tar pots sent up plumes of wavering black smoke that obscured the sun for hours at a time. Out of nowhere we had arrived on the scene as if by divine fiat, a motley army of mingled races led by a bearded giant, a beautiful woman, and a boy, and our presence conjured up a face to occupy every window that faced the river. Apparently, the city was not entirely empty after all—those who remained had simply gone to ground. They found us fascinating because our work was unfathomable, our aim was inscrutable, and our origins were unknowable. Most outlandish of all, we dared to brave the open air.

Among the faces watching our progress was that of the Pasha himself, who peered at us from the safety of his tower. Sometimes a second or third figure appeared there too, although the distance to the palace was so great that I could make out nothing but vague shapes. No doubt that they were all wearing wrappings about their faces anyway.

We soldiered on, baking under the sun by day and seared beneath the heat of our torches by night. We cooled off only in the hour before dawn, when our unbidden audience was asleep and the lamps behind each inhabited window had guttered out like constellations obscured by clouds. At a whispered word from me the men would put down their tools and tread stealthily to the water's edge, lay their clothing on the bank, and ease into the water as silently as otters. James would join them, and Sarah and I would find a secluded spot of our own. For fifteen or twenty minutes we would paddle about in water as fresh and cold as an alpine lake, and then we would climb out and dry off before the sun could rise and illuminate our deception.

*

"BELZONI!" IT WAS GIBRALTAR, who'd lost interest in my project and now spent his days hiding out below the waterline in the cool belly of the *Cleopatra.* "The Pasha has requested the pleasure of your company."

"Not now." I was bent over at the waist, clamping two lengths of bamboo end to end, while a pair of less-than-jolly tars lashed them with reeds into one long conduit. "Tell him I'm busy granting his wishes."

"That's the problem. He doesn't want the river purified anymore."

"Really?" I didn't quite believe him. Besides, I was distracted by one of my helpers, who was methodically wrapping my left thumb up in his lashings.

"Really. He thinks you're manipulating him."

"I believe that I might come to like this fellow. He's getting smarter by the minute."

"To tell you the truth, it wasn't his idea. The French Consul whispered it in his ear."

"There's a Frenchman involved?" I wondered for a second if Napoleon had raised his army with the sole purpose of pursuing me from continent to continent—perhaps out of jealousy over our relative sizes.

"He arrived at dawn. A positively awful man, well known in these parts as a silver-tongued parasite, but he has the Pasha's ear. I must say, though, that he doesn't sound French. Not in the least."

What did I care about the interloper's accent? I yanked my thumb loose and sucked on it.

Gibraltar went on musing. "No sir. He doesn't sound French in the least. And he goes by the name Bernardino Drovetti."

Bernardino Drovetti! It would have been just like that sleek little preening house-cat to have risen up through Napoleon's ranks with the express aim of thwarting my progress in Egypt. But my inclination at that moment was not to worry about myself. I thought instead of Serafina Randazzo, whose heart must even then have been lying shattered upon the flagstones of her shady patio alongside the Piazza Barbieri. Faithless cad! Heartless heel! I realized too late that I was gripping the bamboo pipe as if it were Drovetti's neck. The frail thing exploded into shards, and my assistants cursed like the sailors they were.

The Pasha was pacing his bedchamber when we arrived, his long silken robe swirling about his feet and threatening to trip him. He leaned forward as if into a sandstorm, and fury radiated from his figure in waves. He spoke not a word as I entered behind Gibraltar. He did, however, snap his fingers, which caused a brace of Nubian warriors to leap from behind a tapestry with the speed and precision of striking cobras. They forced my elbows behind my back and stood me up to attention—not an encouraging spectacle for the pair of them to take in, brave as they may have been feeling a moment prior—and although their combined strength was as nothing to me, the polished scimitars hanging from their waistbands were estimable indeed. In other words, I cooperated.

Not that I would have resisted for all the mummies in the Valley of the Kings. Far from it. Instead, I collected myself and put on my most agreeable face. "Your highness!" I said. "For whom are we staging this little performance?"

He narrowed his eyes at me and buried them partly behind lowered black brows.

Craning my neck, I tried to see behind the tapestry that had yielded up the two guards. "Drovetti wouldn't be back there, would he?"

That surprised the Pasha into speech. "I am not in the habit of concealing my friends behind the tapestries."

"Perhaps you should be. They might get an education."

"Not from the likes of you."

"Certainly not, your highness. From you, however, I suspect they could learn a great deal."

"Sadly, I am far more accustomed to flattery than you can imagine." He took two steps toward me and glared up into my face. His guards did their best to drag me down to his level, but I hoisted my shoulders and lifted the pair of them—scimitars and all—a foot off the tile floor. "It will do you no good."

"I shouldn't think that flattery would be necessary. Not given our arrangement."

"Our arrangement?"

I lowered the Nubians until their slippers brushed the floor, and after letting them hover there for a second or two I relented and let them down the rest of the way. Then I leaned over and whispered into the Pasha's ear—confidentially, but loud enough to be heard behind the tapestry or under the bed or wherever it was that Drovetti was hiding. All the way into the next room, if necessary. "The arrangement," I lied, "by which you would cunningly obtain three valuable properties in one—a prototype of your irrigation pump, a lasting monument to your genius, and the undying love of a grateful nation."

"Oh," said the Pasha, tugging at his lip, "*that* arrangement."

"It was all your idea, as I remember."

"Yes. Yes, it was."

I went on, lying through my teeth for Drovetti's benefit, trusting the Pasha to continue playing along. "Although you knew that your city had been in quarantine for sufficient time to drive out the contagion, you intuited how deeply your subjects required something extra. Something theatrical and impressive. A *grand gesture,* designed to make a lasting impression."

"Oh, absolutely. Making a powerful impression is the first principle of leadership." He stood up a little straighter.

I shook off his Nubians. "That's another thing I've learned from you, your majesty. You really should think about giving lessons."

We agreed to meet in three days, down by the apparatus, at the stroke of noon—the Egyptians were still head over heels in love with the sun, even after all those millennia, and why not?—for the ceremonial starting of the pump. I advised him to wear his brightest and most regal clothing, and to come alone. This idea had particular appeal for his guards, who had no interest in leaving the palace anyhow—not with a plague on. Then I dashed off to finish the waterworks and build a reviewing stand upon which the Pasha could take his place of everlasting honor.

*

WHEN IN HUMAN MEMORY had such a fountain ever leapt skyward over the city of Cairo? What individual had ever dreamed of seeing the Pasha himself brave that city's plague-emptied streets on foot and unaccompanied? And how on earth could word of the great man's passage have leapt from house to house to house when every door in the city was barred?

We had visited Cairo to accomplish one miracle, and along the way we had accomplished many more.

The Pasha strode the boulevards as if he were leading a procession, which in a way he was: an invisible procession of his subjects, rising up at least in spirit to wrest their city from the plaguey grip of the dead. His expression was impassive, his pace was stately, and his footsteps left shallow impressions in the sand which the wind instantly filled back up. A ruler of a different character might have paused to consider that as a sign, but not Mohammed 'Ali. His mind was on other things, and he'd seen sand do its work before.

I had lined up the *Cleopatra's* sailors on either side of the boulevard leading to the reviewing stand, and although they presented a sight that surely would have alarmed a lesser man—they were a rag bin of Africans, Chinamen, Indians, and picturesque indecipherable mixed breeds, many of whom advertised their exotic origins with uncouth tattoos, outlandish haircuts, barbaric war paint, ridiculous breechcloths, and more—the Pasha instinctively understood them as his honor guard and strutted past undismayed. Once he had gained the top of the reviewing stand they doubled back behind him and took their seats. Only Sarah and I remained standing—the two of us and James, that is, who was out of sight on the riverbank, leaning upon his waterwheel—and we bowed to Mohammed 'Ali with all the pent-up theatricality of a troupe of Shakespeareans. He took his seat, I whistled my signal to James, and our performance began.

I expected that the audience, jammed by then into every window for miles around, would grow restless while the pipes filled and the rams built up pressure. During such an interlude at Sadler's Wells I'd have been juggling hogsheads of ale or balancing tentpoles on my back in order to keep the paying customers occupied. But alas I had planned no such distraction for that day, and as it happened I didn't need one. The reasons were several. First, the event unfolding before their eyes involved the presence of the Pasha, an individual normally as invisible as a god. Second, the work we'd been carrying on for the last week had served as its own irresistible foreshadowing. And third—the most difficult of all to admit for a showman like myself, but true all the same—the people of Cairo were absolutely starved for any entertainment better than watching shadows creep across their walls. I could have been paring my fingernails, and they'd have been enraptured. The plague, as it happened, was an easy act to follow.

Finally the rams were filled and James stepped clear of the wheel. With my back to the crowd I indicated to the Pasha that the time had arrived for him to do his part. He rose slowly to his feet, and with great ceremony he lifted his arms to the sun. While his arms were upraised, the loose sleeves of his robe shimmering in a light breeze from the river, I let open the valve.

The rest is history, miracle, and—fitting for the desert where it happened—mirage. The fountain sent up a column of water to shatter the sky, the far-flung crowd gasped, and those of us involved in the project withdrew the rags and scarves from our faces. At which the crowd gasped even more loudly than before, and sang out as one the immortal name of their beloved savior, Pasha Mohammed 'Ali.

One eruption would not be sufficient, of course—not to slake the crowd's thirst for drama, and not to purge the Nile of its strictly theoretical contagion. Rather than permit James to wear himself down needlessly, I gave orders for the sailors to line up and operate the waterwheel in turn, one after another. It was mid-afternoon before the crowds permitted us to stop, and we gave off then only because the streets had grown so thronged that returning the Pasha home promised to require every bit of manpower we could muster. We formed ourselves into a wedge—myself in the lead, sailors of diminishing bulk tapering back on either side—and plowed through the streets to the safety of the palace, his highness concealed within our ranks like a pearl within an oyster.

*

IMAGINE THE GRANDEUR of the next evening's state dinner, an affair at which I—as guest of honor—was introduced to the highest ranks of the society that I had so recently delivered. Sarah and I sat at the Pasha's right hand, James sat at his left, and Victor beamed down upon us from a high shelf like a cloud-borne *putto*. The evening that unfolded combined the finest elements of a bacchanal, a rodeo, an eating contest, and Guy Fawkes Day. Speaking of which: believe me when I say that had there been gunpowder available, I'd have had difficulty resisting the urge to blow a certain sleek little faux Frenchman all the way back to his native Barbaria.

All through supper the Pasha chattered at us like a magpie. Everything about me was of interest to him—one detail, it turned out, in particular: "When Gibraltar wrote that he'd found my Nile man," he said between bites, "he never mentioned anything about your delightful companion!"

For a moment I thought that he was talking about Sarah, and then I decided that he was talking about James, and at last I realized that he was talking about Victor. He raised his glass in the direction of the shelf to offer him a toast. "You must bring him around more often!"

"It shall be my pleasure."

"What is his function, exactly? Does he sing? Does he tell fortunes?"

"His singing would empty this room in a heartbeat, your majesty. And as for his knowledge of the future..."

"The less said, the better?"

"As is the case with most such claims, be they true or false."

"You, Signor Belzoni, are a man of wisdom."

I nodded to him, tipping an imaginary hat.

"Is your little friend a man of wisdom as well?"

I raised my own glass in Victor's direction, thinking of Sarah and the encouragement he had given me regarding her pursuit. "I can assure your majesty that he has never favored me with anything but the best of advice."

After supper I was presented with a hastily lettered proclamation (illegible), a fancy silk robe (too short), and certain objects symbolizing the nation's gratitude (newly minted, and therefore worthless in this land of antiquities). In short I was feted and toasted and waited upon so fawningly that a more credulous man would have believed himself risen to a place second only to the Pasha, a position I knew to be nothing but a dangerous and transient illusion.

Drovetti was seated, along with a Babel of other nations' representatives—Tunis Van Doek of Holland, Henry Salt of Britain, and a dozen others—at the foot of our table. "Greetings to you, Signor Drovetti!" I called out during a lull in the praise. "Or should I say '*Monsieur*' Drovetti?"

"As you wish, Belzoni." He raised his glass toward me and spoke with a smile, floating the words out into the silence that had suddenly prevailed in the great hall. Oh, he was an imperturbable one. And he possessed no accent whatsoever. Neither French nor Italian nor anything in between. He sounded as if he'd replaced himself with a blank spot.

The Pasha spoke up. "You gentlemen are acquainted?"

"Most assuredly." I hoisted a leg of lamb from a nearby platter and brandished it at Drovetti. "This gentleman and I were born within a morning's ride of each other."

"I had no idea!"

"Why should you? I am but a strongman and an engineer, while he is a creature of sophistication and refinement. I am but a mechanic for hire, while he is the respected emissary of a foreign government."

Drovetti was enjoying the attention. I believe that for a moment he thought I'd picked up some manners somewhere.

"I am but a poor Italian," I went on, "while he has made himself over into something far greater: a Frenchman."

"Now, now, Belzoni." The Pasha patted my arm, quieting a certain nervous laughter that had begun to make its way around the table. "Nationality isn't everything in our modern world. Why, take a look at yourself: an Italian, imported by way of Great Britain, to become a national hero in Egypt."

To show our listeners that I knew which side of my bread was buttered, I acquiesced. "I suppose you're correct," I said. I took a great mouthful of lamb, and gave a show of ruminating while I chewed. "Besides, now that I recall my history with Consul Drovetti—how he stole my first love and betrayed my country to save his own skin—I realize that there's been something of the Frenchman in him all along."

*

WHAT DID SARAH MAKE OF THAT? Had I sacrificed something of my heart—the greater and truer portion of my heart, I mean, which beat not in my own breast but in hers—merely to deliver a blow to Drovetti's reputation? Hardly, although to tell the whole truth I must admit that that incautious reference to *my first love* did require a certain amount of explanation.

Truthful as I am in all things, I had nonetheless never mentioned Serafina Randazzo's name to my wife. How would I have explained to her that once, long ago, I had yearned to give my heart to a lovely child and yet somehow managed to fail, time and time again? To tell a story of such sad yearning and frustrated inaction would have been as disastrous as relating the details of some headlong conquest. Well, perhaps not quite so disastrous. But pointless all the same. And uncomfortable.

So, with Sarah stalking about our makeshift stateroom demanding the truth about my first love, I did as generations of men have done before me and will no doubt do for as long as there are tales to be told of broken hearts or ruined reputations. I lied.

"Oh," I said with a wave of my hand. "I was making that part up."

"I'm sure."

"Honest." I patted a spot on the rude bunk beside me. "Now come. Sit."

She crossed her arms and retreated into a corner.

"It was right off the top of my head. I swear."

"You're not that skilled an actor. Believe me, I know."

"Ow. Now be nice."

"If it wasn't true, then what if he'd called you on it?"

"I'd have brazened it out. I'd have outwitted him."

"Fine," she said. "Let's give it a try. I'll be Drovetti. 'I recall betraying your country, but I don't seem to recall stealing your true love. Refresh my memory, if you would be so kind.'" She had his supercilious manner down cold.

I leapt from the bed in mock dismay, waving a phantom leg of lamb. "Cad! How like you to have forgotten her!" And then I bowed to the audience at the imaginary table. "The Frenchman is heartless. My argument is concluded, is it not?"

"'Hardly,'" she said, still Drovetti in the flesh. "'Grant my request, and tell me the name of the girl.'"

"Very well. Her name was Serafina. Serafina Randazzo."

Sarah could tell by a quaver in my tone that I had invented neither the girl, the event, nor the broken heart. Such are the ways of love. I threw myself upon her mercy, of course. And she understood.

*

DROVETTI BROUGHT ME A GIFT the following day—a gift which, whether intended to convey his grudging respect for my status or to show his veiled contempt for my person, was to set me on the remainder of my life's course.

I was lounging with a notebook on the deck of the *Cleopatra*, making plans for the agricultural use of my hydraulics and basking in a balmy admixture of sunshine and adulation. My silhouette was unmistakable up there, and I reclined in plain sight like a relic set out for public display. The crowds milling around the harbor, set free from their long imprisonment, kept me occupied returning their *salaams* and salutes.

Drovetti emerged from among them with a long tubular leather case under his arm. He climbed aboard the *Cleopatra* as if he owned the vessel and meant to dispose of it at the earliest opportunity, his nose in the air and his feet barely touching the ground. Sarah emerged from below decks as he passed the rail, and they very nearly collided. He would have been the worse for it, you can count on that, for Sarah was taller by a head and far better constructed. She stopped in the doorway and let him pass, giving him a look of withering disdain. The look that he returned was hungry.

I hailed him from my chaise. "Try your luck, Drovetti, and see if you haven't met your match."

He froze, one toe on the first step to my platform, and then he removed that toe with infinite slowness and turned to present Sarah with his most brilliant smile. He held it before her for a second or two as if it were a maritime signal, and he then doubled over into a deep bow.

When he came up for air, he introduced himself. "Excuse my discourtesy. You are Madame Belzoni, are you not? I am Bernardino Drovetti, Consul of France."

"Your reputation has preceded you."

He squeaked out a disconcerting little chuckle. "So they say, Madame. So they say—thanks in great degree to your husband. Nonetheless, I am charmed to make your acquaintance."

"I'm sure you are," said Sarah with a toss of her head. "I've had that affect on better men."

His smile showing no sign of faltering, Drovetti nodded his well-groomed head and turned toward me. "You seem to have met your match as well!" he called. And this I did not for a moment deny. He climbed to my platform and leaned against the rail and examined me with the eye of a jeweler. "You are looking well, Belzoni. Married life agrees with you."

I nodded.

"Civilian life, too."

I knew where he was headed, so I threw back my head and laughed. "We cannot all be traitors."

"Nor can we all be pragmatists."

"As you wish," I said.

He remembered the leather case, and passed it to me with an off-hand flourish. "From the Embassy, in honor of your achievement." He lifted an ironic eyebrow for punctuation. "It is also from me personally, in recognition of your superb maneuvering with the Pasha. I believe you would have made a fine soldier after all, Belzoni. Difficult to fit with a uniform, but a fine soldier nonetheless."

I didn't know what to make of his remarks, but I accepted the case and unfastened its cap. Within was something that I took at first for an etching—a tightly-rolled sheet of thin paper perhaps six feet wide by nine feet long, depicting from head to toe the fantastically detailed lid of a sarcophagus. The paper was battered and curled, torn in places and folded back upon itself in others as if it had been a long time in the saddlebag of some weary traveler. Down along its bottom were an array of official-looking marks, some flamboyant handwriting, and a single great seal made of red wax. I knelt on the deck and spread the thing out before me, weighing down its four corners with such bits of tackle and hardware as came to hand. "Well," I said, "it's large enough."

"They are all more or less that size," said Drovetti. "Nothing unusual about it, really."

I looked up at him from down upon my knees, an act as unusual for me as for a king. Then I looked back at the engraving and realized that it was not an engraving at all. It was a rubbing. The image of the sarcophagus was life sized—that's what Drovetti meant—having been transferred to the paper with a graphite stick. With new interest I studied its every line and contour. The thing traced was clearly the work of a fanatical master craftsman, or more likely the joint work of a dozen of them. Its subject was obviously royalty, to judge from the beauty of his noble features and the panoply of costly-looking merchandise that surrounded him. Gemstones and vases and staffs. Urns and reeds and amphorae. Not to mention cats.

"I should like very much to see the original."

"Look there," said Drovetti, indicating the text at the bottom with the toe of one elegant shoe. "I should say that it is yours to admire at your leisure."

My French was a trifle rusty, but what I read practically knocked me off my haunches. "Let it be known by all men, according to the seal affixed below, that the sarcophagus whose lid is here depicted, belonging to King Amenhotep of the Eighteenth Dynasty, has been presented by the Republic of France to Monsieur Giovanni Battista Belzoni upon this date in recognition of his contributions to our mutual friends the state and people of Egypt etc. etc. etc." You can imagine the rest. The text was florid and verbose, and the signature at the bottom of it was executed by an individual who sought to conceal his identity within a stunning artifice of ink.

I leapt to my feet, ready to run off to whatever storeroom or warehouse or museum case held the sarcophagus of King Amenhotep. "Good God, Drovetti—the thing must be worth a fortune. All is forgiven." I hardly knew what I was saying. But I knew what I meant, and I came right out with it. "So. Where's the prize?"

"Three days' ride from here," he said, "due south along the Nile in a well-protected spot just outside the city of Luxor—formerly known as Thebes, if you have read your history books."

"And when is it due here?"

"It is not. I fear that our diggers have moved on to other sites, regrettably leaving poor Amenhotep right where he has lain for the better part of human history."

"You'll send them back to fetch it soon, of course."

"It cannot be done. The Pasha has granted us permits to dig in a dozen new locations, and we find ourselves stretched rather thin." He spoke apologetically and even showed me his supplicating palms, but there was a certain merry sparkle in his eyes.

"Very well," I said. "One can't ask for everything. I see that I shall have to run the errand myself." Half of me wanted to embrace Drovetti and his French masters for their generosity, and the other half wanted to sock him in the jaw. Little did I know.

By the time he quit the *Cleopatra* a handful of sailors had gathered around to eye my prize. James had come running too, and he was quick to translate for himself the text at the bottom. His dead father, as I have mentioned, was a scholar. Instantly he ran off to bring Sarah. "What's this about our being rich?" she asked when she arrived.

"You know James," I said. "If Amenhotep had pockets, he'd try to pick them."

"Who's Amenhotep?"

"A king of the Eighteenth Dynasty. We now seem to own his corpse, along with whatever merchandise he arranged to have buried with it. Riches galore, no doubt. Jewels and carvings and hammered gold and papyri. All the things that a king would require in the afterlife."

"Courtesy of Drovetti."

"After a fashion."

"There must be a catch."

No one on earth was ever more insightful than Sarah. No wonder I loved her so; no wonder I still do. I will carry that love all the way to the grave, whether my final place of rest is a grave on the road to Timbuctoo or an uncharted spot in the blue waters between here and the coast of Africa. May God grant me the strength to complete the story of my life—or, failing that, may He grant me the wisdom to make clear, in whatever portion of time and health he may permit me, that the purpose and power of this life of mine came from no source less sublime than my love for Sarah Banne Belzoni. "A catch?" I answered that glorious soul. "Most certainly there's a catch. The sarcophagus of Amenhotep, you see, has not been transported to these precincts. Yet."

*

EGYPT IS A LAND OF INFINITIES, where the aims of one human being matter less than the intent of a single grain of sand. A grain of sand can go anywhere it likes, you see—it can skitter like a thief across the threshold of the palace, sift into the pages of a book like the very substance of time on its constant downward spiral, insinuate itself like an unspeakable curse beneath the tongue of a beggar or a prince—while a man, for all of his furious planning and plotting, must ultimately face a thousand insurmountable obstacles. And as an ordinary man surpasses a grain of sand in size, so my grand scale attracted to me a legion of obstacles proportionately more stubborn.

To begin with, in order to earn my paycheck—for man does not live by adulation and state dinners alone—I had to get the Pasha's irrigation pump running. Easier said than done, since we'd consumed most of the hardware we'd brought from Malta in building his plague eradicator *cum* municipal fountain *cum* public monument. I've never been one to shy from a challenge, but this one was more in the line of a scavenger hunt than a proper sourcing operation. I drew up my specifications in triplicate, one copy for James and one for Captain Gibraltar and one for myself, and we began ransacking every marketplace and warehouse and shipyard in northern Egypt. At the end of each day we would meet to compare notes—James had found a gentleman in possession of five hundred gallons of pitch; Gibraltar had come upon a blacksmith capable of forging our valves and nozzles; I had located the remains of a shipwrecked Indian freighter whose creosote-saturated timbers were ours for the taking. The fact that we were about the Pasha's business opened some doors, but as often as not any invocation of that notable's name caused prices to rise and inventories to diminish. We learned—very much as a physician learns to apply the leech only after careful assessment of his patient—to invoke the name of Mohammed 'Ali only when all other remedies had failed. Before long, in other words, I found myself yearning for the old days at Sadler's Wells, when my operations were profitable enough that even the useless and recalcitrant Frankie Malone would do my bidding.

Meanwhile Sarah, eyeing our retrieval of the sarcophagus of Amenhotep, set out to arrange travel to Luxor. Gibraltar introduced her to Henry Salt, the British Consul. An unprepossessing individual of modest size and a pale complexion immune to the effects of the Egyptian sun, a lifelong functionary whose mustaches preceded him into any room and overshadowed his presence there once he'd arrived, Salt was at once charged with facilitating the activities of his countrymen and constitutionally disinterested in doing so.

Seated like a supplicant before the desk in his enormous office—the place was hung with tapestries showing romanticized views of the English countryside, and Salt himself offered her cup after cup of meticulously brewed tea; say what you like, at least the man hadn't gone native—Sarah explained that we'd need a crew of strong laborers, a dozen horses or camels, and a sufficiently sturdy wagon. (I'd resisted the idea of hiring a boat, since I hadn't a clue as to how much the sarcophagus might weigh. Best not to risk it without a scouting expedition, and there was no time for that.)

He advised her that she was getting ahead of herself. We'd need nothing of the sort, he said. No men, no horses, no camels, no wagon. What we *would* need, he explained, was something he called a *firman*—which Sarah took to be a tribal elder or some sort of specialized excavating equipment.

A firman, Salt explained, would make the undertaking as simple as it could be. Without a firman, on the other hand, nothing was possible. Nothing at all.

Could he help her obtain one?

Perhaps. But he'd never before dealt directly with such things. The French, it turned out, had the firman business pretty well sewn up.

Why the French?

Because of their well-documented interest in antiquities. His opposite number, Drovetti, was himself in the field at least two weeks out of three, overseeing crew after crew of diggers. And when he wasn't in the Valley of the Kings or Karnak or some other desert spot, he was back home in Cairo, conniving through secret channels for additional firmen or firmans or firmani or whatever you called the damned things in the plural. As he'd said, you couldn't expect to haul the slightest thing out of the desert without one.

Sarah decided that a firman must be a hybrid, an individual somehow half shaman and half digger. In her mind she pictured a swarthy giant dressed in a turban and robe and sandals, operating a specialized divining rod with which he could locate the buried tombs of the glorious dead. Where did men like these get their training? Was it a skill passed down from father to son? More to the point, would these primitive people believe anything, anything at all? Egypt was a land of mystery, that was for certain.

"I don't care for such mumbo-jumbo," she told Salt, "but if a firman is what it takes to get things done around here, then I want you to hire us the best one in the city. Hang the cost."

No, no, no, Salt explained with a shake of his head. A firman, far from being symptomatic of a primitive society grounded in magic and mystery, was in fact emblematic of a sophisticated culture lubricated by favoritism, politics, and endless paperwork. For a firman was nothing more and nothing less than a permit—a permit to dig within a certain sector of Egypt's otherwise borderless sands, and then to extract whatever treasures might be located beneath that undifferentiated and arid ocean.

He scratched his chin and gave Sarah a weary look. "If there's a firman to be had for the tomb of Amenhotep—and no doubt there is—you can bet that it's in Drovetti's name. And it's probably dated to expire shortly after the Second Coming of the Lord Christ Jesus."

Sarah wasn't having any of that. "The sarcophagus," she said, "belongs to us."

"Alas, the right to move it does not."

"We have the document. The rubbing. Signed by the French Ambassador, I think."

"You think."

She was unapologetic. "The man has inexcusable handwriting. It's not my fault. Anyhow, who else could have signed it?"

"I'm sure I can't imagine." Salt raised his hand and began ticking off alternatives. "Our friend Drovetti? Some embassy underling? A beggar on a Cairo streetcorner? Your husband himself, not to put too fine a point on it?"

Sarah struck him with a look that could have drawn blood.

"No offense intended, Mrs. Belzoni. And regardless: as I have tried to suggest, it wouldn't matter if the signature at the bottom of that sheet of paper were that of Napoleon himself. Or the Pope, for that matter. In the absence of a duly issued firman, that document is as useless as a nose on the Sphinx."

When Sarah came home—we had by this time traded our microscopic cabin aboard the *Cleopatra* for a shabby flat behind the high wooden gates of the European Quarter—when Sarah came home and told me of her frustrations with Henry Salt, I gave her a bit of practical advice. "If the fellow isn't going to help us," I said, "then by God don't let him get in the way."

"But what about obtaining a firman?"

"You went to him for camels and men and a wagon, didn't you?"

"Yes, but."

"You requested transport, and in return he has denied you a firman. Clever individual that he is, the fellow has changed the subject and sent you home empty-handed."

"Yes, but."

"So never mind about Salt. Tomorrow, without the help of the British Embassy, look into hiring a wagon, employing a dozen men, and obtaining some camels." Camels were everywhere in that city. They were as thick as fleas on—well, as thick as fleas on camels.

"But what of the firman?"

"I've never heard of such a thing. As far as I know, Salt is pulling your leg."

"But he's not."

"Never mind about that. Obtain men and camels, and we'll obtain the sarcophagus that is rightly ours."

Then, just as she was getting accustomed to the idea of entering the desert without the proper paperwork, she recognized a hurdle considerably more immediate. "What am I supposed to do about funds?"

"Promise a share of the fortune we gain by selling the sarcophagus," I said. And then I gave her my warmest smile, straight from my heart. "Think big, my love."

*

SARAH PROVED ONCE MORE to be a natural. By the end of the week we didn't have just a few ornery men and a handful of ill-tempered camels and a lone rickety wagon with impacted sand grinding its axles into dust, we had an entire expedition. Eighteen camels and twice as many horses, vehicles both covered and uncovered, hogsheads full of food and water, sufficient drivers and too many porters and a swarm of miscellaneous hungry boys, along with two former army officers (still bearing their long rifles) and a Macedonian cook equipped with a faraway squint and a peg leg, who claimed to know precisely where the sarcophagus of Amenhotep lay. Rumor had it that he'd done some cooking for the French expedition, although he had acquired nothing in the way of recipe ideas. During our time in the desert, we were to subsist entirely on a regimen of eggplant and chickpeas.

Exactly what use each of these individuals would be I could not have told you under oath. Sarah insisted that no more than half of them were actually on the payroll, and to judge by their lackadaisical behavior I hoped that she was right. Their nerve-wracking presence—by day and night they milled about in the square before our apartment, smoking and spitting and neglecting the animals—made me more eager than ever to complete the irrigation pump and begin the recovery of Amenhotep. Nothing, however, increased my urgency more than the occasional presence of the Pasha himself at our site by the river. His advisors had directed us to a spot on the margins of the city, where the veneer of modern Cairo crumbled away and the real Egypt crawled out from beneath in all of its grandeur, cruelty, and barbarism. It was a land of scorpions and snakes and hissing sand, a land of naked children and starving adults and emaciated elders, a land of desiccated desperation where man maintained a tenuous grip against the longest of odds.

"Do you see the burdens under which my people must live?" said the Pasha from the cool depths of his sedan chair. "There is nothing like this in London, correct?"

"Oh, there is squalor aplenty, if that's what you mean. But it's a damp kind of squalor for the most part. If a rat dies in a London dustbin, he'll be a sticky puddle of putrefaction within the week. Let a rat die in these parts, and he'll be a mummy before you can say 'Amenhotep.'"

"*'Amenhotep,'*" he sighed. "His burial site is quite a find, they say."

"Just so! And it was exceedingly generous of Drovetti to honor me with the sarcophagus. As you can imagine, you could have knocked me over with a feather!"

The Pasha gave me a puzzled smile and changed the subject. He cared nothing for my treasure-hunting aspirations, you see, only for my utility as a kind of gigantic dowsing device. "The traditional pumping mechanisms we use here are poor and ineffectual, are they not?"

I shaded my eyes and looked downstream, past our burgeoning water works, to an embankment where a single skinny boy was operating a *shadoof,* that indigenous mechanism for lifting water by means of a pole, a prop, a bucket, and a counterweight. The boy bobbed and dangled from one end of the pole like a savage marionette, and I wondered about the ratio of the energy he was expending to the nourishment that his family would eventually obtain from their unforgiving little hectare of dust. Perhaps, I thought, they'd be better off roasting the poor sinewy child and eating him for supper. At least his earthly troubles would cease.

I may have thought all of that, but the only remark that I made was to repeat after the Pasha, "Poor and ineffectual, yes."

"You, Belzoni, by merely placing a midget inside a barrel, can raise more water than a hundred of my starving boys."

"He's not a midget."

"That is no concern of mine."

"He's a boy. An orphan boy."

"I do not care if he's a jinni. I do not care if he's a dog you have trained to walk upright." He fluttered a robed arm toward my apparatus. "With the aid of this machinery, you have given that miserable creature the power of a giant such as yourself."

What a snake charmer he was! What an assault he had made upon my overweening vanity of mind and body! All of my urgent lust for the sarcophagus of King Amenhotep, every thought of its mysterious contents and the ease with which I would soon be recovering them, vanished like the heat of the desert at sundown. I redoubled my efforts to complete the pump, which of course produced the result of bringing me closer to Amenhotep with each passing moment. That was all to the good, because the various paid and volunteer members of our incipient expedition were growing restless.

I decided that James Curtin would stay behind in my place once the waterworks was mostly complete. While Sarah and I sallied off to Luxor, he would remain in Cairo to adjust the various valves and rams and pipes, to answer the Pasha's constant questions, and perhaps—with the assistance of Captain Gibraltar—to begin expanding our test project into a real working operation. No one knew better than James the mechanics of the Belzoni pump. No one other than Sarah and myself, that is, and we weren't about to separate. Not then. Not with the treasures of King Amenhotep awaiting us in the desert.

When I brought up the idea, it didn't sit well. "Ye can't leave me here," James said, with his eyes grown wide and a plaintive little catch in his voice. It sounded to me like filial affection wronged, but I couldn't be sure. My own father hadn't left any of us boys alone for a moment, so I'd had no experience with that kind of thing. Besides, even though I loved my father like the earth itself, his world of scissors and razors and steaming hot towels had held no appeal for me. To have been excluded from his adventures in the barber shop on the Campo de Fiori would have been a far different thing from being excluded from a trip down the Nile to prize open the sarcophagus of a pharaoh.

I was all business, though, and I looked James in the eye. "Who better to leave behind than you? Someone has to take care of the pump. Someone has to take care of Victor."

He gave me a look that suggested Victor could take care of himself.

"And besides, it's a great honor."

He looked at his shoes.

"Plenty of other boys would leap at such an opportunity."

"Name one."

Rather than admit that at that moment my knowledge of the great range of boyhood was lacking, I extemporized a detailed report on how I had once saved a Capuchin monastery and half of Rome's starving poor by means of a pumping apparatus far simpler than the one that I was about to bequeath to him, and how the feat had not only made me the apple of a certain Serafina Randazzo's eye but thus the envy—that's correct: the *envy*, a certain well-known list of deadly sins notwithstanding—the envy of every man and boy for miles around. From the students and the struggling novices all the way up to fiery little Brother Ruggiero, whom I swore then and I swear now had appeared more than once gazing out the kitchen window to observe Serafina lingering at her balcony rail. This last revelation, by the way, did not shock James half so profoundly as it had shocked me.

"You'll be a hero just as I was," I concluded. "You'll be the toast of all Cairo."

"Why can't ye just wait a bit longer, and when the pump's running we'll all go to Luxor together?"

My answer had to do with our impatient traveling party, our dwindling funds, my desire that we never leave the pumping apparatus unattended, and some vague and completely fabricated malarkey (I admit it now, to you and to myself, while the disease that I harbor gnaws inexorably through my guts) about changing weather conditions and Nile flooding and a possible threat of sandstorms. The result was that James stayed behind to man the pump, in a dutiful compromise that would teach me a lesson about the relative values of true love and buried treasure.

PART FIVE:

Luxor

"When Belzoni opened the tomb of Amenhotep, he gave mankind the keys to a world far darker than any we had ever known before."

— R. Kingsley Watts, *La Maldición de la Momia*, Buenos Aires, 1953

*

THE JOURNEY TO LUXOR!

If only I had brought my old journal with me, I should invite you to consult the relevant pages for yourself. Alas, that crumbling volume is housed now in my Piccadilly museum, preserved under glass as if it were the equal of the antiquities that crowd around it. I should be under glass myself by now, I think—under glass for preservation, instead of out here on an angry sea, tending my belly on the deck of a warship and hoping against all odds for the best.

We set out before sunrise, when the sand underfoot was cold as a snowdrift and the breath of our animals escaped in great white gusts. The desert is alive at that hour. Lizards and snakes make their languorous way from the ridge of one dune to the next. Scorpions and tarantulas scuttle about checking their traps. Bandits—larger and more flamboyant than their eight-legged brethren, but far less to be feared in the end—slink back to their roosts to stroke their black beards and plot the next night's mischief. We would have no trouble from their kind; my reputation and imposing figure, along with the ready rifles of our two former army officers, saw to that.

Never has an expedition of that size moved so silently. Credit the sand, which muffles all things, even history. I had hoped to make the entire march on foot so as to give my assembled army a lesson in leadership by example, but I soon discovered that despite my legendary might and extraordinary lung capacity the sand underfoot made progress difficult. I began to sink once we passed the outskirts of the city—even when we took special care to stay on such roads as presented themselves. My legs became a pair of clumsy stone pillars, my torso a slab of granite carved into my likeness, and the whole lot of me threatened to sink beneath the sand where I might await discovery in a thousand years or so. Rather than risk becoming an example of the buried treasure that I sought, I took refuge upon the largest of our camels.

The journey took three days, as Drovetti had predicted. Very different from Cairo, which was a bustling metropolis at constant war with the desert, Luxor was an outpost that had long ago surrendered. Its buildings were one and all the color of the sand that encroached from every direction. Making our camp on the edge of town, I had the feeling that bits of old Luxor—Thebes, I mean—lay hidden everywhere beneath our feet. Drive a peg to stake down a tent, and it might clang against the capstone of a buried pyramid. That night, while Sarah and I lay awake upon a bed of sand and the sudden cold desert winds buffeted our tent, I felt as I had felt long before in the shop of my father, suspended there over the historic murder of Julius Caesar. Ghosts passed beneath us, ghosts that floated from room to drifted-shut room in an utter darkness that closed their world to me. In the morning I awoke with sand in my fists and a hole clawed beside me deep enough to bury a man.

I should like to say that I was strictly purposeful in the retrieval of Amenhotep's sarcophagus. I had intended to be. I had intended to go directly about my business, retrieve that which was mine, and return to

Cairo straightaway. Dawn, however, dissuaded me. For as the sun rose that first morning, it sent the shadows of a dozen curious structures racing toward me across the desert. Monoliths and markers, lone obelisks and fragments of once-mighty temples, they thrust themselves upright into the shimmering air and probed across the waste with black fingers, seeking me out.

I strolled to the edge of the camp where Akbar, our Macedonian cook, was preparing breakfast over a fire that was forever threatening to consume his wooden leg. "Tell me," I said, pointing to the east where two matched silhouettes broke the horizon. "Is that a pair of monuments I see in the distance, or only one? I could be persuaded that one of them is mirage."

Akbar looked up from a cauldron of oil in which little balls of falafel smoked and swirled. "Two, Sahib. Rest assured, neither is a mirage—although one of them has been known to sing, and the other remains mute." He thrust a huge slotted spoon into the oil and fished out a sizzling heap of falafel, noticed that the tip of his peg leg was starting to smoke a bit, and ground the sparks out in the sand. "My implement," he said with an apologetic grin, indicating with his free hand the artificial leg, "was once much longer."

I wasn't distracted by the shenanigans with his leg. "What do you mean, *one of them has been known to sing*"?

"Nothing, Sahib. Loose talk. Superstition. How could a statue sing, I ask you? And why?" He emptied the contents of his spoon onto a flat rock, and I helped myself.

By this time the men had begun to gather, and their opinions on the singing statue were as numerous and slippery as grains of sand.

"The statue isn't really singing," someone offered. "It's talking."

"Whispering, to be precise."

"Without words, though."

"How would you know so much about it? Until this week, you'd never set foot outside Cairo."

"Say what you like, it has a kind of music to it. It's as if someone were whispering through a flute."

"It's true that only one of them sings, though."

"Talks."

"Anything you say. Only one of them does it, whatever it is."

"The other one has nothing whatsoever to say."

"You should learn a lesson from him."

"From who?"

"From whom?"

"King Memnon. That's the statue. The statues, I mean."

"How big are they?"

"Two hundred and fifty feet tall."

"Sixty-five or seventy. No more."

"The sand has worn them down."

"Wasn't he the Son of the Dawn?"

"Who?"

"King Memnon of Ethiopia."

"Something like that."

"'Son of the Dawn,' eh? Perhaps that's the reason he sings at sunrise."

"Sunrise? Only at sunrise?"

"So they say."

"Really?"

"I think it's a trick. The high priests are behind the whole thing. They throw their voices through a tube somewhere. It fattens up the offerings."

"Nonsense. There hasn't been a high priest there in a hundred years."

"Not according to my brother-in-law."

At which point a certain percentage of the group descended into name-calling and petty recrimination, while the rest busied themselves consuming what was left of the falafel.

Need I say that the mention of passing sound through a tube caused my very heart to leap? Although my usual medium was pressurized water—not the spoken word compressed into some kind of long-distance ventriloquism—it seemed to me that my understanding might be applied to unraveling the riddle of the singing tower. So after a consultation with Akbar, who assured me that we had sufficient provisions to stretch our trip out by a few days, I resolved to take a handful of men on a sight-seeing expedition before we recovered our treasure.

*

THE STATUES, AS DESCRIBED by the less enthusiastic but more practical of their promoters, were some seventy feet high. They sat apart and at a slight angle to one another, flanking a pile of rubble that had once been the burial place of a king. Time, robbers, and the elements had been unkind to the tomb itself—which was collapsed well beyond entry, even by an explorer as determined as myself—but the colossi had held up surprisingly well. Their crowns had tumbled off and disintegrated who knows how long ago, and the years had worn their visages down to an assemblage of ghastly lumps, but their forms were still visibly human and they sat astride their matched thrones with grim authority. I could have taken either of their massive laps as my sleeping pallet, and been as comfortable as if I had been dozing on my little threadbare rug at Jaundyce's. Soon enough I would do exactly that. But in the meantime I was thrilled to have stumbled into a land inhabited by statuary that made me feel positively puny. How refreshing it was! Like a draft of cool water in the desert heat.

On the subject of which—the desert heat, I mean—between the sun and the sand and the great carved rocks, that blast furnace of a country in which I found myself was positively roaring by the time our little party thundered up to the statues. (The colossi were situated just off a well-traveled road leading to the Valley of the Kings, and people came and went within their shadow as if they were of no more interest than a pair of elm trees. A pair of elm trees would have been of far greater interest, come to think of it, and for good reason.) I slid off my camel and knelt at the foot of the more northern colossus, digging my hands into the sand at its base. It was like the sand everywhere else, only slightly more coarse—studded with stubborn little knobs and crystals of quartz that had not yet completed their transformation from statuary to undifferentiated dust. As with the collapsing city of Luxor, it was impossible to tell if the desert were reclaiming the work of man or if the work of man were reasserting its God-given right to be desert.

If the statue had been talking earlier—or singing, or humming, or whatever it was that it did these days—it had given off by the time we arrived. I dug in the sand for a few futile minutes, scraping around the base of its carved throne with my hands as if I might unearth the secret of its operation so easily, but I soon gave off. It didn't strike me that there could be any high priests behind this mischief, since there wasn't a priest in sight—much less an offering box, their unmistakable sign and signifier. Just a handful of my men and a troop of forlorn-looking tourists. Two or three of the travelers were nuns, as I recall, martyring themselves under habits of thick black wool.

Satisfied that the sand concealed nothing of any import, we addressed ourselves to the communicative statue itself. I drew upon my experience at Sadler's Wells, arranging my men into sturdy pyramids that I could climb like so much scaffolding. I would clamber up to a rocky perch, haul the men up after me one by one, and there begin the process over again. Ropes took me to the highest and narrowest reaches. I scoured every inch of that monument, and in the end I saw not the slightest sign of any cunning noisemaker.

At sundown I sent the men back to our camp, keeping only my camel, some ropes and blankets, a canteen, my pistol, and a sackful of some edible compound that Akbar had prepared for the outing. It was gritty between my teeth and hot on my tongue; like most of his cooking, it felt like pulverized refractory cement and tasted like burning walnut shells mixed with horse liniment—but I made a supper of it and climbed up into Memnon's lap to take my rest. The view from that spot, looking westward toward the horizon, was fit for a king. Night bloomed over the desert as I watched, and the silence deepened as it always does in darkness. Old Memnon creaked and groaned beneath me as the stars flickered to luminous life overhead, and I dreamed that I was rocked upon a ship at sea.

*

MORNING BROUGHT ILLUMINATION.

I awoke flat on my back in Memnon's lap, shivering beneath my thin blanket. I'd slept under worse conditions many times, so it wasn't the temperature that had awakened me. What had awakened me was a vibration against the back of my head, insistent and penetrating enough to rattle my skull and make my vision wobble. It was dark down in Memnon's lap, but as I sat up and peered over the edge I could see that the sun had been up for some time. My high perch cast a long shadow toward the horizon, and with the shadow of the southern colossus it formed a pair of swords that penetrated the desert.

I sat there in the cold, feeling the buzzing continue beneath the base of my spine. A tiny movement in a shadowy recess of Memnon's stony lap caught my eye—I thought at first it was a spider—and as I focused on it I realized that the entire floor was alive with quivering flakes of quartz and grains of sand, each one hopping and sizzling like a droplet of water on a hot griddle.

And then, as I came up on one knee and started gathering my equipment, the colossus began to sing. It was more like a deep whistling, actually, with a sort of a scratchy muffled hum overlaid upon it. The sound began softly, at a volume hardly louder than a stage whisper, but soon it acquired the vigorous and resonant tone of a pipe organ. More curiously, it seemed to be coming from hard by the very spot where I was kneeling.

I studied the vibrating particles of sand, and saw that as a group they were taking on a curious radial pattern, just as iron filings will arrange themselves in the presence of a powerful magnet. At the center of their various dancing three-quarter-circles was a small fissure where a bit of rock had crumbled away centuries ago, and I bent instinctively to place my ear upon it.

Yes! Precisely as you have imagined! Victory!

The thing boomed into my ear like a musical cannon, and the air upon which its voice floated was several degrees warmer than the stones surrounding it.

The Great Belzoni, hydraulicist to the Pasha, had proven himself the man for the job after all. I leapt to my feet, scrambled down to the desert floor unaided by ropes, and dashed around to the eastern side of the colossus where the sun was hot and the possibilities were hotter still.

The sound was less loud there, more diffuse and mysterious. It swelled and sank and seemed to emanate from every corner of the compass at once. The difference between this music—which already had the morning's fresh handful of tourists all aswoon—and the blast that I'd heard in my stony bed was the difference between a hunting horn piping somewhere across the moors and a steam whistle pressed against your eardrum.

I dropped my equipment, bowed to the tourists—who seemed to believe that I was part of the show—and began feeling my way along the wall. Father Mullooly would have been proud of the cautious way I proceeded, patient as history, all senses on the alert. I was searching for a telltale crack in the stonework, and indeed I located it in no time. The air rushing into it tugged at the hairs of my beard like a high wind. It was just as I'd thought: some accident of architecture and decay had provided the colossus with a chimney. And as the stonework began to warm each morning, it drew in air that resonated in the hidden hollow space. I put my hand against the opening—it was no bigger than my palm—and the singing stopped, just like that. The tourists gasped. I lifted my hand again, and the singing started up once more. Great relief all around. And so it was that I spent an hour or so experimenting with the thing, variously modulating it with my palm and the fabric of my clothing and bits of crumbled stone, attempting to tame its pitch. Had I been a musician instead of a strongman, I might have played a concerto upon that colossal instrument. Eventually the tourists grew bored and wandered off in groups of two and three to study the other colossus, to poke at the ruined gravesite with their walking sticks, and to scratch themselves while staring blankly at the horizon. As for me, I tried one last experiment as the sun reached its zenith and the song of the colossus began to taper off. I took a handful of Akbar's refractory cement, wet it with a splash of water from my canteen, and used it to plug up the aperture. The statue wheezed into silence, and to the best of my knowledge it has never since made so much as a peep.

*

THE NEXT MORNING, leaving only Sarah and a single armed soldier behind to guard our camp, we set off to retrieve the sarcophagus of Amenhotep. I wanted our expedition to be at full strength, since there was no telling how much the sarcophagus would weigh and no anticipating the difficulties we might encounter in bringing it to light.

As a trickle of water running down a pane of glass will gather other droplets to itself, so our caravan gained strength as it passed through villages and desert encampments. Half-naked boys, hard-muscled men, crippled old blind wizards and deeply shrouded women of unknowable age attached themselves to us instinctively, no doubt because we were the most interesting thing to pass by in ages. We were the Egyptian equivalent of a circus parade, and we grew more irresistibly colorful as the journey went on. I led the way, mounted high upon my camel like a figurehead. Only Akbar, with the camel's rope wound in his hands, preceded me.

He led us straight to the tomb, which was accessible by a dark little stairway hidden between two conical dunes. As I drew nearer I realized that the dunes were recent additions to the scene, the results of massive excavations. Leave it to the French, and their well-known obsession with the female form, to have piled up their waste so suggestively. Little wonder the local women wrapped their burnooses tighter if any one of us happened to so much as glance in their direction.

Akbar looped my camel's rope around a pile of rock. "This way," he said, and he vanished down the stairs.

I scrambled down from my camel, took a moment to light a torch, and followed. Drovetti had promised that the sarcophagus was in a secure spot, but this certainly didn't look like one. Not if a fellow could come and go so easily. I half hoped that the thing weighed the better part of a ton, and had been thus protected from pillage by its own unassailable bulk. Akbar scampered ahead as if he knew the place by heart, which I supposed he did, while I followed behind as cautiously as I dared. The air at the bottom of the stairs was comparatively cool, but my torch and the pressure of antiquity conspired to draw some of the freshness out of it.

The main tunnel ran straight as a ray of sunlight—no wonder Akbar could make such haste in the dark, even with that peg leg!—and every inch of it was decorated with fantastically complex patterns both incised and painted. Geometric shapes, figures human and half-human, representations of gods and beasts and gods with the heads of beasts and beasts with the heads of gods, they flickered around me in the light of my torch, appearing and vanishing and reappearing again in the unnerving manner of faces glimpsed behind darkened windows. I hadn't found myself in a spot so crowded with mystery since I'd last set foot in Brother Silvestro's boneyard. A portion of me wanted to stop and study every inch of that tunnel, but the greater part of me desired to lay my hands upon the treasure of Amenhotep.

"This way, Sahib!" It was Akbar, his voice an urgent whisper amplified by the stony walls of a side passage down which he'd slipped.

I paused, looked back over my shoulder to see the wavering light of other torches moving in my direction, and ducked down the passage. Within a dozen paces Akbar appeared to me out of nowhere, looming from the darkness with his face contorted into a hideous grin and sweat pouring down from beneath his turban. With one hand—I hadn't noticed how powerful an individual he was—he took my shoulder and spun me about to face into a low alcove.

"Behold!" he cried. "The sarcophagus of King Amenhotep!"

Well. It was big all right, just as big as I'd seen it depicted on Drovetti's rubbing, and it was certainly impressive. Roughly the size and proportions of a double door, the sarcophagus lid stood upright and gleamed in the flickering torchlight. It was manufactured of cut stone, incised with figures and objects of all kinds, and encrusted with a king's ransom in dusty, dusky gemstones. Just how we should move it from its resting place I did not know, but my mind ran quickly to systems of ropes and rollers, levers and pulleys. I stepped forward—the assembled torch-bearers held their breath and leaned inward with me—and placed my hand tenderly upon the impassive face of King Amenhotep. A bit of gilt flaked off upon my damp hand, and I brushed it away onto the floor. There would be plenty more where that came from.

I left Akbar in charge of fixing torches into whatever crevices he could locate or manufacture in the walls, and returned to the caravan with perhaps half of the men. We armed ourselves with ropes, lumber, shovels and pry bars, a few likely-looking rocks that might serve as fulcrums, and some long wooden rods that the wagon's previous user had left behind. The alcove was lit like a theater when we returned, and I fell to my knees before the sarcophagus. In the time-honored manner of Father Mullooly I bent double, shielded my eyes against the dust, and blew. Odd, I thought. The seam between the bottom lip of the sarcophagus and the floor upon which it rested was tight enough to have held water. Where I'd been expecting loose bits of stone and an edge made jagged by the gouging of pickaxes and crowbars, I saw instead a meticulously made and undisturbed union. I studied it from edge to edge: no markings anywhere, none at all. There were no markings on the floor in the vicinity, either; now that the light was good I could see that the sarcophagus hadn't been dragged or levered into its place against the wall at any time in human memory. I drew slowly to my feet. There were telltale marks around both sides—the kind of thing I'd been expecting to see at the bottom, spots where I might have wedged in my pry bar and set to work—but they weren't confined to the sarcophagus itself. Not in the least. On the contrary, the walls themselves were chipped and battered and ground to powder, as if the sarcophagus were embedded in the rock and some great beast had exhausted itself scrabbling to pry it free.

"Surprise, surprise, Sahib." Akbar grinned at me from the shadows where he'd concealed himself.

"Drovetti failed to move this, didn't he? And you knew all along."

"I had an idea."

"And you didn't tell me."

"Would you have changed your mind? Would you have abandoned Amenhotep to the grave robbers, and been content with nothing but your rubbing?" He rolled his "R" like a Frenchman.

Akbar knew me well, I had to grant him that.

*

WE WORKED THE REST OF THE DAY and into the night. The men took turns, but I kept at it without ceasing, laboring with a furious and mounting desperation—as if each hour that I spent extracting Amenhotep represented another eternity that my immortal soul should be required to spend in Hades. The burial alcove took on a certain hellish

quality of its own, thanks to the oily smoke of the torches and the thick-
ening cloud of chalky dust and the sweat-streaked faces of the laborers
who toiled beside me in the flickering light of the torches. Men who
hadn't removed their turbans in years unfurled them now, and re-
wrapped them tightly about their mouths and noses. When their shifts
ended they raced to the surface and lay gasping in the sand, for all the
world like men resurrected and uncertain as to their prospects.

I observed them laid out there each time I stormed up the stairs for
another rod, another rope, another unwilling assistant. What a sight
they must have made when Sarah—yes, Sarah, my one and only—s-
tepped out of the desert and found them strewn about like corpses in
the moonlight!

What was she doing there at that time of night? How had she found
her way to us unguided and alone? How had she wrangled a long rifle
free from the soldier keeping watch over what remained of our encampment? None of these questions mattered—none of them, I tell
you—when I set my eyes on her. I was slaving in the alcove, sweating in
torrents and coughing without letup and bloodying my fingers against
the stubborn sarcophagus of Amenhotep. Her appearance before me in
that place, an immaculate seraph radiant amid the fumes and the filth,
was stunning enough on its own—to say nothing of the explosive weight
of the message she bore.

"It's James," she said. "He's been hurt. A messenger arrived this
noon, but I couldn't understand half of what he said. An accident.
Something to do with the pump."

A thousand nightmarish images flashed through my mind, every
one of them appallingly tragic and every one of them entirely my fault.
If Father Mullooly had been available, I'd have had confessions enough
to last the remainder of my lifetime. Instinctively I reached to embrace
Sarah, and instinctively she leaned toward me in her distress, but discre-
tion before the men and awareness of my filthy state overwhelmed our

natural inclinations. Frustrated, I turned with a wail and slammed my fist against the sarcophagus.

Something grated. Something crunched. Something *moved.* And I stood there like a man preparing to be drawn and quartered in the public square: Sarah and James tugging in one direction, Amenhotep in the other.

"Perhaps," I hazarded with as much nonchalance as I could summon, "we should wait until dawn before we set out."

But Sarah knew what I was up to. "I didn't walk all this way in the dark just to cool my heels until morning."

"Of course not." With one furtive finger I traced the edge of the sarcophagus, and detected a gap where none had been before. "All the same, you must be exhausted."

"Not too exhausted to ride a horse, I should think."

She had me. And as frustrated as I was, I was ten times as ashamed. How could I have thought of lingering to salvage Amenhotep at a time like this? Had I no sense of propriety? Hating myself, I turned my back on Sarah, spanned the width of the sarcophagus with my arms, gripped its edges with the bloody remnants of my fingertips, and pulled.

The men gasped to hear the high grating sound of stone upon stone. The liberating angel of Easter, with his appearance like lightning and his raiment white as snow, could not have impressed them more. I took a deep breath and pulled again, and this time the gap around the edge permitted a little puff of air to reach us from across the centuries. Its scent spoke to us of spice and decay and the desiccated nests of arachnids.

"Sarah," I said, before bracing myself for one last attempt that would certainly bring the lid free of its moorings, "I'm going to need a half-dozen of those long rods."

Did she know exactly where to arrange them? Absolutely. One after another on the floor, parallel and evenly spaced, in between the place where I stood and the open doorway. Did she think that I would be able to wrangle the lid onto them all by myself? Who knows? I certainly didn't believe that such a feat was within my powers. But the men of my crew were fixed in their places around the gallery, impassive and useless as gentlemen come to witness a hanging. I was left alone to do the heavy work. Such has always been my lot. And I rose, as always, to the challenge.

I folded my hands and bowed my head and rapidly uttered a little prayer, although why I hadn't done the same when I'd heard word of James's accident I cannot say. When I opened my eyes again I saw that the men had folded their hands in unconscious imitation of me. They were bobbing their heads up and down in a kind of rhythmic trance, and muttering to themselves in a tongue that I did not understand. The impression that they made there in the murky torchlight had a dark and primitive quality, as if they were up to something far deeper than merely encouraging me to remove the lid and were instead summoning up some ancient force that had been imprisoned behind that stone barrier since the beginning of time.

Sarah cringed, either from a soul-deep dread or from a practical fear that I was about to throw my back out and ruin myself for our return to Cairo.

Regardless of the consequences—a mummy's curse, a week's agony and bed rest—I applied myself with all due haste to the sarcophagus. And assisted by my own God and by whatever half-beast deities the workmen were busy invoking, I had its lid positioned on the rollers in little more than an instant. It fell with a crash that brought down rock from the ceiling and dimmed the chamber beneath a cloud of dust, and the velocity of its movement set up a windstorm that rapidly extinguished the torches. We lit them all again, our ready lucifers filling the place with the stink of brimstone, and were met by the vision of Amenhotep upright in the niche where he had stood for centuries without number. Poor old Amenhotep! Just a pathetic skeleton encased in rawhide, gripping in its folded claws a scroll of papyrus.

I snatched up the scroll for safekeeping, along with a pair of stone amphorae and something that looked as if it once had been a bundle of reeds, and jammed it all into my pack before giving instructions on how to get the rest of it—the sarcophagus of Amenhotep, leathery old Amenhotep himself, and the remainder of his belongings (which I inventoried on the spot with only the most cursory of glances)—up the stairs and onto the wagon.

Then, without a look back, Sarah and I lit out for Cairo under stars that were just then beginning to fade.

*

JAMES, JAMES, JAMES! Permit me to say that the disease ravaging my vitals right now—worsened by the yawing of this wretched ship and the revolting victuals that the British Navy serves to even its most honored guests—was nothing in comparison to the ache that I felt when we entered the presence of that poor crippled child. I feared that it would knock me over, and that once down I would never rise again.

But he was a fighter, our boy James. For that he had his father's heart to thank, not to mention his own street-honed resilience and his adoptive Uncle Giovanni's legendary strength. Even this soon after the accident, he struggled up from his sickbed and hobbled forward to greet us as we entered his room at the royal palace.

"The Pasha wouldn't let me go home," he explained around Sarah's embrace. "Not with this."

"Not *without* this" might have been the more apt expression, for our James had lost his right leg from a point just above the knee. The poor creature weighed nothing—less than nothing—as I stepped in and lifted him up into my arms. A touching scene, as you can imagine. But it was not strictly necessary. As I have said, James was a fighter. He'd have no more been willing to be carted around by yours truly than I'd have been eager to be trotted about in a sedan chair by a team of eunuchs.

Over supper he explained how he had come to this tragic state. The pumping apparatus. The successful demonstration. The rejoicing crowds. And above all, the gang of chattering men who'd persuaded him to give them each a turn in the wheel. They'd entered first one by one and then two by two and finally three by three, a merry mob well beyond his control, and as the hours went by their combined force must have placed unanticipated strains on the machinery, weakening the safeguards that we had so cautiously engineered. Something snapped when James finally took his place again, and the weight of the accumulated water spun the wheel in reverse, sending him spiraling out on a collision course with the hull of a boat drifting in the shallows of the Nile. He hit, the bones of his leg snapped and pierced his flesh like so many knives, and he tumbled headfirst into the water, unconscious. He was lucky that he didn't drown.

"In ancient times," the Pasha interrupted, "a damaged youth such as he might have been sacrificed to guarantee a good harvest. See how far your contributions have brought us, Signor Belzoni?"

Far enough that my truest friend had sacrificed a leg on the altar of my carelessness and greed. Which was altogether too far for my liking.

*

"WHEREVER YOU'RE GOING," James said, "I'm better off staying here. I'll be fine."

It was a blistering hot day—what day in Cairo wasn't? the place was barbarous, sulfurous, like unto hell itself—and the boy was sitting up in bed wearing a pair of borrowed linen pajamas and a visible film of sweat.

I was in my traveling clothes. Sarah and I had spent the night in our little flat in the European Quarter, breathing the familiar scents of Italian and French cooking and feeling powerfully the absence of our orphan from his bed in the next room. Guilt and compassion notwithstanding, though, it was time to return to the desert and meet Amenhotep's incoming caravan.

"Go on without me," said James.

"I've made myself a vow. I shall never again leave you behind."

"Ye'd make us into circus freaks, joined together at the hip."

"There are worse fates. I will bear you up."

"It's no way to live."

"Fine. Then I won't go. I'll stay right here instead." I plumped down on the bed beside him.

"Really, boss," he winced. "Ye've got work to do."

I cast a curious gaze around the room. "Have you any playing cards?"

"I don't think so."

"Dice?"

"Please."

"A good book, then. I'll read to you. Or you to me. It will be just like old times." I sprang from the bed and went to a shelf by the window, but the books there were inscribed in strange characters that flamed across the page like armies of battling dragons. The mysterious and exotic beauty of that writing reminded me—I may as well own up to it now—of what I'd be giving up by lingering with James in his sickroom. I gazed out the window for a minute, letting my eyes take in the desert and a small plume of dust that was forming on the horizon. "You're certain that you don't want to come along? Yours could be the first European eyes to see that sarcophagus by the light of day."

"Amenhotep has gotten by without me for this long. It won't hurt him to wait a bit longer."

He was a philosopher, our James Curtin.

"Besides, me leg hurts."

"I see. Of course. Very well."

"And I need to sleep."

"I am sorry."

"Don't apologize."

"Can I draw the curtains?"

"No. It gets too hot."

"Anything else? Water?"

"No. Thank you. Please."

"You're sure?"

"Positive. Just come back and tell me all about it, won't ye?"

"Every last detail."

*

SARAH AND I GALLOPED out of the city and into the desert, taking dead aim at the gathering cloud of dust I'd spied from the palace window. It had to be our caravan, come bearing my prize—although frankly, judging from volume of dust it sent up, it seemed to have grown a bit since I'd last seen it.

"It looks like an army," was what Sarah said.

She was correct. It looked very much like an army. And the closer we drew to it, the more it looked like one army in particular. Napoleon's.

We rode to the crest of a nearby dune for a better look. The formation must have consisted of a hundred and fifty men, stiff and stoic in their gritty uniforms, mounted on the most magnificent horses you've ever seen. There were so many soldiers, and they rode so closely together rank upon rank, that they had digested my little caravan the way a snake swallows a rat. I could discern one particular wagon of mine in the center of it all, though, laboring along under the burden of Amenhotep's sarcophagus.

At the head of the column, unmistakable on account of his puffed-up posture, rode Drovetti. And not far behind, swilling from a bottle of wine that cost more than most Egyptian men would earn in a month, rode Akbar.

I reined in my horse and took up my pistol. Sarah pulled up along-side and placed a hand upon my elbow.

"Easy there, Atlas..."

"I'm not about to take on the French army. Not today. But I do mean to get their attention." I removed her hand and raised my weapon to the sky, but before I could squeeze off a shot Drovetti was calling my name from the desert floor.

The simultaneous clicking of the one hundred and fifty rifles at his command sounded like a forest of very angry crickets.

"Belzoni!" he cried, perfectly at ease and pointing with a genteel fin-ger toward the wagon and the prize lashed down upon it. "I understand that you have made the acquaintance of my friend Amenhotep!"

"Your friend? Hah! You seem to have trouble keeping track of your friends, Drovetti. As I recall, you made quite a show of presenting Amenhotep to me."

Drovetti pulled something out of his pocket—not a weapon, at least not a conventional one—and held it up into the sunlight. It was flat, squarish, and pale, the size of an envelope. He laughed into his scarf as Sarah and I rode down to get a better look. "It is you, Belzoni, who seem to have trouble keeping track of your friends. According to this firman, issued by agents of Pasha Mohammed 'Ali and bearing his signature, I am the only individual authorized to remove artifacts from anywhere within ten miles of that tomb. Any such work is to be carried out only on my behalf and by my agents, whose acquaintance I understand you have also made."

Akbar raised his bottle in a sly greeting.

"You're lucky I came along when I did, Belzoni. The Pasha isn't showing much patience with grave robbers lately. And I understand that the Egyptian prisons are less comfortable than ever."

I clenched a useless fist. "What of my rubbing? What of the inscrip-tion and the signature and the seal?"

"In France, they might be worth something. They might be worth great deal, in fact. But here..." he gave a Gallic shrug that seemed to refer to this entire inscrutable country.

"You scoundrel."

"It is out of my hands, Belzoni. I am terribly sorry, believe me." He spurred his horse, and the formation began to lurch forward. "Most kind of you to have dug him out, though. Really. I shall be forever grateful."

I pointed a finger. "If you dare take him to Paris, he's mine."

He turned in his saddle and gave me a big smile, which was apparently all I was going to get out of this transaction. "Oh, there's not a chance in the world of that," he said. "I mean to present him to the Pasha as a gift."

*

HENRY SALT WAS A DIFFICULT MAN to get moving. As many complaints as I put before him—I went so far as to drag him to the ceremony where Drovetti turned over Amenhotep's sarcophagus, *my* sarcophagus, to the Pasha—he was all recalcitrance and delay when it came to obtaining a trifling firman or two on behalf of England. There was little I could do. I paced outside his office—and inside, when he gave me the opportunity. I monopolized the sofa in his waiting room for days at a time. I drank up half of his tea. I stamped my feet and shook my fist. All for nothing.

In the end, motivating him required nothing less than a directive straight from Lord Elgin himself. England's legendary demolition man had just finished helping himself to a good portion of the Parthenon, and the spoils were such an ornament to the British Museum that he had sent out for more. I was present when the order arrived, and every word of it fell upon my ears like music. "'...*you are hereby instructed to obtain with all haste any such firman as may...*'" Salt stopped reading and scratched his head. "What does Elgin know about the paperwork in a

217

godforsaken outpost like this?" He lowered his brows and eyed me as if I'd been going over his head, sneaking uncomplimentary information back to London.

"Elgin," I reminded him, "had a firman that covered most of Athens." I may have been an innocent on this subject just a few weeks prior, but I've always been a quick study. And lately the newspapers had been positively loaded with details of Elgin's work.

Salt cursed and balled the letter in his fist. And then, with that ready bureaucratic embarrassment that both propels and hobbles every servant of the crown, he began smoothing it out again. "Very well, sir. Very well. You shall have your damned firman."

That "*sir*" gave me pause, for I couldn't tell if he were grumbling to me or apostrophizing the absent Lord Elgin. Either way, as long as he was aiming to get us a digging permit of our very own, I hoped he'd get his hands on a good one.

*

TIME WENT BY. Cairo became my prison. I refined my pump, built a half-dozen more, and then spent my days teaching their operation and manufacture to rapt gangs of natives. Captain Gibraltar collected a colossal bonus from the Pasha and vanished aboard the *Cleopatra* for parts undisclosed. Sarah grew bored and began teaching poetry to a surprisingly docile pack of children—each of whom, prior to my arrival, had been doomed to spend his days dangling like a spider from the long arm of the family *shadoof*. And James developed a searing fever, lost another portion of his leg, very nearly died, and came home to us at last.

The Pasha was reluctant to see him go. He stood in the grand foyer surrounded by his entourage (which now included Victor, perched upon a tall rolling platform built exclusively for his use) and he wrung his hands as James hobbled past. "It has been my pleasure and my honor to care for your friend, Signor Belzoni. He is a fine boy. I regret that I once presumed him a midget, and also that I once suggested that work such as his might be accomplished by a trained dog."

James turned upon his crutches and looked hurt, but I calmed him with a glance.

"I should not let him go at all," the Pasha went on, "but for my understanding that his powers of recuperation will be increased by exposure to a person of your great dimensions and vigorous character."

I had no idea where he'd gotten so ridiculous an idea. I smiled at him the way you'd smile at a lunatic or a mad dog, and I reached a steadying hand to James's elbow.

"As you see, Belzoni, I am acquainted with the latest Western medical thought—including Professor Dibdin's *Theory of Proximity* and the Doctor Schmidtka's *The Transfer of Vital Particles.*"

Professor Dibdin. Doctor Schmidtka. I glanced up at Victor, who was turning a pale shade of purple. He looked desperate for a pair of hands behind which he could hide his face.

*

MY OWN *THEORY OF PROXIMITY* is that too many people gathered into too little space are certain to generate discomfort. Especially in a place as crowded as Cairo, and even if they love one another as much as Sarah and James and I. So although the boy's plight very nearly killed me, I was as eager to thrust myself beyond the confines of the city as any man has ever been. The good news of our liberation came at last from Henry Salt.

"You're not going to like this much." Salt had a great fondness for starting conversations that way, as if by lowering your expectations from the start he might cast his lackluster performance in a more favorable light.

"Tell me."

"It's a firman. An actual firman, right here in my hand."

I leaned toward it, but he snatched it away .

"Alas, it covers a site that's been thoroughly picked over. A place not far from Luxor. You remember Luxor? The scene of your triumph in recovering Amenhotep?"

I bit my tongue.

"There's a temple there. Quite an enormous one."

"Demolished, I suppose?"

"Absolutely."

"Ransacked?"

"So thoroughly that even the French abandoned it long ago."

"There's nothing left, then?"

"Nothing a person could take away."

Nothing a person could take away. I said not a word to Salt, but it sounded exactly like the sort of place where I did my finest work.

*

THE FIRMAN WAS FOR THE TEMPLE of Ramesses II, a great pile of rocks located, as Salt had said, just outside the city of Luxor. (Some call Ramesses II by another name, *The Young Memnon.* Was this the same Memnon whose colossus I'd silenced with a fistful of Akbar's horrible cooking? Your guess is as good as mine.)

The document wasn't valid until the end of the month, and until then my French nemesis still held the digging rights to the place. I advised Salt to keep mum as to our developing plans, and I set out quietly to make the rounds of the marketplace and the docks, hoping to hire a stout boat and round up a handful of men who could be counted upon to keep their mouths shut. Easier said than done, considering the poor rewards I'd had for those we'd employed the last time around. And I certainly had no desire to allow turncoats like Akbar to infiltrate our party. Yet I persevered.

The men I found were a sorry lot, a ragged coven of malnourished wraiths whose expectations in life were as thin as their bellies, but they had heard stories of my accomplishments and seemed as a result to share an almost superstitious faith in me. I found them huddled around a fire on the edge of town, sucking hot *sahlab* through the gaps in their teeth. Flecks of coconut clung to their upper lips, furnishing each with a snowy mustache that gleamed in the darkness. Addressing them was like speaking before a convention of glowworms.

"Signor Belzoni!" The ringleader leapt to his feet as I approached, as if he'd been waiting for me to arrive. Perhaps he had. By the look in his eye, he may have been of the opinion that he'd actually conjured me. No sooner had he gained his feet than he bent himself double in a panicky *salaam*, spilling his beverage into the sand. I reached out my hand to him as if I were setting a child's broken plaything upright. His breath stank of rotted molars, curdled milk, and the ground bulbs of orchids. "Signor Belzoni!" he repeated. "We were just speaking of you!"

I was the talk of the town, at least among a certain class of character.

"We were speculating," he said, and with the word a rancid stew of milk and grated coconut and orchid powder sprayed from between his teeth, "we were speculating, the lot of us, over the source of your powers. Speculating fruitlessly, I might add."

The other men either gaped at me or shielded their eyes as if I were brightly aflame.

"About the source of my powers?"

"Just so. The manipulation of water, for one example. The juggling of great stones as if they were pebbles, for another. They say that in opening the sarcophagus, you were assisted by a mighty wind that rose up and devoured the flames of a thousand torches."

"Well, it was more on the order of..."

"As for me," he said, "I believe that you have acquired control of a powerful jinni." A muttered undercurrent of mingled assent and derision went around the fire, along with a shuffling of sandaled feet.

"Umar, on the other hand," and here the ringleader pointed to one of the gentlemen who shaded their eyes rather than look directly upon me, "holds the opinion that you are in fact a jinni yourself." Somebody on the other side of the fire gulped his sahlab and gagged audibly.

The talkative fellow bowed again. "Although I do not pretend to know who or even what you are, Signor Belzoni, I assure you that I am at your service for as long as you shall permit me to be so." He gave the impression that to offer anything less would show astonishing stupidity and invite grave personal risk, and of this I was not about to dissuade him.

He offered me a steaming mug of sahlab, and told me that his name was Hakim. I declined the beverage—the better to preserve something of the mysterious about my nature—but I knew at that moment that he and his men were about to become as valuable to me as my own limbs. I squatted before their fire and took them into my confidence. "Very soon I shall be starting operations at the tomb of Ramesses II. Are any of you familiar with it?"

Hands up all around.

A voice: "There's a big statue there."

"How big?" I asked the darkness.

Another voice: "It's just a head, really. Not a statue, technically speaking."

And another: "I'd say it's more on the order of a bust."

I repeated my question with a touch of theatrical impatience. No sense letting the conversation escape my control. *"How big?"*

"Oh, my. How big, yes. Well. Six feet tall, at the least."

"Eight."

"Nine."

"Carved out of solid granite."

"Solid quartz."

"Absolutely immovable."

That last one hurt, and I snapped my head in the speaker's direction to let him know just how much. It was Umar, the poor pious deluded fellow who suspected me of being a jinni. The gentlemen to his left and right clamped hands upon his shoulders to keep him from flying off or turning to stone from sheer terror.

"Immovable?" I growled. "We shall see about that."

*

MY FINANCIAL PROBLEMS may have been over, but my personnel difficulties were just beginning. I put Hakim in charge of obtaining the use of a boat, and I rewarded Umar's fear of me by making him our quartermaster.

He may have been frightened, but that didn't keep him from being recalcitrant and lazy. From the very start he had a million useless ideas. "Couldn't you just conjure up what we need when we get to Luxor?" That sort of thing. He was impossible. I thanked God I hadn't put him in charge of acquiring transportation.

Early one morning I got a message from Victor asking me to drop by the palace at my earliest convenience. I set aside my work and found him on a shaded balcony overlooking the city's rooftops. Someone had set him up with a hookah, for which he seemed to have developed a dangerous affinity. He drew on it again and again while we talked, and in between pulls he coughed like a tubercular. He didn't look well. He looked enormously contented, but not well.

"Have you put on weight?" I knew it wasn't the kindest way to start a conversation, but a person could always be direct with Victor.

"Maybe a little. I don't get out much."

"Are you doing your exercises?"

"When I think of it."

"Don't go soft, Victor. That's not like you."

"And the food around here! Incredible."

"No doubt, but still. I'm just looking after your best interests."

Victor coughed, sucked on the tube, and looked through watery eyes at the roofs below. "Enough about me, Sammy. How about you? You all set for Luxor?"

"Another few days should do it. We're having some trouble with provisions, but other than that..." I trailed off, guessing that he was about to ask if he could go along on the expedition. It would be just like the old days in London, except with him in a backpack instead of his perambulator. Or so I imagined it. Victor, however, had a surprise in store.

"Go now." He whispered it through a mouthful of smoke, as if to hide his words from anyone but me. "Leave today."

"We're not half ready. Well, perhaps *half* ready. But..."

"Take my word for it. Leave now, and push up the river as fast as you can. Your firman isn't good until what, Wednesday? Midnight Wednesday?"

"You seem to know everything these days, Victor."

"You can't expect me to cover up my ears."

I smiled. "That's four days from now. It's a three-day voyage up the river. And with provisions as short as they are, there's no sense arriving early."

Victor coughed, and he coughed again, and it wasn't a cough developed from drawing on the hookah. It signified that he'd said his last word on the subject, and I knew that it was time to head for Luxor.

*

WE LEFT AT NIGHTFALL with almost enough food, a rag-bin of frayed ropes and bent rollers, and an old tub of a barge less suited to navigating the Nile than to fueling a bonfire. Sarah and James and I sat on the bow to let the spray cool our ankles as darkness settled over the desert and the lights of Cairo faded behind us. It was the first chance we'd had to talk all day.

"Since when," she asked me, "have you become the impulsive, 'God will provide' type?"

"Since I had a little chat with Victor. He's all ears, that one. And he gave me the distinct impression that we ought to make haste."

"He gave you 'the distinct impression.'"

"Oh, yes. Distinct. Absolutely distinct."

"It's not the *distinct* part that worries me. It's the *impression* part."

"Oh, he couldn't talk. Not at any length. The walls have ears, as you can imagine."

"I can imagine."

"And besides, if anyone can recover that bust with less than ideal equipment, it would be the Great Belzoni."

She put her arm in mine and lay her head on my bicep. "Atlas," she said, "I love a man with plenty of self-confidence."

"I know," I said. "Lucky me."

*

IF SARAH STILL HARBORED any doubts about Victor's veiled communication, they dissolved when we reached the temple of Ramesses II three mornings later—for that awe-inspiring ruin was surrounded by an army of Frenchmen.

We piloted the barge into the shallows and ran her aground beneath the cocked rifles of our enemies. I instructed everyone to remain on board, and slipped over the far side into the water. I was dripping as I climbed the sandbank to the perimeter of the temple grounds, but the desert heat soon seared every drop of moisture from my clothing and me.

"I hope you're preparing to leave," I said to a sentry who looked very much like one of the men I'd taken into the desert previously—it wasn't

Akbar, for this individual was in possession of both of his legs, but it might have been Akbar's twin. "My firman will take effect at midnight." I tapped my breast pocket as if I had the document folded up in there, although the truth was that Salt had barely let me see the thing before he'd whisked it into his safe.

"You'll have to take that up with the consul," said the sentry, whom I was beginning to think of as Akbar II.

"Oh really? I'm afraid I have no time to return to Cairo."

"No need." The sentry nodded toward the great temple, where Drovetti himself idled while workmen scrambled around a gigantic sculpture of a man's head. "Tell me," I said before I took my leave. "Is that Ramesses II?"

"It's either him or Young Memnon. Or maybe it's that Amenhotep. I can't tell them apart, to tell you the truth."

I signaled my men to remain in the boat, although it seemed un-likely that they would elect to join me on my walk into the nest of spi-ders. Then I made my way over jumbled rocks and through crowds of laborers to the foot of the statue.

"Ho there, Belzoni!" It was Drovetti, slumped against a wall, sucking for nourishment upon a narrow cigarette. "Have you come for the show? If you have, you've arrived just in time."

"I didn't expect to find you here, Drovetti. Salt told me you'd aban-doned this dig long ago."

"We did. Bigger fish to fry. A man can't do everything."

"What changed your mind?"

He crushed out his cigarette on the rocks, and inhaled as if there were something sweet in the air. The smell of hyacinths, perhaps, or per-fume. "Oh, you know how it is."

"Tell me."

He drew coy little half-circles in the sand with the toe of his boot. "My dear Belzoni," he said to the ground. "'Jealousy' is such a strong word, don't you think? But there you have it. There you have it in a nut-shell."

"Jealousy."

"Loath as I am to admit it."

"Come, come, Drovetti. You and jealousy are old friends. There's no shame in that."

He ran his fingers through his hair and gave me a wan smile.

"This time, though, you're not going to get what's mine." I knew what I was talking about, too, because I could see from where I stood that Ramesses wasn't going anywhere—at least not before sundown. The head stood there like the seven tons of stubborn rock it was, half of its headdress missing and a mysterious little smile dancing about its lips, surrounded by men pushing useless little carts and shouldering wooden trunks. Not a ramp or a rope or a roller in sight.

"We shall see," said Drovetti.

"May I?" I indicated the statue with a tilt of my head.

"Be my guest." He waved me on, and scratched a lucifer against the rock to fire up another cigarette.

His men were busy, but not in the sprawling industrious way that indicates an army of ants at work on the carcass of a butterfly or a team of men preparing to move a gigantic piece of rock across the desert floor. They were concentrated, one would almost say that they were drawn to a point, and at the focus of their congested bustling was a tall thin man on a ladder set by Ramesses' right shoulder. Even from the ground I could see that he was laboring mightily—with a brace and bit, a twelve-pound sledgehammer, and a three-foot rod of tempered iron—to drill a hole in the statue's shoulder.

The men scattered as I approached. They weren't armed—the armed guards were at some distance, spaced along the perimeter of the site. These individuals, some of whom I recognized as they fumbled with their turbans or coughed into their fists, showing me their backs, were lowly diggers as terrified of Drovetti and me as they were of what they might be called upon to unleash from some ghost-haunted tomb. I ignored them one and all, and called out directly to the man on the ladder.

"You'll be attaching a fitting there, I suppose? A hook of some sort?"

"No." He didn't even look back over his shoulder.

"A pulley, then? For running tackle?"

"No." He put down his bit and picked up his hammer.

I stood and scratched my head, watching him work. Sweat flew from him.

"What, then?"

"Since you asked," he said, "we're about ready to fill this old boy up with black powder."

I stuck a finger in my ear and ran it around a couple of times. I couldn't possibly have heard him correctly. "Black powder, you say? As in—?"

"Righto." Finally he turned, and for a moment he grinned down at me from his perch like a merry skull. "Kaboom!" he said, and his eyes lit up.

*

HOW MANY MORE DAYS until we reach Africa, do you suppose? I don't know whether to wish for more or fewer, given the uncertain condition of my poor tormented belly. More days in transit, and I should be required to endure this ship's incessant pitching that much longer— although I should also continue to enjoy the best medical services that the Royal Navy can offer. Fewer days in transit, and I should be free of this rocking tub before it kills me—but left subsequently to my own devices, abandoned and friendless upon the shore of Africa, bound alone for Benin and, God willing, from there to Timbuctoo and the source of the Niger.

Never in my life have I known such uncertainty. Not even on that night when I stood trapped in a tomb filling steadily with poison gas.

Not even on that afternoon by the banks of the Nile, when I drew my pistol and ordered that jolly skeleton of a workman down from his ladder. Who was there to stop me, after all? As I have said, the workmen in the vicinity were tame as housecats—and the armed soldiers on the perimeter were too busy keeping watch on my barge to pay attention to me.

"You might want to reconsider," suggested the skeleton. He indicated Drovetti's army by means of a quick look over my shoulder.

"And let you blow Ramesses' head to bits? Just to prevent me from having it?"

"I don't believe that's the point, exactly."

"No?"

"It's more a matter of making light work of him, I should think." He dared shift on his heel a bit, and let one of his hands point toward the statue's shoulder. "There's a fault just there, you see, in the granite. It goes across to the right, and then up? Do you see it? Good. Well, precisely enough powder—that's my job—and this old boy should fall into fifty or sixty convenient bits."

Drovetti's voice came from behind me: "We'll reassemble them in Paris. I have people."

By God, it was brilliant. I could have kissed the man, if I hadn't been of a mind to kill him. "You'll never get the pieces out of here by tomorrow. It'll all be mine. It'll be in pieces, but it'll be mine."

"So you would think, if not for the reinforcements." He shaded his eyes and looked upriver, from whence came three ships overflowing with men and equipment. "We have many other projects going, but I have pulled some people over here for the rest of the afternoon. Once the fireworks are over, they're certain to prove useful."

My shoulders dropped, and all the breath went out of me. I, the Great Belzoni, felt about six inches tall.

"Now put away that little gun of yours," he said. "Before somebody gets hurt."

*

DROVETTI DECIDED THAT the best way to torment me was to require that I watch the proceedings. I was made a prisoner within the grounds of the temple, although you wouldn't have known it from appearances. He gave me the run of the place, so long as I didn't get too close to the armed soldiers or attempt to signal my men. All I could do was wander about, admire the organization of the French army and their local hirelings, and wait for the destruction of Ramesses.

I plotted like a demon, but there was no profit in it.

Can you imagine the schemes that a person might cook up under conditions so impossibly desperate? I considered everything—from tying myself to Ramesses' shoulder as a daring human shield (too dramatic, too hopeless, and far too accommodating of Drovetti's rabid hatred of me) to micturating upon the skeleton's supply of gunpowder (easier said than done, given that I hadn't downed a sip of water since breakfast). In the end there was nothing for me to do but watch while Drovetti's men unloaded miles of rope and acres of bamboo and several tons of lumber. They had a series of long shallow ramps built in no time, each one running from the lip of the temple wall to the spot where their boats were aground at the edge of the Nile. Getting Ramesses to the river, once they had him in pieces, was going to be light work.

And there was nothing I could do about it. From time to time I'd throw a glance in the direction of my barge, but no one aboard showed any sign of alarm. They barely showed any sign of life, come to that. Most of them just lolled about on the deck or napped in the hammocks they'd strung in the open air, fanning one another with palm leaves and watching with undisguised disinterest as the French went about their dirty business.

Only once, when I caught Sarah and James taking the air on a little afternoon hobble around the deck, did something approaching communication take place. James leaned a crutch against the rail and scratched the very top of his head, pantomiming curiosity.

I pointed to Drovetti, pointed to the head, and signified with my hands the rolling motion that its pieces would soon make down the ramps. (There was no use miming an explosion; I'd been a theatrical professional, but I knew my limitations.) Then I shrugged and lifted my palms, hopeless.

James got the idea. He lifted the crutch as if it were a long rifle and he the cavalry.

I shook my head and waved my hands as violently as I dared. There were no more than dozen guns on board the ship, just about enough to get the whole lot of us killed.

At this point Sarah interrupted with an upraised hand that beckoned me home, and I signified my sad inability to return by wiping away a tear. She could not have known that it was genuine.

Dusk had fallen before the ramps were complete and reinforced with sandbags, and by then Drovetti was satisfied with the skeleton's preliminary surgery on Ramesses' shoulder. At his order, and without ceremony or hesitation, the tall man packed the hole full of gunpowder, ran a fuse, and scurried back down the ladder.

There were plenty of rocks for hiding behind, great cut stones as tall and wide as a man and jumbled about the site like nursery blocks, but I decided to wait until the last instant before ducking out of harm's way. If I weren't going to take Ramesses home, then I would do my best to possess the sight of him until the very end. Everyone else, except for the skeleton, made himself scarce.

The first fuse was an unlightable dud. The second, which burned as if Satan himself had set it aflame and were personally pursuing its sizzling business end across the stones, fell out of Ramesses' shoulder before the spark could reach the charge. The third took. I was still standing when the powder exploded, which explains two curious things that endured well past that brief burst of smoke and flame.

First, my silhouette appeared on the blackened stone against which I stood—a pale ghost in the shape of a man, surrounded by scorched rock. It was a huge thing, made even slightly larger than life by means of geometry, and I have no doubt that distant generations will understand it to represent some outsized spirit or ragged god. I should think that it will remain on those premises forever, or at least until some opportunist steals it on behalf of a museum.

Second, the men on my barge sent up a cheer the likes of which I had never heard before. Not because Ramesses was destroyed and they could go home, but because they assumed that the explosion was the doing of their hero and deity, the Great Belzoni.

When the smoke dissipated and the moonlight revealed the gleaming head of Ramesses in all its intact glory, the only other figure standing in that wild tableau was I—which suggested to my credulous crew that I had willed the explosion as a demonstration of my powers. Seeing the French army and their native diggers all down upon their knees only reinforced the idea.

"Huzzah!" they cried, and, "Three cheers for Belzoni!"

Drovetti and his frustrated skeleton repeated their attempted demolition three or four more times before midnight, and each experiment went the same way. A burst of light and a crash like thunder, a slowly clearing haze of smoke and dust, and a triumphant cheer from my band of believers. In the end, not so much as a single granite chip fell from the stubborn head of Ramesses.

When the moon was at its zenith I advised Drovetti that he'd better move along or else be subject to legal sanctions at the whim of the Pasha, and with a wave of his hand he caused his crews to vanish into the night like gypsies. I generously gave them permission to leave their ropes and ramps and rollers, since there wouldn't be an opportunity to remove them while vacating the premises in time. They dropped everything, boarded their ships, and shoved off. Not a single man of them so much as looked back. They were true professionals, one and all.

*

WHICH BRINGS ME TO my own men.

If there is any power on earth superior to a company of true professionals, it's a company of true believers. Man by man they were worthless. Less than worthless. They were incalculable liabilities, one and all, good only for luxuriating in the shade and consuming copious amounts of food and water. But together, united by the irrational love and crippling fear with which they regarded their leader, they were unstoppable.

I needed only to nod my head, wink my eye, or otherwise signify that I desired something accomplished, and it was under way. I had to watch them closely, though, for having that group of incompetents under my direction was like commanding a troop of chimpanzees.

By noon we had the bust of Ramesses lashed into a makeshift cat's cradle. Had I followed in the footsteps of my ancient Roman forbears and built a catapult as outsized as my own figure, I could have flung the head straight down the Nile and clear back to Cairo, saving us all a great deal of trouble. And if I'd had proper targeting equipment, I might have smashed one of Drovetti's ships to the bottom of the river in the bargain. Sometimes, however, it just does not pay to think big. Sometimes a vision of greatness serves only to frustrate a man, especially a man who's doomed to doing business with an army of monkeys.

The head secured, I set the men to work dismantling one of the ramps and building a wheeled cart with the salvaged lumber. I sketched the general outlines I had in mind upon a convenient rock, pointed to a pile of carpenter's tools, and left Hakim in charge of things. I told him—Hakim, who after the explosions of the previous night believed more than ever that I had acquired power over a jinni—that today he would have the honor of serving as my obliging spirit, and he obeyed my wishes with a vengeance. Good old terrified Hakim. You'd have thought I had threatened to bottle him up inside a lamp.

Sarah and James and I attended to Ramesses. The job required only the three of us—the three of us and some lumber and a wheelbarrow full of rocks and a crowbar or two—thanks to our long experience with all things mechanical and theatrical. The bottom rear edge of the bust had acquired some ragged gashes, a couple of them just right for the insertion of a pry bar and, after a brief struggle, the end of a long wooden plank.

By mid-afternoon we had an enormous lever arranged behind the head. The sight took me straight back to the old days at Sadler's Wells, when little James would send me flying across the stage to the delight of the paying customers. I instructed Hakim to draw the cart into position, divided the most able of the men into teams for steadying the ropes that bound the bust, and then shooed the loiterers to safety. Next I took up my own position, high on a pile of rubble from which I could oversee everything, and with a theatrical combination of drama and deliberation I began to count off. With each increment Sarah and James took a step outward on the lever. They went slowly, testing their balance inch by inch, cautious as a pair of judges walking to court on ice. And by the time I reached twenty, the head of Ramesses had begun to tilt.

The thrill that passed through my men was great enough to make them drop their ropes and throw up their hands in terror and awe. Only a dire look from me, augmented by a few black words in an Italian dialect that they probably took to be some supernatural tongue, got them back to work. And just in time, too. For once the thing had begun to tip past its point of equilibrium, there would be no stopping it. Sarah and James did their part with the grace of swans, at each instant edging outward on the lever precisely as much as Ramesses required and no more. When the crucial point came, they stepped off the far end as if their perch had never been more elevated or perilous than the nap of a Turkish carpet. And as they stepped down, the head of Ramesses settled itself upon the cart that Hakim had built to my exact specification.

I can't say which pleased me more: Acquiring the bust that had stymied Drovetti, cementing the superstitious loyalty of my men, or demonstrating to James that even in his reduced condition—suspended like a marionette between a pair of crutches—he could still be as useful to me as ever.

*

VICTORIOUS, WE LEFT RAMESSES where he lay and spent the evening in celebration. We feasted on great misshapen balls of deep-fried falafel, on a muddy pottage of stewed fuul beans, and on bowls of red-hot kashary—that unlikely Egyptian stew of macaroni, lentils, chick peas, onions, garlic, rice, tomatoes, and combustible chili peppers. An Italian of lesser digestive powers might have fished out the macaroni and made do, but not the Great Belzoni. I ate like a king. I ate like a pharaoh. I ate until my belly rang like a gong and complained even more loudly than it complains now. And I drank too, gallon after gallon of some bitter black concoction that caused me to sweat like a boar and gave me nightmares in which Drovetti took everything in the world that had ever belonged to me, including my life and my love.

*

I AWOKE STRETCHED OUT beneath my hammock, with the grain of the planking embossed upon my face. Sarah dreamed on above me, and at my feet James added his snore to the chorus set up by the men. They sang in that early dawn light like an army of bullfrogs, and from the margins of the river an army of bullfrogs answered them back.

I sat up, regained my orientation, drew a deep breath or two, and peered over the rail to make sure that the head of Ramesses was still where we'd left it the night before. Then, as stealthily as possible for a creature of my size, I went about waking Sarah and James.

So far as I know, none of the great artists has ever painted an angel in repose. The sight is perhaps beyond their earthbound imaginations—but it is not beyond mine. Not anymore. Not since that early morning on the Nile when starlight and sunrise painted Sarah's cheeks a pale golden pink and turned her hair exactly one hundred and fifteen distinguishable shades of gold. I remember the scene to this day. I need not even close my eyes to see her before me.

Sarah was awake the instant I breathed upon her. She had declined the vile black alcohol that I had drunk so recklessly the night before, and as soon as she opened her eyes she was ready for adventure and action. She kissed me with enthusiasm—despite the seething residue of that black fluid I'd consumed the night before—and exited the hammock as gracefully as a cheetah. A naval man yourself, you know how rare an accomplishment that is.

I lifted James in my arms and shushed him as he came awake. Sarah took up his crutches and, silent as thieves, we crept along the deck toward shore. The footing was uncertain and perilous, for crewmen were flung everywhere, but that black liquor had done its work so well that I could have marched over the lot of them like a swami over hot coals and not disturbed a single man's slumber.

We trooped up the ramp to the temple, and there we rested while I outlined our next feat. "I intend," I said, "to have old Ramesses at the foot of the ramp when our friends wake up."

"This has gone beyond impressing the natives," said Sarah, uncharacteristically peeved. "You don't know when to quit, do you?"

"Adulation is a powerful motivator."

"One of these days, you're going to have to stop doing all the work and give the help a chance to pull their own weight."

More precisely, she might have been thinking about requiring the help to *restrain* some weight—in this case the dead and downward-bound mass of Ramesses' seven-ton head. Anyone could see that the ponderous thing, lying on its wheeled cart, would be unstoppable once it began making its way down the ramp. It would charge the boat like a battering ram, and come to rest at the bottom of the Nile as a monument to my hubris.

And so it might have gone even if we had engaged the entire crew in a tug of war with it. From the ledge where we sat, with the head looming beside us and the ramp aimed at the barge like the barrel of a gun, the project all at once seemed absurd—as impossible as moving hot water from the Vatican kitchens to the Pope's washroom without the efforts of one hundred toiling children. "Did I ever tell you about the time I helped shave the neck of the Pope?" I asked James. And of course I had. But he heard me out nonetheless, attentive as a robin in springtime, with his one leg dangling over the ledge and the other one, the blunted one, wrapped in a pantleg whose cunning origami revealed more than it hid.

But all the while his mind—may God love that boy as much as I do—his mind was active elsewhere. For when I finished my story, he revealed that he had in the meantime been inspired by a brainstorm. "Do you remember how you laid out those rollers for Amenhotep's sarcophagus?" He asked the question as nonchalantly as if he'd seen the thing with his own eyes. I had described the scene for him so often and in so much detail, moved by my apologetic fury to erase or at least to atone for his fateful absence from that trip, that he recalled certain events better than I did. As a sailor yourself, no doubt a most excellent spinner of yarns in your own right, you surely know what I mean.

"Sarah laid them out, actually." I patted James on the knee and smiled brightly at my wife over the top of his head. Best to give credit where credit was due.

"We could try the same thing here," he said. "Except with rocks instead of rods. They'd act as brakes, a whole series of them."

I finished his thought. "All the way down to the boat." It was brilliant.

"We could knock them out one by one."

"Two by two."

"Just like Noah. Sort of."

What a fine boy. Imaginative and practical and metaphorically-minded all at once. He'd have made his father proud. He'd have made any father proud.

I was the only mule available to handle stones of the dimensions we'd need, but I didn't mind. The morning was newborn, the night air still drifted cool from the river, and I leapt about the temple grounds as if part of James's plan called been for me to become weightless with joy.

With the crew deeply hung over and sound asleep, no one heard us as we lowered the head of Ramesses foot by foot from the temple to the river. The work proceeded two blocks at a time. I took up my sledge-hammer on one side and Sarah and James took up a pair of them on the other, and together we synchronously struck at the rocks I'd arranged like stair steps down the ramp. It was like playing croquet, with the added dangers of ricocheting stone shards and a lurching granite head the size of a house. The stones gave thunderous cracks as they shattered and flew, and the cart groaned with every downward lurch. But in spite of the noise, by the time we reached the barge there was only one pair of eyes open and sufficiently alert to have focused upon us—a bleary pair of dark eyes blinking from below decks with disappointed incredulity at the show of hard labor I'd soon be passing off as a miracle.

*

HOW CAN I EXPLAIN what happened next? Irresistible gravitational forces. Inexorable hydrodynamics. Incalculable complications involving displacement and weight and depth.

The head of Ramesses was sized to fit perfectly in the center of the barge, and Hakim oversaw the building of a wall of sandbags to keep it from rolling overboard. We rigged great levers and ropes to ease the cart off the ramp and onto the deck. The only thing we didn't anticipate was that the weight of the head might force the barge straight to the bottom of the Nile.

It dropped by a foot as soon as the cart touched the deck, and amid the shouting of the crew and the creaking of the timbers the over-matched tub sank until it came to rest on the river bottom. I ran to the rail and peered over the side, noting with some satisfaction that there was still plenty of timber above the waterline. The problem, I saw immediately, was not that the barge was overloaded but that the Nile was too low. With enough rope and sufficient timber, a team of men might build a mechanism powerful enough to raise the barge and float it to deeper water.

"You could do that," Sarah advised me as we paced together in the shade of Ramesses' head. "Or you could just wait until the rainy season."

How could I have tolerated such inaction? Was there in all the world a strategy less suited to the methods and reputation of the Great Belzoni?

"Feel free to do as you like," she said. "But I'm flagging down the next boat and heading back to Cairo."

Blackmailed by my own beloved! She would have done it, too. That woman fears nothing. No bandit, no white slaver, no band of murderous fiends could have discouraged her or thwarted her efforts to make it back to the European Quarter. Nonetheless, I'd have been a poor protector indeed if I had let her go alone. So we abandoned ship—all of us except Hakim, a pair of his best men (such as they were), and James Curtin. That's correct. James stayed behind to throw his inconsequential weight into the defense of our liberated head, committing himself to guarding that thing with a long rifle until the rains came and the river rose and Hakim could navigate the lot of them safely home to Cairo. It was to be his rite of passage, or at least that was what I told myself. This time it was his idea, and this time nothing could go wrong. He had little to do aboard ship but to exercise his good leg and wait for nature to do her work.

The rest of us bought our transport home with artifacts that we gleaned in haste from the ruins. There was nothing of any real value—just broken-up rubbish and half-cracked castoffs that generations of grave robbers had dropped in favor of bigger prizes. A carved cat, missing one ear and both forelegs. A dozen scarabs. A fistful of desiccated flowers and a broken vase and a round chunk of something that looked like alabaster. These objects, although worthless to the serious collector or museum, nonetheless had a certain value to the watermen plying the river, and with them we financed our journey back to Cairo.

PART SIX:
Abu Simbel

"As little as Belzoni actually grasped about archaeology, he seems to have grasped far less about human nature."

— Reginald Untermeyer, *The Riddle of Belzoni*, New York, 1914

*

AT LAST, HENRY SALT acquired a proper and properly valuable firman—one that any competent digger could have made use of, and one that in the hands of the Great Belzoni would become the raw material of legend. He beamed at me from behind his mustaches, clearly proud of the ease with which he'd negotiated the black waters of palace intrigue. "I'll have you know that I've obtained quite the prize," he said. "Please do make the most of it. No explosions, no sunken transports, and no messing about with the French army if you can help it."

"Where am I going?"

"Abu Simbel."

Abu Simbel. It was a dream come true. Abu Simbel was a rumored complex of temples, granaries, and gravesites, illuminated with vast friezes and guarded by gigantic statues buried up to their necks in sand. There was treasure there for certain. Treasure aplenty. More than any living man could properly imagine.

And thanks to the potential of the find, this expedition was to be the real thing: a fleet of boats, two hundred men familiar with the ways of the desert and the culinary requirements of civilized individuals, provisions galore, plenty of lumber and rope and weaponry, and quantities of near-worthless baubles for appeasing whatever local authorities might present their barren palms along the way.

*

"ATLAS," THE LOVE OF MY LIFE began over breakfast one morning, during the period when we were making our preparations. "I think I'm going to sit this one out."

"Really?" I believed that if I kept my reactions small, she'd reconsider. Perhaps there was nothing to it. Perhaps she was just testing the waters.

"Really."

"But what shall I do without you?"

"Something tells me you'll keep busy."

"What shall *you* do without *me?*" I freely admit it: the notion that Sarah's life might come to revolve around some other focal point, if only for the months that I'd be excavating the sands of Abu Simbel, unnerved me to no end. Wouldn't she miss me? Her Atlas? Her Great Belzoni? Apparently not.

"I thought maybe I'd start a school," was her ready answer.

"A school. *A school.*" Saying it twice didn't help it sink in any further, and it didn't improve my position with Sarah. "What kind of school?"

"Oh, you know. English language. A little history. Some literature. That sort of thing." She plunged her teeth into a date. "For the poor Egyptian children, I mean. Not for the consulate brats."

"Just so." I blew steam from my teacup and watched it vanish into the dry desert air. "I just hope you're not counting on this as a source of income."

"If I were, I'd have to take in the Europeans. In which case I wouldn't do it at all."

I could see her point. I understood the benevolent impulse. Hadn't I raised up an orphan of my own?

"I've had every advantage in life," she said.

"I won't deny it." Even though the condition of our flat might have suggested otherwise. Luxury isn't everything.

"Just look at the man I married."

She had me in the palm of her hand. We talked for a while longer, about how Salt's money would keep our little family afloat whether she traveled with me or not, and about the ignorance and poverty and superstition that lay ahead for the children of Cairo's streets as long as they remained unsaved by the likes of Sarah. "Look at the men of your last crew!" she reminded me. "What hope do these children have, if they're all to grow up like Umar and Hakim?"

"You're right. I can't come along and pull every one of them up by the tatters of his turban. It will be best if you get a head start on a few."

*

THE PATH OF MY CAREER having sloped upward without interruption, I grew accustomed to cutting a fine and heroic figure in the streets of Cairo. I could not so much as walk to the grocer's without collecting a throng of curiosity-seekers and hangers-on. Soon word got out that the consulate was hiring men for my expedition, and more than a few of my old crewmen began lingering at the gates of the European Quarter in hopes of pouncing upon me. And why not? I was their ideal superior: a slave driver who could be counted upon to do all of the heavy work himself.

Hakim met me at the gates one morning with an especially pathetic story. It seems he'd gone straight to the consul's office and appealed to Henry Salt's secretary—Mr. Bascombe, a withered purple fig of a man with the vigor of a corpse and the personal charm of a puff adder—for employment on my expedition. Bascombe demanded that he fill out several reams of paperwork, a task that poor illiterate Hakim was as likely to complete as he was to sprout wings and fly in circles around the Sphinx. Frustrated, he flung the papers aside and pleaded to Bascombe upon his knees, explaining how useful he'd been to me on the expedition to Luxor. Bascombe was unmoved. Not that I blame him. He required some means for separating the wheat from the chaff, and the ability to fill out a lengthy form was as good a test as any.

But could I intercede? That was what Hakim had in mind. "Come on, boss," he said. "You know I'd never let you down."

Well, maybe not. At least not as long as I kept my eye on him. So I agreed.

I found Bascombe behind his desk, upright and stiff as a mummy, patiently copying something from a sheet of paper into a ledger book the size of a headstone. His handwriting was tiny, immaculate, and per-fectly legible to anyone with a sufficiently powerful magnifying glass. Between the size of the ledger and the size of his script, I got the idea that he had made a crafty agreement with some god or other to finish filling this book before his soul could be swept off to damnation—pro-vided the universe lasted long enough.

"Take it from me," he sniffed when I'd made my request. "It's unwise to engage these individuals personally. The less you know about them—and the less they know about you—the better the outcome for all par-ties."

"But—"

He raised a hand. "Now, now, Belzoni. A certain distance is required in all employer-employee relations." Bascombe himself was a fine exam-ple of that principle. It's said that he once found himself in an opera box with Henry Salt, and the two never made eye contact.

"But I made the man a promise."

"A promise that due to circumstances you shall be unable to keep. There's no dishonor in that."

"Perhaps not for you."

"Pshaw. There's more at stake here than your reputation, Belzoni. And more at stake than the employment of one individual Arab, worthy or not. Remember this: if you insist that I offer this fellow a job, the men of this city will be upon you like wild dogs. They'll smell blood. They won't be able to help themselves."

"I shall take that risk."

"It's your funeral," said Bascombe. Coming from him, any reference to things funerary carried particular weight.

"Let us hope not."

Bascombe tore a half-sheet of paper from his notebook, erected upon it an edifice of words and figures, signed his name, and handed it over. "Give this to him. Then watch your back. There'll be hungry Egyptians crawling in through your windows by nightfall."

The results weren't half so dramatic as Bascombe had predicted, but only because I'd already had Egyptians crawling in through my windows. Or I would have had them, if the gates of the European Quarter hadn't kept them out. I remained firm throughout the assault nonetheless, and left the remainder of the hiring to Bascombe's systematized whims. Not even poor terrified Umar, who saw a jinni each time he saw me, succeeded in taking advantage of our history together—although it might have gone better for everyone if he had.

*

WHEN WE SET OUT AT LAST for Abu Simbel, the harbor at Cairo spontaneously erupted into twin festivals. For no sooner had I kissed Sarah goodbye and leapt aboard my broad-beamed ship than Hakim's barge hove into view from upriver. Amidships, borne down the Nile with stately slowness befitting a king, rode the massive head of Ramesses.

Every breath in Cairo, even the searing breath of the desert itself, famous for battering the gates of the city without letup in its horrifying animal urge to bury the place for eternity under a mile of sand, every breath in the ancient and world-weary capital city of Cairo, a place that had witnessed everything under the sun and then some, was instantly suspended. For not even Cairo was prepared for the sight of that seven-ton head afloat upon the face of the waters, or for the added attraction of a one-legged Irish orphan boy balanced upon the lip of its tall stone headdress. James waved and salaamed to the crowd with an easy showmanship that he'd learned from the best in the business. They repaid him—and me—with a torrent of applause.

For they knew, one and all, that as shocking and magnificent as the scene in the harbor was, its maker was embarking on an adventure of even more epic scale. In the tombs and temples of Abu Simbel I would unleash mysteries as yet uncalculated. I would bring back to light a past that mankind had buried deeper than its own most guilty nightmares.

Not that I lacked for detractors. Any character as outsized as mine is always bound to collect a few. And just as I could always pick out a distracted tobacco-chewing half-asleep unbeliever at Sadler's Wells without so much as turning my eyes in his direction, I felt upon me that morning the jealous gaze of my rival in all things, Consul Bernardino Drovetti. (Poor Drovetti! How the tables had turned! Here he was remaining in Cairo, while I embarked for the desert in a roar of adulation and my assistant rode the head of Ramesses homeward as if it were a tamed dolphin.) As soon as I felt his eyes upon me, I turned. But Drovetti was not where I had expected to find him. He was not among the dignitaries seated upon the reviewing stand. He was deep within the crowd, buried among turbaned and robed figures like a mummy among mummies, and he was whispering into the ear of an individual whose back was turned to me.

Very well, I thought. Let him have his little intrigues. I possessed the head of Ramesses. I possessed a firman for Abu Simbel. I had the entire history of Egypt laid out before me like a crumpled map.

Throwing a salute to James and a kiss to Sarah, I set out.

248

*

THE VOYAGE UP THE NILE! Ah, never mind. It was in every respect exactly like the last voyage up the Nile, only with more men and a superior ship. Nothing of any consequence happened. I stayed in my cabin more than was my custom, perhaps, and I had my orders executed through a pair of servants assigned to the job by Bascombe. The crewmen luxuriated day and night in dreams of the pay they would receive when the expedition was done, and the Nile beneath us maintained her comfortably elevated level in anticipation of our fully-laden return trip. Let that suffice to depict the voyage upstream. Fill in such gaps as you detect with whatever information or conjecture you see fit.

The details matter not to me. Were I to narrate every single thing that I remember, this story of mine would still have us deep in the Mithraic ruins below the church of San Clemente, which would never do. On the contrary. With the passage of each day I see more and more clearly that I have no choice but to telescope my tale so as to cover the rest of it before this warship reaches Africa, where you and I must go our several ways.

Not to mention, God forbid, before I succumb.

So. Onward.

You have no doubt seen Abu Simbel for yourself, at least in the popular engravings. That huge facade carved out of solid sandstone. Those four mighty statues confined within it like chess pieces in a box. The little entranceway secreted between the central colossi as if to remind visitors of their own inconsequential scale. Unburied from the sands of the ages, the place looks today as if it had thrust itself whole from the sandstone cliffs, or as if it were some kind of uncanny natural formation, coaxed out of the rock by the wind and whistled very nearly to life. More than once during the excavations I felt as if I were sculpting those colossi myself—and in some manner of speaking, I believe now that I was. Sympathetic energy of that sort is the hallmark of true genius. Consider, for example, this story that we are telling together, you and I. Although the words are mine, I dare not take full responsibility for where they may take us.

While my crews penetrated the deep sands of Abu Simbel, I would go roving across the desert with a couple of stout-hearted fellows for days at a time. I was restless, itching for discovery, ill at ease from days spent watching progress that seemed every bit as slow as the passage of sand through an hourglass. Now and then my traveling partners and I would come across an abandoned excavation that Drovetti's men had pillaged and forsaken. We'd add our footprints to those already present, pushing at likely looking rocks and blowing into suspicious crevices, untroubled by our lack of a proper firman.

Somewhere near the oasis at Bahira—I kept no specific records of these things, lest the authorities retrace my steps and strip me of my souvenirs—I observed a vertical crack in a cliff wall into which crept a slow trickle of sand from the surrounding dunes. Just how slow? Five or six grains per hour, according to my best estimate. Nothing to attract the attention of anyone with less than history's most magnificent eye for the errant archaeological detail. But I, the Great Belzoni, took note indeed and paused to ask myself: where was all of that sand going? I reasoned that there must be a huge space of some kind beneath that cliff wall, a man-made chamber perhaps even larger than the one we were unearthing at Abu Simbel, and I resolved that I would return one day and find out for certain.

I was never to make the trip, alas, for chance and opportunity conspired to distract me from it again and again. But that crevice and its patient drip of sand remain right where I found them, there in that secret place in the desert near Bahira, and somewhere behind that fissured wall lies treasure. Remind me to write down its coordinates. Someone ought to have the benefit of my experience, and it might as well be you.

Weeks passed in this mode of idle wandering and opportunistic pillage. I'd assembled an impressive collection of relics, which I kept locked
in crates at our encampment. Whenever we returned there, our packs
jammed with off-the-record artifacts, I assessed the unreinforced mountains of sand growing on either side of my tent and wondered how long
it might be before they finally caved in, turning me and my own cache
into buried treasure all over again.

No wonder I spent so few nights sleeping in that perilous place! No
wonder I was so relieved when at last we cleared the temple entrance
and prepared to move inside!

*

PERMIT ME TO TELL YOU a secret: there are few pleasures in life greater
than firing off a matched pair of pistols inside the burial chamber of an
Egyptian king. The noise, first of all, is like nothing else on earth—or
within it, for that matter. You must be sure to select a large chamber, in
order to guarantee both optimum resonance and some measure of personal safety. And because of the danger posed by ricocheting bullets, you
must choose your targets as carefully as if you were playing billiards with
live grenades.

The entrance to Abu Simbel led to a space that could have been
built to order for this magnificent sport. Gigantic, vaulted, ringed about
with a maze of statues and half-flooded with loose sand perfect for ab-
sorbing errant shots, the place called out to me with a voice sufficient to
overwhelm my urge for exploration. I ordered the men to set up a ring
of torches around the central vault, shooed them back out the door to
safety, and drew my pistols.

I fired at the carved statuary. I fired at the chiseled columns. I fired
and I fired until the shattered stones of the ceiling pelted down around
my feet and the mighty room rang with a din sufficient to wake the
dead. Or very nearly, anyhow. Mad with joy, I kept going until I ran

short of ammunition—and then I poked my head out the door and ordered a fresh supply brought up from the ship.

It was a festive occasion, that entry into Abu Simbel. It was my first truly virgin find. I shall never forget it.

*

I VERY NEARLY DIED on that expedition, but not from gunfire. And not from some ridiculous curse or imaginary booby-trap, either, no matter what dire predictions old d'Outremeuse would have made. The place was actually fairly clean and well laid-out, orderly as a box of bonbons and just as richly packed.

The principal chamber was devoted exclusively to those columns and statues I mentioned, giant things towering four or five stories tall, arrayed in long corridors like Englishmen queued up at Sadler's Wells. We brought in ladders to study them more closely, and to examine the various hieroglyphics and pictographs incised into the walls. Give him credit: Bascombe had hired a team of artists and technicians whose charge was to record every detail in graphite and chalk and watercolor. I'd never have thought of such a thing.

At the far end was a passage sealed with a massive stone half again my height. Long-dead workmen had chiseled into its surface the unsettling likenesses of strange dog-headed warriors and bird-headed gods, dozens of them, interspersed with evil-looking women whose faces bore the fixed expressions of adders. Those figures not seated on thrones or standing in niches marched around the perimeter of the tableau with that sideways gait so favored by the ancient Egyptians. All in all, glimmering there in the first torchlight they'd seen for thousands of years, the carvings presented a display of singular and threatening beauty. I had one of the men prepare a graphite rubbing, while I sent four others out to locate a palm trunk that would make a suitable battering ram.

The door, you see—if a door it was—would simply not budge otherwise. All around its edge was a lip of solid stone perfectly built to exclude the tip of a pry bar, so we charged the thing with a twenty-foot tree trunk manned by thirty or more diggers. It was a fine idea. It would have been a better idea if sturdier and heavier trees had been available. For as it was, we accomplished little beyond reducing the palm trunk to flinders, scraping the raw flesh from our palms, and bringing down a cloud of dust from every elevated surface.

What little we did accomplish, however, proved to be sufficient. Because even though we didn't manage to batter down the door, our pounding did jar loose some compacted sand from around *another* door, a previously *undiscovered* door, just a few feet from where we were working. This portal was far more cooperative. I tested its perimeter by inserting a barley stalk, which penetrated a full six inches before I lost my grip and let it disappear into the black unknown. There was plenty of room back there. We would begin our excavations in the morning.

I slept that night on the threshold of discovery in the great temple chamber, surrounded on all sides by menacing statuary. My brain still echoed with the shockwaves of our battering ram and the sharp reports of my pistol. Outside the doorway, deep in the cool desert night, the furtive whispering of men served as my lullaby.

*

WE HAD THAT SECOND DOOR down before the sun was up, but have no fear: I won't bore you with the details of rod and rope and pulley. I will, however, describe to you what we discovered within: a long and downward-sloping tunnel, carved out of solid stone. The walls were free of decoration and so rudely cut as to give the impression that the tunnel was merely a natural fissure in the rock.

"This," I told the men, "is a very good sign."

Right away I understood the hidden door and the unadorned passage to be evidence of the highest cunning—the kind of sophisticated misdirection that a pharaoh would employ in order to protect his bones from plunderers. I felt a kinship with that dead king, whoever he was, as we hurried down his long and chilly tunnel. Clearly this fellow had been an imaginative showman in his own right. I flattered myself that only the Great Belzoni could have found him out.

Torchless, I rushed ahead into the dark. The men were having trouble keeping up with my headlong strides, so I called over my shoulder to cheer them on. "You can bet the ancients didn't want us finding this place, boys. And once we did, they wanted us to turn back. *'There's nothing down there for us!'* is what we're supposed to be saying right now. *'The show's over! Nothing but a dead end!'* But we're smarter than that, aren't we?"

They murmured and whispered among themselves, and they panted from their efforts to match my furious speed, and I could almost feel their desperate hot breathing in that cold underground space.

The tunnel ended in a stairway leading down—I took the steps two at a time even in the dark, running on pure instinct—and the stairway ended at a small chamber with three blank stone walls. The place had all of the appeal of that hidden stair under San Clemente where Lorenzo and I had incinerated the nest of rats. And piled upon the floor, knee-deep, were shards of crockery and scraps of linen and—wonder of wonders—the broken remains of somewhere between twenty-five and thirty pathetic old mummies. Someone had stacked them down there like cordwood, and over the years they'd crumbled and shifted until their bones were mingled together into one great and undifferentiated pile. I made the sign of the cross over them, and then kneeled to sift through their dust for anything of value.

Sad to say, the trick behind this hidden passageway was that there was no trick at all. No ruby-encrusted king, no bronze-plated sarcophagus, not so much as an alabaster jar or a mummified cat. Just some trash, really, and a secret boneyard surely built for the slaves who'd perished building the temple in whose sub-basement they slept. It was no kind of place to spend any amount of time. And it was certainly no kind of place to be lingering with your employees. The cruel implications were just too plain for comfort.

Have I mentioned that from birth I have possessed an unreliable sense of smell? It's a failing that served me well during my years in Egypt, and I could see from the obvious discomfort of my men that it was still serving me as I sifted through the bone pile for a ring or a scroll or some little stone scarab. I slept that night among the statues of the main chamber on a pillow of rags—winding sheets and tattered bits of turban and the like—which I'd collected from the trash at the bottom of the stairway. In all candor, I'd have slept better if a certain something hadn't been gnawing at my consciousness.

*

WHAT KEPT ME AWAKE was the noise made by a thin trickle of sand. To judge by the sound of it, it was even smaller than the trickle I'd seen passing through that tiny crevice at Bahira, but as the night wore on it became an absolute torment. The high chamber fairly echoed as grain after grain fell to the floor, each one landing with the impact of a boulder thrown from a great height. I jammed my ears full of rags and lay twitching until dawn.

Before the men awoke I was out prowling their camp like a sneak thief, in search of a certain someone who owed me a favor: Hakim. I found him curled up in a tent with a dozen other indistinguishable figures—the sight reminded me for a distressing second of those mummies at the bottom of the stairs—and I roused him without a word.

"Grab a torch," I whispered when we were clear of the tents. "Grab a couple of them while you're at it, and follow me."

With Hakim at my side I plunged back into the dimly dawn-lit temple, certain that finding the drip would be short work if only I followed my ears. But the carvings and pillars and statues set up a confusing maze of echoes, and soon I gave off. We lighted the torches next, but their crackling overwhelmed the auditory evidence while their illumination did nothing to reveal its source. Stymied, I sat down in the center of the chamber and sank the base of my torch into a convenient pile of sand. I ruminated for a while. Hakim lay down and went back to sleep. The desert outside the door was quiet and absolutely still. And soon enough, a miracle occurred.

An inky tendril of smoke from the torch began to move purposefully across the room. I watched it go, scarcely daring to breathe as it snaked its wavering way through the great chamber like the airborne spirit of a cobra. Perhaps d'Outremeuse was right, I thought. Perhaps that old fabricator knew what he was talking about with his fairy stories of fumigation: a stick of incense, or in my case a single oily torch, might be the key to finding a concealed passage after all.

My hopes rose and fell with the movement of that finger of smoke. The temperamental thing did not, however, seek out some unexpected crevice as I'd trusted it would, but instead made straight for the decorated door that we'd already scourged. There would be no surprises there, I told myself. Which was, of course, incorrect. For the smoke disappeared not to one side of the door or the other, but into the crevice above it.

I woke Hakim and dashed to the spot, where I learned that the smoke had found my trickle of sand after all—and that my trickle of sand was issuing from a spot somewhere up behind the lintel. I rummaged for a barley stalk and poked it upward into the crevice, and it disappeared entirely. For a second, a little more sand streamed out through the space it had opened. Then it stopped.

"What we have here," I said to Hakim, "is a sliding door. Only it doesn't go from side to side."

"No, Signor Belzoni. I can see that. It goes *up.*" He was a sharp one after all, that Hakim. And I think that right at that moment his belief in jinn came to its end. Who, after all, could require a supernatural spirit—when he could rely upon me instead?

*

I HAVE NO IDEA how the rest of the men spent their morning, but Hakim and a few of his favorites and I labored like demons to raise that door. It was a game of inches, played with levers and pry bars and slivers of stone.

"It's a pity that we wasted such effort with that battering ram," Hakim said at one point.

"Not at all. Our efforts were what shook loose the seal and got the sand flowing from above. Sometimes," I advised him, "the path ahead is simply not so straight as we might like."

We were starving by the time we'd raised the thing far enough to insert a finger beneath it (one of Hakim's, not mine—and just his scrawny pinkie at that). As we broke for lunch and stepped out the door into the desert heat, a cheer went up among the men in the camp. Flushed with our minuscule success, I presumed that it was a spontaneous sign of their devotion to their leader, but when each one of them turned his back to me and made for the banks of the Nile I realized that something more prosaic was at work. The arrival of a boat, as it turned out, a wobbly little tub half-filled with vegetables and salted sardines and such other goods as characterized trade along the river. I gave a whoop of my own when I observed that sitting atop a mountain of dried garbanzos was my friend, my protégé, and my adopted son—the one-legged James Curtin.

I hurried to help him down, but he didn't need my assistance. In the time that had intervened since he and I had last been together, he seemed to have recovered much of his old vigor. He leapt from the crates with the agility of a cricket, and he sprang toward me without even stopping to gather up his crutches. *Crutch,* I should say, for I soon learned that he'd reduced by half his dependency on the things. We embraced like the dear old comrades we were, and then I shouted an order to buy up the contents of the trading boat and prepare a feast. James was no prodigal, and I was the one who'd been doing most of the wandering, but I desired all the same to sacrifice the fattest calf around—even if it were only a crate of dried figs.

We ate a little, and then we tried to loaf for a while in the shade of the four seated colossi who guarded the temple entrance, but neither one of us had his heart in it. Not with the black temple door yawning open right behind us. So we decided to do our catching up while I took him on the grand tour.

Sarah was well indeed, he told me. In fact, he was certain that he hadn't seen her so well since we'd left London. I should rest assured that she longed for my presence every hour of the day. She'd adopted several dozen urchins from the street and given them the run of the flat in exchange for their promise to endure daily instruction in history and mathematics and English and so on. Then she'd recruited the volunteer help of every knowledgeable individual in the city—Henry Salt for British history, one of the Pasha's carpenters for woodworking, and so forth—and turned the place into a regular university where classes went on day and night.

I could only shake my head. "If anyone has the persuasive powers to pull it off," I said, picturing her and wishing that I were in her presence myself, "it would be Sarah."

"True, true, true. She could tame a lion, that Sarah could, and have him serving tea just as nicely as ye please."

We wandered around the great chamber, admiring the statues and the columns and the carvings, while some of the men gave solemn tours of the premises to the traders who'd arrived on the boat. Turbaned and cloaked figures they all were, as like one another—visitors and guests, I mean—as matchsticks in a carton. They bent their heads and whispered together in a reverential way, as if by setting foot in this once-holy place they'd reacquired the primitive beliefs of their forbears. Let Sarah do as she pleased, I thought, her disciples were sure to fall victim to these same atavistic tendencies once they left her care.

"And how about Victor?" I asked. "Do you see him much?"

"These days ye don't see him but in the company of that Pasha."

"When I spoke with him last, he'd picked up some bad habits."

"It's all a matter of who ye spend yer time with, innit?"

I nodded, seeing that if I spent more time with James I might grow wiser myself. "He's done me a great favor or two, that Victor."

"And you him. Don't forget."

"True. Still, I worry about the poor creature. A pasha's palace can be more treacherous than a pharaoh's tomb."

The boneyard at the bottom of the stairs troubled James far more than it had troubled me, for he was younger and less comfortable with the notion of mortality. Besides, his olfactory organs (unlike mine) were reliably functional. Mummies and statues aside, though, the thing that excited him the most was the fantastically carved door—and the mechanism by which Hakim and I were inching its terrible weight upwards. James, like me, was always thrilled by the unknown. And he had a fine head for geometry, too.

*

I CONFESS THAT I NEVER even saw the traders' boat leave. Time, as you can imagine, is difficult to gauge in a place as dim as the chambers of Abu Simbel, and night had long since fallen when we thought to lay off work. Supper, what there was left of it, was a cold cauldron of fiery kashary and a hot mug of vile sahlab. The men huddled at the water's edge, smacking their lips and savoring that whitish brew as if it were the veriest nectar, while several stinking gallons of it bubbled and burped away over the fire. Apparently the traders had been well supplied with goat's milk and orchid bulbs and coconuts.

"First thing in the morning," I announced when I'd cleaned my plate, "we shall be making our entrance into the second chamber."

A cheer went up, especially among the still-vigorous masses who'd spent the day malingering while my little team handled the rough work.

"Our plan is to send one man through the opening with a torch. His job will be to assess the potential of the room beyond, before we expend any further effort in raising the door."

As if I'd asked for volunteers, every hand in that encampment went up. But I already knew the only individual whom I could trust with the job.

*

"JESUS AND MARY AND Holy S'int Joseph."

To judge from his opening remarks, James Curtin must have gotten quite an eyeful when he finally got his torch lit.

"What? What is it? What do you see?"

"Oh," he sang out, "not so much, really. Only the realization of every dream ye've ever dreamed."

After substantial urging on my part, he came scrambling back out. Upon his face was the dazed look of a child who'd seen a ghost, mingled with the hungry look of a man who desires nothing more than to see that same ghost again.

With James's expert technical assistance we finished raising the door, propped it up on either side with some provisional masonry, and ducked inside without another second's hesitation. The room beyond was a gold mine. A treasure trove. A cache of riches the likes of which mankind hadn't seen since Ali Baba last uttered his *"Open Sesame."*

In the center stood a cluster of massive stone sarcophagi suited for accommodating only the most elevated of royalty. We flung the stone top from the first that came to hand, revealing a gilded and richly varnished mummy case of sycamore—within which lay in turn a mummy who appeared richly varnished himself. The garland of flowers around his neck was remarkably preserved, although the blossoms crumbled to dust under my eager fingers. All around were packets and bundles and jars containing an array of unguessable substances, as a rule either a once-fragrant preservative or a desiccated internal organ. Sometimes both. And sometimes, appallingly enough, we couldn't tell the difference.

Cache after cache of scarabs and jars and carvings and amphorae filled the room, making investigation as difficult as it was profitable. And once we managed to look away from the sarcophagi and their bedding of scattered riches, we discovered upon the walls a treasure every bit as magnificent, although considerably less portable: enormous friezes, carved in subtle detail and painted with a sure and artful hand, celebrating the lives of the poor creatures who'd come to rest here. All around the high walls of the crypt, immediate physical evidence to the contrary notwithstanding, these kings and queens went on eating and dancing and sitting in judgment. They went on transmogrifying into snakes and dogs and cat-headed beasts. They went on battling hideous monsters and ferocious bulls and one another. In those primitive images was a sense of eternity that I found deeply touching, especially when combined with the proximity of corpse after preserved corpse, their hopeful viscera arranged all about the premises in papyrus packets and alabaster jars.

We brought in ladders—the room was even higher than the main chamber, since it was farther back inside the cliffs—so that Bascombe's artists could start tracing the friezes onto long scrolls of paper. Then James and I began to catalog the treasure and transfer the smaller pieces to the main chamber where they could be wrapped and crated for the trip to Cairo. Only once, when one of the pencil-men pointed out a horizontal aperture near the ceiling that gave out onto the cliff wall like a gun slit, did we pause to look up and to marvel and to rest.

*

THAT NIGHT, JAMES AND I made up our pallets on the floor of the inner chamber—right in the thick of things, down among the gaping sarcophagi. Exhausted as I was, mainly from excitement, I found myself in no condition to resume the old conversational habits we'd established at Jaundyce's boarding house. James, on the other hand, could have jabbered away for half the night. My head spun with mummies and treasures and fortune, and the longer I lay there the less sense he made. His voice came to me in the darkness like a whisper in a dream, and before long that was precisely what it was.

Time passed. I had no idea how much of it.

And then this: "Hey! Belzoni!" His hand was on my shoulder, and he hissed directly into my ear. "Did ye hear that?"

"It's nothing. Go back to sleep." I'd been dreaming of mummies, and I suspected that he had been doing the same. It would have been only natural.

But James wasn't to be so easily deterred. He squeezed my shoulder with a grip that I realized even in my half-slumber had become, while I wasn't paying attention, the grip of a man. "No," he said. "It's footsteps, in the main chamber. Very slow, and very cautious. As if someone don't want us to know he's out there. Listen."

If he was correct, I didn't need to listen. What I needed to do was act quickly to stop my riches from being spirited away by a pack of thieves. A pack of thieves, I thought even then—do you see how rapidly my mind was clearing?—who were almost surely in the employ of a certain jealous-minded French consul.

I tensed, fully alert. "Get a torch, but don't light it until I say so. And at all costs, don't make a sound." He removed his hand from my shoulder and we separated into the thick darkness, each of us rising in his own direction. A model of grace despite my size, I made straight for the sliding door and crouched there to listen.

There were indeed footsteps in the main chamber. More precisely, there was a sound that had the alternating cadence of footsteps without their clear individuation. It was more on the order of a soft sort of scuffling, as if an individual were moving about very stealthily upon his knees. It was not, in other words, the sound of a thief carrying an armload of loot, and so it gave me pause.

James came up from behind and nearly knocked me over, but we recovered our balance at the last instant and stood listening together in the menacing dark. The feats of balance with which we'd awed the crowds at Sadler's Wells served to unite us yet, as if we were still but two parts of one remarkable machine.

Something—I knew not what it was or where it had come from at that second or if even it had been there all along and I had simply bumbled into it while I was off balance—something touched the tip of my bare toe. It was hard, glassy, and cool. Gingerly, I reached one hand down to feel of it.

It was a bowl, filled to the brim with liquid. This was a poor time of night to start feeding cats, I thought, so it probably wasn't milk. I permitted my hand to retreat, and was shocked to discover another hand hovering directly over mine. I snatched at it instinctively and got it by the wrist, a brown and emaciated wrist, as I was to see for myself in the light of James's sudden matchstick.

"Umar!" The fellow was as shocked to see me as I was to see him.

In his hand he held a vial—the cork was in his teeth, but it vanished down his throat with a gasp that made his eyes pop—in his hand, as I was saying, he held an open glass vial, and it fell into the bowl the instant that I snatched his wrist. There was no recovering it, and no recapturing the sickly green fluid that crept from its mouth like a serpent to merge with whatever was already in the bowl.

James began to cough, and my eyes started to water. An acrid cloud of gray-green gas rose into the air. Umar had not come to take my treasure, I realized. He had come to take my life.

"Ye know him?" said James between coughs, striking another match. He'd dropped the torch, and in his panic he was having difficulty locating it.

"Too well," I answered, or something on that order. There was no time for explanation.

As for Umar, he said nothing—thanks no doubt to the cork lodged in his windpipe. Instead he threw himself backward and kicked madly at the piled-up rocks supporting the stone door. Whether he only meant to make good his escape or desired to imprison us in the burial chamber, I cannot say. But he was no equal for my strength and speed, and when the door did come crashing down a certain portion of his body remained pinned beneath it.

*

I WAS DIZZY, my eyes ran with tears, and thanks to the concussion made by the falling door my ears would not stop ringing. James had lit his torch and jammed it into a crevice in the wall so that he might resume choking to death unburdened, and by its gleam I watched the sinister gray-green gas boil out of the bowl and commence filling the chamber. I let go of Umar's twitching hand and drew myself—with some effort and uncertainty—to my feet. The air was clearer up at my natural elevation, but I could see that it would not remain so for long. Down below, where the gas had had a chance to accumulate in thicker strata, my dismasted friend James was clutching at his throat and threatening to collapse upon his one remaining knee.

I held my breath, dove to the floor, and spilled the contents of the bowl out upon the stones in hopes of stopping the chemical reaction already under way. Alas, I only succeeded in accelerating it by maximizing its surface area. A certain amount of the boiling liquid spilled out the doorway through a crack kept open by some stray stones and the ruined body of Umar, but that was the extent of my achievement. I stood again, hoisted James up into air as fresh as air can possibly be in a roomful of rotting mummies, and tried to give us both one final opportunity to think.

"The slit," James said, "up by the ceiling." I believe that he pointed, but between the rising fog and the tears in my eyes and the failings of memory I cannot say for certain.

"We'll never make it. That ladder's only fit for mice to climb." Or fellows James's size, I could have added—at least those still blessed with both of their God-given legs. My mind raced through a catalog of acrobatic possibilities, since we had plenty of the conventional equipment at hand: wood for levers, stone for fulcrums, and an endless quantity of rope. But nothing I could envision would lift the pair of us up to that little aperture. And once we'd gotten there, what were we to do? Breathe through the slit until the gas dissipated, which might take days? Hang there like starving bats while the men outside mourned my would-be assassin and tried—without a mechanically-inclined brain among the lot of them—to raise the door again?

The gas reached my chest, and I hoisted James higher still.

"Did I mention," he said between gasps, with the panicky determination of a man delivering his last confession, "that Sarah's students are studying French as well as the rest of it?"

"French?" I nearly dropped him to the floor out of shock. "*Drovetti*."

"The very same." His body shook with a cough that seemed to struggle all the way up from the sole of his one remaining foot. I noticed that his clothes were wringing wet. Mine were as well.

The mention of my rival's name struck me like a blow to the solar plexus and a slap to the face. I found myself agonized and energized all at once, to an extent that would have gratified Drovetti and terrified him too. I saw everything in that smoky chamber in a new light—including the invisible slit at the top of the unclimbable ladder.

"God bless you, James; you've hit upon it."

"I have?"

The gas was eddying right beneath my nose, and I showed my airborne partner how it swirled even higher in the vicinity of the burning torch. "We may be trapped," I said, "but at least we've had the good fortune to be trapped inside a chimney."

I hoisted him to my shoulders, took up the torch, and dashed about the chamber setting fire to anything that would burn. That moment's work cost mankind the full acquaintance of seven royal mummies, along with the opportunity to appreciate their linen wrappings and their sycamore cases and their explosive stuffings of dried flowers, but it saved the living pair of us.

We could always find more mummies. The desert was infested with them back in those days.

The clutch of sarcophagi blossomed straightaway into an inferno. And when the last corpse had caught fire we threw ourselves at the crack below the door. There we sucked air from the spaces around Umar's body—it rushed in, cool and fresh, as the room heated up—until the chimney had done its work and the fire had died out and the room was clear of gas. At last we slept. In the morning we began prying our way back into the world of living men.

*

IF WE HADN'T ALREADY been itching to light out for Cairo, one final surprise awaiting discovery in that blackened chamber would have set us in motion.

James found it quite by accident. He'd pushed Umar back into the main chamber and was down on his knee, attempting to fit his own head underneath the doorway, when his gaze fell upon the glass vial that had fallen during the night from our assailant's hand. It was intact still, sticky all over, and blackened with the soot of sacrificed riches. Upon its face it bore a label written in the unmistakable language of the Gauls.

Just here I would like to interrupt the facts and explain how, in a burst of superhuman power fueled by despairing love and impotent rage, I lifted the stone door with nothing more than the strength of my own broad back. Samson indeed. But every man has his limits. All that James and I could do was to redouble our efforts. Men arrived by and by from the encampment by the river, and we fabricated on their behalf a more or less palatable death for Umar, who I understood from their the sound of their voices wasn't looking quite himself.

I shouted instructions under the slab of the door, and with the men's help we raised it in record time. James and I squeezed underneath, black as a pair of coal miners and still smelling of something acrid that would make our eyes water and keep the flies away for a week. And then, with the damning vial in my pocket and James under my arm—his crutch was one more thing lost in the blaze—I bolted for the ship and ordered her downriver to Cairo.

*

JAMES AND I WERE RESTING in the shade of the canvas, drying off from a dunking we'd taken in a futile attempt to scrub off the soot and the residue of poison. The acrid compound was still in my nose, and I was lightheaded either from its continuing effects or from sleeplessness. "You seemed surprised that I knew Umar," I said, my eyes closed against the glare of the morning sun off the water.

"Surely I was. He came south on the trading boat. With the vegetables."

"He was working?"

"Not at all. He'd paid his way with honest piasters. Just like me."

"In his case, 'honest' may be an overstatement."

We drifted north. Hungry insects terrorized everyone on board except the two of us, until the boat vibrated with enough slapping to fill a concert hall and gratify the most narcissistic impresario.

"So when were you going to tell me about Drovetti?"

James yawned. "I only mentioned it on account of I thought ye could use a bit more motivation. It's nothing, really. Best if ye don't give it another thought."

"It's *nothing*? The man invades my home in my absence, and it's nothing? He hires an assassin to murder me, and it's nothing?"

"I didn't mean that. Not about the part with the assassin, anyhow."

"Still, you propose an interesting point of view."

"And what point of view would that be?"

"A rather generous one, I think. One suggesting that just because strong and blameless women like Sarah exist in this world, wretches like Drovetti should be permitted to insinuate themselves into their presence as freely as they see fit."

"She'd never do ye wrong, boss. Ye can count on that."

"Even after my death? The cause of which she'd never know?"

"I suppose ye're right."

"You suppose? Then it's been far too long since you've read your Homer. We'll have to rectify that when we return to London."

*

BUT FIRST THERE WAS the matter of Cairo.

We arrived in the dead of night, creeping unnoticed toward the city upon waters as unruffled and black as a pool of oil. A high overcast obscured the stars, and my crew worked the oars so cunningly that we could have been a boatload of ghosts. Finding the harbor deserted, we tied up where we pleased.

If not for James's various impediments, I'd have taken a running start and leapt to the wharf while the ship was still six or eight feet out.

Conditions being as they were, however, I checked my eagerness and helped him ashore.

The gates to the European Quarter were locked, but scaling them was short work even with James clinging to my neck. We found the door to our flat far less carefully secured, although every square foot of the premises was booby-trapped with the sleeping bodies of two or three collapsed urchins, not to mention an accompanying delegation of mongrel dogs and feral cats, every invisible one of the latter wide awake and fixing us with a suspicious yellow gaze. I could almost have navigated by them, as by a roomful of tiny candles.

The place stank. It stank of filthy children and filthier animals, it stank of poor ventilation and vigorous activity, and it stank of whatever appalling food these juveniles desired to gorge themselves upon now that it was free of charge and in plentiful supply. It did not, however, stink of French cologne. This I took for a good sign, as if I required one.

Sarah was sound asleep in our marriage bed, snoring away happily beneath six woolen blankets and an afghan she'd knitted on our voyage from Malta. She could never get enough heat when it came time for bed—not even in Cairo—and she could sleep properly only beneath a pile of blankets sufficient to suffocate an army. She looked like an igloo, and she slept like a contented angel.

All traces of children and animals were absent from this room, as if they had been excluded by means of a spell. Here all was my Sarah: her warmth and her breath and her body and her hair. I bent, intending to place the gentlest of kisses upon her brow before setting out to surprise Drovetti in his own slumber, but as I drew near she awoke with a magnetic urge.

"Giovanni!" I may have been Atlas in public and in jest, but in her heart of hearts I was always and only her dear sweet Giovanni. "You've come to find Victor," she said as if from somewhere deep inside a dream. "I knew that you would."

"Victor? What's become of him?" I said, suddenly as alert and ready for action as I have been at any time in my life.

She put a finger to my lips and muttered something about there being plenty of time to track him down come morning, and then she threw her arms about my neck and drew me sleepily down.

*

THE SUN WAS UP and Cairo's outline was beginning to waver beneath it when I extricated myself and went to knock on Drovetti's door. His man answered—butler, factotum, manservant, or something else altogether—a well-groomed and supercilious insect whose speech was confined to a variety of French as thick as Béarnaise and twice as opaque. Monsieur Drovetti, I believe he suggested, was either indisposed or on a journey to Siberia. I indicated that I would prefer seeing about that for myself—a bit of cross-cultural communication I accomplished by lifting the insect by his armpits and depositing him in a spot that gave me more convenient access to the door.

Drovetti was upstairs at his breakfast—coffee, cheese, bread, and olives, a tribute to his Barbarian background. His eyes, downcast upon some bit of paper, showed a flicker of annoyance as I entered. At last he looked up and identified me—a walking ghost and one surely bent on revenge, for despite my reunion with Sarah I was still rumpled and turbaned and covered all over with soot, still creepily redolent of mummies and fire and futile poison—and in his startlement he dropped a fat green imported Bella Di Cerignola olive into his lap.

I paused to see what he'd do about it—nothing whatsoever, it turned out; he just let the thing lie there and soak its brine into his expensive dressing gown—and then I waited another second or two purely for the drama of it. Finally, convinced that my entry had been sufficiently theatrical, I hailed him in the most sepulchral tones I could summon.

"Greetings," I said. "Greetings from the tomb!"

Drovetti scrambled to his feet, losing his balance in the process and knocking over his chair. The olive—forgive me for concentrating on something as inconsequential as a single succulent Bella Di Cerignola olive at a time like this, but you must remember that I'd been in the desert for weeks, subsisting upon a diet of falafel and kashary and figs— the olive rolled into the darkness beneath an enormous carved sideboard, never to be seen again.

"Belzoni!" He snatched the napkin from around his neck. "However did you...?"

I held my ground and waited for him to finish his sentence, hoping to learn whether he was asking how I'd gotten into his breakfast room or how I'd survived his hireling's attempt on my life. Soon it grew apparent that he did not intend to clarify.

I pointed a finger as big and as black as the barrel of a gun straight at his sleek little head. "I would come back from the grave to guard what's mine from the likes of you," I said. "And thanks to your intervention, such a feat was very nearly necessary."

"I have no idea of what you're talking about, I assure you."

"On your honor?"

"On my honor." He believed that he was absolutely credible. I could tell from the way he lifted his shoulders and cocked one corner of his mouth up in a pale imitation of a smile.

"Would that be your honor as a son of Barbaria, or your honor as a Frenchman?"

"Please." He was at his courtly worst. I feared that he was about to bow, and then I would have had to bash his head in from pure frustration. "Please, Signor Belzoni. Why do you despise me so?"

I reached into the folds of my garment and drew out the evidence: the vial that Umar had dropped in the closing seconds of his misdirected life, its inner surface still powdered with the dried residue of death and its outside still bearing that damning French label. I placed it before Drovetti, who pursed his lips and shrugged. "And this would be—?"

"The poison with which you arranged to have me killed."

"Your imagination is even larger than you are."

"So a person might think, until he saw the facts for himself." I tapped my finger on the label and give him a knowing grin.

He squinted at it. "This proves nothing."

"So you say."

"Anyone could have obtained that material," he sniffed. "Whatever it is."

"If you insist, I'm sure that we can trace its origin to a point somewhere within your sphere of influence."

"Tut-tut, Belzoni. Half of the world's great poisoners have been French. The rest, alas, have been Italian."

"So much the worse for you, eh?"

He lifted the vial and scrutinized it as if it were a mediocre gemstone. "So tell me: Exactly how did I attempt to do you in with this?"

Frankly, I'd expected a confession by this point. But since one didn't seem to be forthcoming, I suggested the story in only the most cursory of ways: "Umar," I said. "I saw you with him on the wharf that day."

"Umar? Yes, I believe I know a gentleman by that name."

We were making progress.

"He quite despises you, Belzoni, if memory serves."

"Make that *despised.*"

Drovetti clucked and shook his head and then, with a shiver of relief, returned the vial to me. "Hoist by his own petard, was he?"

"By someone's petard."

"A shame, but it shows where treachery will get you." He wiped his hand, the one that had touched the vial, on his pantleg. "He sought me out because he was disappointed in you."

"Disappointed?" I'm a fool for a good story, and in spite of myself Drovetti had me hooked.

"He'd put a great deal of primitive faith in you, and he was heartbroken when you dashed that faith to the ground."

"He believed me to be a jinni."

"And then he learned the truth, I understand. Quite by accident."

I squinted at the ceiling, trying to picture the moment.

"It happened at the Temple of Ramesses II. On the morning of your great victory."

I remembered, of course: the bust of Ramesses on its wheeled cart; the brutal work of lowering it stone by stone to the waiting boat; the pair of dark eyes flashing at us from below decks, drinking in my hard labor and my ingenuity and my pointless prideful deception.

I remembered all of that. And I remembered something else, too.

"You, Monsieur Drovetti, were as disappointed on that day as he was."

"Perhaps. In my own way."

"I'm sure his story touched your heart."

"But there is a difference: Umar never got over his disappointment. And when your people refused to hire him on for Abu Simbel, he lost faith altogether."

"And he came to you for redress."

"Not at all. He came to me for employment."

"And you were happy gave it to him, I see." Eyeing the vial.

"Now, now. Why would I do a thing like that?"

I ticked off some of the reasons on my fingers. "Jealousy. Greed. Pridefulness. A mad thirst for revenge."

"The Seven Deadlies, more or less. Minus what? Sloth, I suppose, of which I've never been accused. Oh, and gluttony." He looked hungrily at his plate. "And lust. Don't forget lust—however that fits into your scheme. Here, help yourself to some olives."

"It will be my pleasure." I was starving, but I surely wasn't about to let his olives and cheese and bread distract me from my mission—or from the specifics, now that he had brought it up, of his transgressions in the lust department. "Lust," I mused around a fat green olive. "I think that one speaks for itself, don't you?"

"You have a long memory."

"Only as long as necessary."

"You're a regular elephant, Belzoni. Do you know that? All those years ago, that plain-faced little girl in the house beside the Piazza Barbieri. I suppose that insulting me before the Pasha wasn't enough. Now it's grounds for an accusation that I plotted murder."

"I'm not thinking of Serafina Randazzo. I hardly ever think of Serafina Randazzo." Which wasn't true, but also wasn't the point. Serafina was hardly plain-faced, as I have told you, but defending her would have been another distraction from the reason I'd come. I let it drop.

A light dawned in his eyes, and he spat the pit of an olive into his palm. "You're thinking of that wife of yours, aren't you? I'd have better luck courting a wolverine. And trust me, Belzoni, I don't mean that as an insult. Not to either one of you."

I was reaching for a bit of cheese when a great thump and a familiar voice emerged from across the hall. "I knew I could count on you, Sammy. This one doesn't know when to quit." After a bit of scuffling, Victor the Human Snail poked his head in through the door. He was bleary-eyed from sleep, but otherwise unhurt and undiminished. "I come between him and that Pasha for two minutes—angle for that firman at Abu Simbel, maybe make a few other suggestions that I'm not at liberty to discuss—and next thing you know he turns kidnapper. And with me in my helpless condition. It just ain't fair."

At the sight of him—and at the realization of the true depths of Drovetti's villainy—I dropped the vial. It shattered to pieces on the floor, spilling out the remainder of its contents. Nearly done in by the stuff last time around and still bearing a healthy respect for it, I jumped as if stung by bees.

Drovetti popped an olive into his mouth and said, just as innocently as you can imagine, "Don't worry, it's harmless in the absence of water."

I nearly choked with rage.

As for Drovetti, he actually did choke—on that enormous Bella Di Cerignola olive, when he realized exactly how much he'd just confessed. He clutched at his throat and fell forward onto the table, scrabbling at the cloth and sending his breakfast tumbling to the floor—including a pot of hot coffee, whose contents ran straight for the last crumbly bits of green powder.

"Drovetti!"

He didn't answer. He couldn't answer. And as I overcame the paralysis induced by the spilling of his poison and stepped forward to help, from the corner of my eye I witnessed a horrifying tableau: long tendrils of sickly green gas, moving straight for Victor. They wavered along the floor, stealthy and purposeful, and he could do nothing but watch them come.

I did my best to assist both my enemy and my friend. If you have envisioned nothing else clearly in this story of mine, you must envision this. The momentum of my first step took me toward Drovetti, and I did not resist it. I permitted myself to fall at his side in my filthy robes, clapping him upon the back with the flat of my hand in hope that I might dislodge the olive. Still he writhed, breathless. I clapped his back again, pressing down this time, driving his stomach toward the floor, and that movement seemed to serve. A little breath escaped his lungs, and he began to stir with more purpose.

I had no time to attend further to him. The gas was spreading. I rose up and strode toward Victor, setting the tendrils of smoke aswirl, and in a heartbeat I had fetched him up to safety. In the same heartbeat, however, poor gasping Drovetti had inhaled something far more treacherous than a Bella Di Cerignola olive. He had inhaled his own poison. I pressed upon his back again, kneeling there beside him with Victor ensconced safely on the tabletop, but it was no use.

"I told him once that he was poor in spirit," I remarked as I trooped down the stairs with Victor under my right arm and Drovetti under my left. "And he assured me that he would see God."

"Oh," said Victor the Human Snail, "I wouldn't be so sure about that."

*

WHAT FOLLOWED? My second reunion with Sarah, where we embraced one another and kissed until the pots boiled over. More journeys up the Nile, each longer and more daring and more gloriously mounted than the last. Pyramids ravaged and tombs plundered and riches dragged into the sunlight in quantities sufficient to make a pharaoh gasp. Antiquities shipped to London by the groaning boatload and displayed there within a museum of my very own, the legendary Egyptian Hall at Piccadilly.

In between I wrote and illustrated the book that guaranteed my fame, my Narrative of the Operations and Recent Discoveries Within the Pyramids, Temples, Tombs and Excavations, in Egypt and Nubia; and of a Journey to the Coast of the Red Sea, in Search of the Ancient Berenice; and Another to the Oasis of Jupiter Ammon. By the length of the title alone I'd surpassed old Jean d'Outremeuse and his paltry *Voiage and Travaile of Sir John Mandeville, Knight.*

And my book was all true.

Yet another Frenchman bested.

POSTLUDE:

The Coast of Africa

"Belzoni...did have a go at Timbuctoo. He was landed at Benin
by a Royal Navy vessel and bade it farewell in inimitable style:
"God bless you, my fine fellows, and send you a happy sight of your
country and friends!" He died on 3 December 1823
of dysentery, having covered only ten miles."

— Fergus Fleming, *Barrow's Boys*, London, 1998

*

ALTHOUGH MAN HAS YET to set his eyes upon the source of the River
Niger, I believe in my heart that that fabled place shall soon enough reveal itself to me. And why not? I have spent my life journeying to locations far more remote, and I have seen sights far more mysterious.

My only wish is that my dear Sarah could be along to serve as my
witness. What a celebration we would have, the two of us! Even in the
absence of decent food or drink. Even in the presence of this fiery afflic-
tion that lays siege to my poor digestive tract.

I have always known how to accomplish much with little. Think of
the broken shovel with which I opened the Mithraic temple. Think of
the damp mouthful of ground chickpeas with which I silenced the singing statue of Memnon. Think of the burning mummies with which
James Curtin and I rescued ourselves from death at the hands of a mad
and broken-hearted murderer.

Think of a poor overgrown boy from Padua, the son of a barber, who made his bed among the bones of kings.

Hidden within my sea chest, tucked behind the frontispiece of *The Voiage,* is a document over which I have been laboring—a document that must find its way home to London regardless of how or when or even whether I return from this expedition. It is a diagram, a minutely detailed plan for the first hydraulic project I've envisioned since my carelessness nearly killed James Curtin on the banks of the Nile. It describes a monumental tower of iron and lead and a mighty cluster of hydraulic rams, all of it linked to a steam engine and a pressurized boiler. I beg you to take this plan, to carry it with you on your return voyage to England, and to see that it gets into the hands of James Curtin.

I can count upon him to know what to do. I can count upon him to free the Pope's band of imprisoned angels once and for all.

And then, my work complete, I shall find peace at last—whether at home in London with my dear faithful Sarah, or alone beneath the African stars.

* * *

Also by Jon Clinch:

Finn
Kings of the Earth
The Thief of Auschwitz
What Came After (writing as Sam Winston)
Into the Silent World (writing as Sam Winston)

*

Jon Clinch is on the web:

Web site: jonclinch.com
Twitter: @jonclinch
Facebook: facebook.com/JonClinchBooks